TOO LATE TO TURN BACK NOW

RYAN CAHILL

TOO LATE TO TURN BACK NOW

Print ISBN: 979-8-35093-000-9

eBook ISBN: 979-8-35093-001-6

TO DARIAN, TORI, AND NEENA.

I love *YOU* more than anybody loves anybody!

haol·e

/ˈhoulē/

noun

often derogatory (in Hawaii) a person who is not a native Hawaiian, especially a white person.

HO'I HOU KE ALOHA -

(LET US FALL IN LOVE ALL OVER AGAIN.)

MAY 2019

"ASHES TO ASHES, DUST TO DUST," THE PRIEST BEGINS, AS mourners gather around Dad's grave. My son stands next to me as we prepare to pitch dirt on the casket. Pops is finally on time for a family gathering. It's his own funeral, and he got a ride.

"Grandpa was the best," Mikey whispers to me, his eyes red from crying. "I'm going to miss him so much."

"Me too, Son. Me too."

Three weeks later, I'm sitting in my favorite chair reading a book. This is a rare Saturday afternoon alone, just me and our new 60" flat screen, showing the Yankee game on mute. Sunlight and a fresh breeze stream through big windows on the back porch, the view getting greener by the day as trees thicken with springtime leaves. Suddenly my tall, handsome son ducks under the doorway, his hat on backward and wearing big floppy shorts. He plops down in a chair next to me, subtle as a firecracker; so much for a little alone time.

"Dad, prom is Saturday. Can I take the Cutlass or not?"

"You can take it, Mikey. Just remember, if anything bad happens, don't come home. Don't ever come home," I joke.

He rolls his eyes and walks to the window, looking out at my car in the driveway. Sun bounds off the perfect blue paint job, it's polished chrome twinkling. "It's just a car, Dad. A dope-ass car, but just a car."

"Ah Son, one day you'll understand. I was your age when Grandpa gave it to me. Did you know I took your mother on our first date in that car?"

"Seriously Dad? You've only told me like a million times."

I fold over my page and put the book down next to me, locking eyes with Mikey. "It's a symbol of my life, Boy. I've had that Olds for thirty years. Hell, I drove it to my own prom. It's a beauty now, but sometimes I look at her and still see the rust and dings she had when I was a kid. I look in the rear-view mirror; my young self is staring back. Every day that car reminds me of how far I've come."

"Okay Pop, it was just a simple question. I don't need the life story of Bryan Grayhill!" my wise-ass kid replies.

"I'm just saying, when me and that car started out together, both of us were a mess, and we didn't get all nice and shiny by osmosis, it took a lot of hard work. So please don't say it's *just* a car."

"I hear you Dad, but I gotta bounce," Michael replies flippantly as he rises from his seat. "Don't worry about your Cutlass, It'll all work out. Aloha, Pops!" he finishes, then breezes out the door.

"*A hui hou kakou,*" I shout in his wake, a Hawaiian saying I learned from my wife. "*Until we meet again.* Love you, Boy."

CHAPTER 1
FALL 1988

I SUCK IN THE LAST DRAG OF WHAT HAS TO BE MY TWENTIETH
Marlboro Red of the day so far and flick it out the window as I park.
Searching through a pile of junk and papers on the seat next to me, I finally
locate my smokes, tuck some matches under the box top and quickly check
myself in the rear-view mirror. Keg parties like the one I'm about to walk into
are for two things, getting drunk with your friends and more importantly,
trying to hook up. I'm 21 years old, my goals are very simple. Lucky me, I
get a spot for my big blue Oldsmobile Cutlass Supreme right in front of the
mailbox. Looking through the passenger side window, I can see a crowd
gathered in the driveway, half in and half out of the open garage. A single
overhead light illuminates an outline of the partygoers, a haze of cigarette
smoke lingering above them.

The fall chill has yet to arrive, so I leave my jacket behind as I exit the
car and slowly walk toward the festivities, not particularly excited to see
anyone here. Most are from my class of 1985 but in the three years since
graduation, gatherings such as this are no longer the norm and I don't know
who is going to show up. Billy Gorman spots me as I get out of the car and
is now walking the length of the driveway to identify who I am. This is his

house party, so Billy is on high alert, making sure no unwanted guests try to slip in uninvited.

"What's up Grayhill?! It's been too long, Brother!" he shouts upon recognizing me, and we share a big but man-acceptable hug. Guy hugs need to be quick, just a pat on the back, any lingering is not good.

"Yeah, it's been a while Dude, how the fuck are you?"

We were inseparable best friends in high school. His strong athletic frame has gotten a bit lumpy since I last saw him, with a rounder face and darker eyes. Billy's odometer is going a lot faster than mine, I think he's been living hard for a while now. Considering we haven't communicated at all in the past three years, this could have been a little awkward, but his enthusiastic greeting takes us right back to the good old days, not that I'm looking to stay there.

"When did you get back from LA?" Billy asks while slapping me on the shoulder.

"Dude, I've been back in Rockland for almost a year. Just been so busy trying to figure shit out," I lie.

The truth is Billy developed a little coke and whatever else habit by the end of high school and became a real dick, unbearable to be around. So, I stopped being around.

"Oh Man, you should have called me, we could have been hanging this whole time," he says, then begins yapping about himself. "I dropped out of UCONN after freshman year, too much partying. My Dad said screw it, just come home and run the plumbing business. I'm going to be making some big-time money, Bro!"

Sure you are Billy; all the Roto-Rooter guys drive a Mercedes. He always has to have the most and is always bragging about how great he thinks his life is. It's a real turn-off.

"Hey man, let's go get a beer," I suggest, already tiring of the conversation. "I need to pound a few before the cops come and break this thing up."

Billy scoffs. "My Dad's buddies with all the cops, they won't be bothering us tonight."

Uh-huh, right, Billy, I forgot you're the king of Rockland.

I shoot the shit with a dozen other people and finally make it to the beer keg, which is chilling in a big tin bucket filled with ice in front of the garage. As always, it's a barrel of the cheapest crap you can buy, like Busch or Meister Brau, something heinous like that. I peek in and see Billy's garage is neatly organized, featuring a speedboat on one half and the other side reserved for motorcycles, tools, and lawn equipment, everything prominently displayed for maximum envy. There is a labeled cubby for each family member; Mom, Dad, and the boys. I'm not familiar with the life being led here at Billy's, but gun to my head, I'm a little jealous. The only thing nuclear about my family is the way my parents blew it up.

People at these parties are always hanging around the beer keg, it's like the office water cooler for the pre-employed. I scan the crowd a bit, looking for a place to settle in. After evaluating the female talent at this shindig, I've found several candidates that merit my further attention. One of the ladies, Sara Addeo, is scoping me out with some pretty direct eye contact. I'll have to investigate this further and without delay. Tall and shapely, with black hair and tan skin, Sara Addeo is an Italian goddess who's at the top of every guy's most wanted list. I give her a sideways glance so as not to be too obvious and I think of a Meatloaf lyric I sang in the Olds on the ride over here. Sara is tonight's *"Ruby in a Mountain of Rocks."*

Making my way closer to her, I mumble "'Sup Sara," while lighting a Marlboro and tossing the match.

"Hey, Bryan Grayhill," she says with a glow. "You're looking all grown up these days!"

I wasn't even sure she knew my name so this is off to a good start. Sara is older than me, always was out of my league and frankly, I don't think I've ever had a conversation with her before right now. My beer full, I dump half into her empty cup and then raise mine in salute. Smooth move, I think proudly to myself, as she cheers me back and we both take a gulp.

"Good to see you, Sara, how's it going? What brings you to our youngster party?"

"Nice to see you too, Bry," she replies with a mischievous grin. "I actually came with my little sister Cara. She's class of '86."

Yeah everybody knows Sara and Cara Addeo, no need to clarify, they are like the hottest sisters in the history of Rockland High School. There is an older Addeo girl as well, named Tara, also a beauty.

"Oh yeah, I know Cara, kinda."

"How's your sister Lauren?" Sara asks. "She used to hang out with Tara all the time in high school but I haven't really seen her since they graduated."

"Lauren's good," I answer vaguely, not wanting to waste time talking about my sister. "So anyway, what have you been up to these last few years?"

"I graduated from Penn State this year and I'm back with my parents now in Congers, not really in a rush to go job hunting yet, just kinda hanging out you know? I've been waitressing a little and working at Jack Lalane's teaching aerobics once in a while, but that's about it."

"Okay, that's cool. Let's get physical!" I say like a moron while dropping my cigarette butt into the bath of ice water cooling the keg. This chick is gorgeous, a college graduate (something I'll never be), and for some reason locking in on me; an interesting situation is starting to develop here.

Just then my fat friend Pat Byrne appears in my face. He's the size of Mean Joe Green and I feel like I'm witnessing a solar eclipse as Sara disappears from my view. Nice timing Patty, can't you see I've got a big fish on the line here? We all call him Patty Funk because he's always sweating and has a little stink to him. He is our school's version of Pigpen.

"Five in a row, Yankees can't win for shit. Even Mattingly sucks this year," Funk chirps with a snicker. Pat is a notorious Mets die-hard, which used to be an embarrassment for him, but sadly The Mets have taken over New York in the last few years, so their fans are all pumped up.

"Shut your face, Patty. Boston choked in '86 and gave you the Series on a silver platter. Same platter Gooden is snorting his coke off now. Your Boys ain't winning shit this year either." This is a lame retort, but it's the best I can come up with. The Mets own the city right now, definitely a hard pill for us Yankee fans to swallow. Anyway, I'm too worried about losing my place in line with Sara to care about baseball right now.

I give Pat a look that says "Get the fuck outta here," and shift the focus back to more pressing matters, returning all my attention to Sara before I lose this chance. I lean into her ear and suggest "Hey, let's take a walk," which she agrees to without hesitation. We shuffle off to a rock wall about 10 feet away and sit down. So much for walking.

"Last I heard about you, you were moving to California. How'd that turn out? When did you get back?" Sara asks.

"Yeah, high school was so screwed up for me I was just like, I need to get as far away from here as possible. I had an Uncle in Cali so I just went for it. I'm hoping to open my own restaurant one day so I was wanting to get some big-time experience but it didn't really pan out. I was out there for two years doing not too much. Lots of work, little school, and mostly just bored, to be honest. I've been back for a while now."

"Still pretty cool that you were in LA. I don't know anybody that went that far after school. Did you see any movie stars?"

"Not really. Danny Devito was shooting a movie on Venice Beach once but that's about it."

We continue on chatting like this for a half hour or so about our lives and whatever else came up. I can barely concentrate on what she is saying. Smitten with her good looks, I still can't believe that she is at all interested in me.

Her sister Cara, also tall, tan, and gorgeous, approaches. "Sara, we gotta book," she interrupts, without acknowledging me. "I have work at 8 tomorrow."

"You can leave, I'm going to hang here for a while. Tell Ma I won't be late."

Ohh K, I like the sound of that. "I can take you home whenever you want," I offer.

"Bet your ass you can, Big Guy! You're the reason I'm staying." Her sister rolls her eyes and walks off without another word.

The party is broken up by the cops soon after, Billy's earlier tough talk notwithstanding.

"Adios, Grayhill," he says while walking around and putting trash in a plastic bag. "See you later, Man."

"Not if I see you first, Billy Boy," I reply with a laugh, but I mean it. Next time I see this kid coming the other way, I'll hide before he sees me. Billy is a real gasbag these days, but thanks to his kegger, I'm about to score my best piece of ass ever.

I grab a few cans of beer floating in the water around the keg and run out to my car, quickly clearing all the crap off the passenger seat as I ready it for Sara. My ride looks like it belongs in the junkyard but Sara doesn't seem to mind.

"Thanks for taking me, Bry. I live on the other side of Christian Herald Road, in the Indian Hills apartments. It's like five minutes away."

"My pleasure, Sara Addeo," I smile flirtatiously. "I wish it was farther so we had more time to talk."

"Oh well, I'm not in a rush to get inside, Bry. We can hang for a while if you want."

"I'm available for the rest of my life," I confirm with a grin.

I've been to Sara's complex many times before. This parking lot is used often as a lover's lane type area for kids from our school and I know exactly where to go; this is not my first rodeo. We sit outside the car on top of some cement chess tables, set up for the old folks from the apartments I suppose.

Smoking butts, drinking, and laughing, it's a done deal that we will be making out very shortly. I'm a little slow on the uptake and always like to be real sure my advances are going to be warmly received before I make a move. I wait probably way longer than necessary but now it's happening, I am tongue to tongue with this *woman*. Hopefully, she can't read my mind because I'm a little intimidated right now. Again, she is way out of my league. Though I don't know how experienced Sara is, I'm pretty sure that it's way more than me. I've made out and messed around with lots of girls, but my actual sexual experience is nothing to brag about.

I keep it together and start making my way around the bases. I can't get this Meatloaf music out of my head; *"He's rounding first and really turning it on now, he's not letting up at all, he's gonna try for second."* Sara has no qualms either and doesn't flinch when I move my hand under her shirt to squeeze the Charmin. Holy shit, who knew? What a rack, very impressive. Sara's so gorgeous, this is a generous bonus.

Unfortunately, our getting-to-know-you exploratory journey is about to end for the night. A police spotlight suddenly shines brightly upon us from a patrol car across the lot. As we scramble to unscramble, a voice comes over a loudspeaker, loud enough for anyone within a mile to hear.

"Playtime is over kids," the cop mockingly announces.

"Ha ha, funny, Asshole," I whisper under my breath, then walk Sara to her door around the corner. The porch light is off, and we kiss for probably ten more minutes.

"Alright, Big Guy (my new nickname?), you're going to suck my face off."

"I can't help myself."

"Give me your hand, Grayhill. Here's my number," she says, reaching inside the door to grab a pen and writing it on my palm, then mine on hers. "Call me anytime."

One last kiss and she slowly eases the door closed. I float back to my car on cloud nine, still not sure of what just happened. I can't get Sara out of my mind for a second on the ride home. When my head hits the pillow that night, I am surprisingly not thinking of Sara's stunning body or reliving our lengthy make-out session, I fall asleep thinking of her smile and laugh. I can't wait to see her again.

CHAPTER 2

A RINGING PHONE WAKES ME UP THE NEXT MORNING, MY HEAD pulsating along with the racket. On and on it blares, but nobody is around to answer it. "Get the phone!" I scream into my pillow, yet it continues uninterrupted. I let it ring on and bury my head deeper, but then suddenly realize it may be Sara calling. I ninja roll of the bed and lunge for the receiver, hopeful to hear her voice on the other end.

"Hello?" I ask, with much more energy than I'm feeling, not wanting to give Sara the impression that I sleep all day. The digital clock reads 1:14. I guess it's not the morning after all.

"Bry Boy, how goes it?" Fuck, it's just my Dad. Well, this sucks.

I pinch the phone between my ear and shoulder while lighting up a Marlboro. Sun and heat pour through the windows. "What's up, Pop?" I mumble, the cig hanging out of my mouth.

My Dad clears his throat before talking. "Ah-hem," he barks loudly as if to signify it's time for me to pay attention, the king is about to speak. "We haven't caught up in a while Bryan, I feel like you never call me. What's so busy about your life that you can't stay in touch with your father?"

"Oh my God Dad, you can't be serious," I shout incredulously. "You're never around. If you want to talk just fucking call me, I don't go anywhere. Why's it always my job to call you?"

He ignores my question and gets to his point. "We have to talk about the car insurance for the Oldsmobile. You haven't given me any money for it. When I gave it to you, I said insurance was 25 dollars a month."

"Yeah, and it's a big piece of shit that I keep having to fix so that's where my money's going. Are you calling to catch up like you said or just looking to collect from me, Dad? I'll put a hundred aside for the next time I see you (which could be months), does that work for you? Anything else you need?"

He doesn't reply, then starts talking to someone else in the room with him. Finally, Dad says absently, "That's it for now, Bryan, I gotta run."

Of course you do. This conversation is par for the course with me and my Dad these days. He's always moving and grooving in his fancy suits, partying with his Wall Street buddies, and running around taking care of number one; himself!

Two weeks later on a sunny Saturday afternoon, I'm relaxing in my room watching baseball's game of the week as the Yanks beat up the Red Sox in Fenway Park. The Yankees suck again this year, but New York vs. Boston is not to be missed by me.

I've been talking to Sara on the phone here and there over the last couple of weeks, sometimes for hours and hours. Unfortunately, she's been unusually busy, and unavailable to get together in person.

Our conversations have been mostly easy, with lots of laughs and banter back and forth, but also deep at times, digging into each other's past.

As with most kids raised in the seventies, we both spent most of our years growing up being outside with friends, unsupervised from dawn till dusk. We talked about everything. Among the hours of details and little nuggets we shared, I told Sara I don't eat vegetables, prefer to always leave my shoes on, and one time I drank my brother's pee (straight from the spigot!) on a dare when we were little. In turn, Sara shared that her first kiss was while playing spin the bottle, she ate anything on her pizza and her most embarrassing moment ever (speaking of little nuggets) was pooping her pants in class when she was 10. "I thought it was going to be a fart!" she laughed.

"Don't worry," I assured her, "I just did that a few weeks ago."

We learned that both of us had lived pretty easy lives so far, with no great tragedies to share. Yes, my parents have been divorced for as long as I can remember, but it's all I know and is my normal. Sara's parents, on the other hand, spend day and night together. They own a karate school in our town and constantly shuffle between work and home. I didn't know Italians were into karate but hey, why not?

"The only thing I know about martial arts I learned from the Karate Kid. Wax on, wax off," I joked.

"Yeah well I know everything and I'm not afraid to use it, so don't make me mad, Grayhill!"

Most of our conversations were filled with laughter but as I mentioned, some took a more serious track. One night recently Sara was telling me her grandparents arrived "fresh off the boat" from Italy during the Great Depression with their three-year-old son, Sara's father. Her grandparents decided after one year that they were better off returning to Italy, the American dream they envisioned didn't include waiting on bread lines and living in a Central Park Hooverville. Sara's Dad Angelo was left behind in New York, raised by his father's brother in a tiny Bronx apartment overcrowded with relatives. He grew up unloved and lonely due to his parent's abandonment. Sara insists he's a good Dad and can be a kind and outgoing man, but still deeply scarred from childhood and therefore sometimes very difficult to please.

"Jesus, that's heartbreaking. We have it so easy compared to our parents and their parents," I told Sara.

"What about you, Bry? What's your family like?"

"Listen, my Dad's no great shakes either, but I'm my own worst enemy. My brother and sister hog up all the good decisions and leave me with the bad ones! I'm a well of untapped potential, let's put it that way. It's definitely time for me to get my shit together, once and for all."

"Maybe I can help you become the man you want to be," Sara said encouragingly.

"Uh, yeah, I would love that," I replied, still having trouble believing little ol' me is worthy of her. I am excited about seeing her again and we decided it would be tonight.

The Red Sox's feeble performance today culminates in a 3-hit shutout by the Yankees, and all is right in the world as I stand up to hit the head. Looking out the window, I see two police cars pulling slowly onto our little tree-lined street, their red and blue lights flashing. This can't be good. Maybe everything's not all right in the world after all.

CHAPTER 3

MY MOM GIVES MY BEDROOM DOOR A QUICK KNOCK AND THEN jerks it open before I can answer. "The police are at the front door looking for you," she reports in a remarkably calm voice, like this is normal, which it most definitely is not. Her eyes are darting back and forth wildly, contradicting the calmness of her tone.

"What are you talking about, Ma?"

Just then, a uniformed officer appears over her shoulder, towering over my tiny mother. "Bryan Grayhill, you're under arrest. Stand up, put your hands behind your back."

"For what, Dude? I haven't been in trouble in years," I cry out as he roughly runs his hands all over me.

"I'm not your fucking dude, first of all. The warrant here says you violated probation."

With that, I'm led out of my house in handcuffs as my poor Mom watches in confusion.

"Do you want me to call Daddy?" she asks as I'm eased into the back of a cop car with more care than I would have expected.

"No Mom, this is not a big deal," I mistakenly declare. "I'll get it figured out as soon as—" and the door shuts in my face mid-sentence. My

Mom is left standing there clueless, watching her son get carted off in a cop car and wondering where she went wrong.

I'm not nervous, though I should be of course. I am handcuffed in the back of a cop car. There is a metal cage in front of me in case I am compelled to attack someone. Right now I'm sitting where killers have sat before me. The cruiser is driving through my neighborhood, just like I do myself on a daily basis, except this time I'm not casually smoking a butt or waving to my friends; I'm hiding from them. The cop passes the police station in town and all of a sudden we are on the highway heading north, and I'm wondering where the hell is this guy taking me.

"I can't remember the last time I knocked on a door to serve a warrant and the Perp didn't try to run or make some bullshit excuse," the officer says to me, the perp.

Ignoring his comment, I ask where we are going. This is turning into a little road trip, without the sing-a-longs and snacks.

"County jail, Mr.Grayhill," he tells me, in what seems like slow motion. "Coooouuuunnnntttttttyyyyy Jaaaaaiiiiilllllll!" The Joint. The Big House. I'm going to the Clink. This I did not expect. Should have, but didn't.

"Oh okay, I see. Interesting," I mutter while keeping a low profile and ignoring the traffic around me. I've traveled these roads free as a bird all my life, but not today. I'm still calm, but the immediate future has no choices, my freedom is lost.

We pass the exit for Sara's town and I instinctively slink even lower in my seat. I imagine her pulling up in the car next to me on the highway and glancing over. She gives a double take and then puts her fingers on her forehead in the shape of an "L." I read her lips as she shakes her head in disapproval and mouths, "You're such a fucking loser," then jams on the gas and speeds off, out of my life forever.

The reason I'm in this situation is so stupid. It was just some high school prank that was not well planned. I rarely thought things out with any care, this is my biggest downfall. On Senior Prank Day, which was over three years ago and happened to fall on my 18th birthday, some buddies and I decided it would be funny to grease the hallway with Canola Oil and pull the fire alarm during detention after school. Turned out it was anything but funny. With only a few teachers and felonious students in the building at 3 p.m., Billy, Pat, and this other kid who we hung with on occasion, Kevin Baker, sprang into action.

"Us three are going to grab mops from the downstairs closet and spread oil over the hall floors," Billy directed. "Bry, you're going to pull the alarm in five minutes. We can all meet up by the stairs, smoke a butt, and act like we don't know shit. We'll be right outside the back doors, so hopefully, everybody comes rushing out, looking like greasy pigs after slipping and sliding on the floor."

It never went through my head that pulling the fire alarm would make me more susceptible to punishment, nor that because this event was occurring on my 18th birthday, I was now an actual adult in this band of misfit children. I never thought about getting caught, what could go wrong? We greased the floor, pulled the alarm, and waited outside.

The first kid out the door, who I did not know (ended up there were only three people on the whole floor, hardly worth the effort), screamed "Call 911! Mr. Timin slipped on the floor and busted his head open. He's gushing blood and the dude is out like a light."

Timin was the assistant principal. Talk about fucked. We turned and booked it out of there like our pants were on fire, and nobody was laughing. Did we kill this guy?

"We are so screwed, I'm fucking dead," Kevin kept babbling on. This kid was losing his shit, he looked ready to cry.

"Take it easy Numb Nuts, relax, nobody knows anything but us," Patty barked at him. Billy, Pat, and I, we've seen and done some shit, stuff much worse. Of all the crazy things, we can't get snagged for this!

Timin ended up being fine. He had a little cut and a headache, nowhere close to dead. The guy was a complete tool anyway, he had it coming as far as I was concerned. But… he was pissed and went on the warpath looking for the culprits.

It didn't take long for that little narc Kevin Baker to name names. So I pulled the alarm. Combine it with the fact that I'm already a pain in the principal's ass and was now 18 years old, they decided to make an example out of me. I got put on three years of probation for that dumb shit. It was all very informal. I had to go to the police station and turn myself in, then got fingerprinted and photographed, but walked in and out on my own, without even having a lawyer.

I went to probation steadily for the next couple of years. I had a good job at the time, especially for a kid my age, didn't do drugs (ever), was well-spoken, and pretty responsible. So after those two years of reporting regularly, amid promises from the probation officer that if I kept on the right track it would end after a year or so, I said fuck it, I'm just not going anymore. I'm cavalier like that. I got probation, which is some serious shit, grew tired of it, and just stopped showing up. Not a good idea.

Now, fast forward to right here and now. Sitting in a cop car, hands cuffed on a beautiful Saturday afternoon. Off to the Pokey we go…

CHAPTER 4

THE COUNTY JAIL IS ON THE CORNER OF MAIN STREET IN NEW City, a dirty old black-bricked building. I always wondered what this place is like on the inside, not that I wanted a personal tour. My arresting officer parks on a hilly side lot next to several other cop cars. He walks around and opens the door, then helps me out of the car. Still cuffed at the wrists, I have a new appreciation for my hands now that I can't use them. "Walk with me inside. You are going to be processed and booked in for the weekend," 1 Adam 12 informs me.

Ah, hello? Did he say the weekend? Bro, I have a date tonight, with Sara Addeo! "Oh shit, I thought this would be a few-hour thing, at the most. Why are you so sure it will be the whole weekend?" For some reason, I think at this moment that I should have packed a bag. I'm going to have nothing to wear.

"It's Saturday afternoon Mr. Grayhill, no judge is going to be available to see you until Monday morning."

Okay, now I'm channeling Matthew Brodrick in WarGames. Take it down to DEFCON 1, or maybe 5, whichever is worse. We walk through the entrance, a heavy black metal door, and are immediately greeted (if you want to call his death stare a greeting) by a jailer guard sitting behind a clear partition, hands on a microphone with a bendy silver cord like the ones they have at Burger King.

The guard looks me up and down, then speaks into the mike, asking "And who do we have here?"

"Bryan Grayhill," I answer with a smile. "I'll have a Whopper with cheese and a Diet Coke."

Once again the guard slowly takes hold of the microphone, and after an uncomfortable pause, threatens me. "What you'll have, fucking Smart Ass, is a shit sandwich shoved so far up your crusty, dirty hole it will come out your nose. Now, let me ask again. Who, prey tell, do we have here?"

"Bryan Grayhill, Sir. Sorry for that," I reply sincerely, deeply regretting my ill-timed attempt at humor.

"Here's the paperwork from Judge Nelson," my police escort steps forward, handing the guard some forms. "Is there anything else you need from me?"

"Nope, that'll do it, thank you, Officer. I'll set up Mr. Grayhill for a nice stay."

"Later, Dude," the cop snickers at me as he barges out the heavy door, still smarting from my disrespectful greeting back at Mom's.

The Burger King guard continues. "We'll see if you're still cracking jokes when you make it back to court. You better not try the comedy act on Judge Nelson, Mr. Grayhill. He will fry your ass."

"Yes, Sir. It won't happen again, Sir." Now I'm thinking prison movie, which in the past I've always enjoyed watching. I never thought I'd be living the real thing. In a minute I'll be crying as I hold my blanket and pillow close to my chest, taking the long walk to my cell. All of the locked-up animals will be hollering from behind the bars, sizing me up for a little ass play. They'll be spitting on me and screaming "Fresh meat!"

Thankfully, that didn't happen. The entire entry procedure is so far well practiced and cordial enough.

"Hey Lumpy, give Grayhill here some new threads," the guard behind the mike orders.

"Height and weight?" a short, round guard behind a counter inquires of me. He is surrounded by orange clothing, stacked floor to ceiling. The clothes are stamped "INMATE" in several different places, in case there is any doubt.

"I'm 6'3, like two-twen—" I began to answer, but before I finish, what has to be three or four sets of shoddy prison garb is slammed onto the counter in front of me. Looks like they know something I don't because I'm getting enough clothing to stick around for a while.

"Pick it up and continue down the hall Mr. Grayhill," instructs Lumpy. I randomly picture kicking this little gnome in his face. I see in my mind's eye the bright red blood pouring out of his nose. What is my problem? I give him a thumbs up instead of a kick.

Well, the easy part of the jail intro is over and it's about to get serious. I carry my new duds into the next room and am greeted by a hulking guard, replete with the prerequisite mustache and bulging muscles.

"Please remove all your clothes and put them on the table."

I see. Getting naked on command from a dude, this also feels like freedom is permanently lost. I'm not a "naked" guy. I don't love my body and certainly don't wish to share it with this bruiser. Before I get dressed in my new jail get-up, I'll have to pass his inspection.

"Feet in the outlines on the floor," directs Muscles the guard. "Lift," he grunts, pointing at my balls. Nothing to lift here as my nuts are snuggling my body in a scared, naked chill. I comply anyway and am then instructed to "turn around and spread 'em." How did I get so fucking lucky? Yes sir, for you, I shall. On second thought I guess I am lucky. I'd much rather spread my asshole than be the one that has to check it for contraband.

Now dressed in the orange jail scrubs, I am escorted to my "cell." A guard walks me down a long hallway, there are no inmates behind bars like

I've seen in the movies. It looks more like an old school, with dark orange tile everywhere. Maybe my new uniform will be camouflaged against the walls at night and I can escape.

A door to what looks like a classroom swings open to reveal what I would call a real shit show. Turns out, this room is the rectory, usually used for church services, but due to overcrowding, it's being used in place of actual cells to house prisoners. Maybe they can open up some space if they didn't, for example, have someone like me in here for the Canola caper, surely the lamest crime in the history of this jail. Yet here I am, yes indeed. Little tiny five-foot by three-foot "mattresses" are abutted against each other all over the floor, there have to be at least thirty of them.

But this isn't the first thing I notice. That would be the twenty or so loud as hell criminals, all smoking, laughing, and seemingly happy as can be. It reminds me more of a summer cookout than jail. These fellas are having a good old time, whooping it up in the slammer! Hmmm, maybe this won't be so bad after all. These cats look like this is exactly where they want to be. Oh yeah, and they are mostly black dudes. I've shared schools and ball fields very amicably with black guys all my life, this doesn't faze me a bit.

Nobody looks twice when I join the party, their loud chatter and laughter continuing uninterrupted. I may as well be invisible; these guys don't give a shit about me. I am assigned a mattress slab, right next to the only other white guy in the room, probably not a mistake. This guy is a little more criminal looking than me, that's for sure, with tattoos and long hair. He is chillin' like everyone else in this weird and happy world they have created.

"What's up, Chump? I'm Junior, welcome to the Rock," he rattles off in a friendly tone, extending a hand. I shake and he rambles on. "First time? It's obvious Cuz. Man believe me Cuz this is the best possible situation in this joint. We don't do nothin' but hang around smoke and bullshit all day. Get yourself some commissary money, buy all the mother fuckin' shit you want and nobody gonna' bother you Cuz."

Junior didn't ask my name, I guess Cuz is going to suffice, which is fine with me. This guy can talk a blue streak, babbling a mile a minute. He doesn't seem too smart like maybe something is a little off with him, probably a high school dropout if I had to guess. But we are both here in the county jail, so who am I to talk? Right now I feel lost like I'm in a foreign land.

"Why'd you call it the Rock?"

"Rockland County Jail. The Rock, Dumb Ass," Junior answers as if this is common knowledge.

"And what's commissary money?"

"Oh Okay well somebody needs to put some money in your account Cuz and then you can buy whatever the fuck you want. Ring Dings, Ding Dongs, fuckin' Doritos, any kind of shit like that. Gotta buy plenty of cigarettes too, seeing if you smoke and all?"

"I do. Can I grub one off you?"

"Oh, you wanna bogart a smoke off Junior? Well, let me explain to you how this is going to go down. I got me a carton of Marlboro in my possession and I'll give you as many as you want Cuz. When you get that money, you gonna be giving Junior back times three! Otherwise, you gonna have ta quit if you don't like that deal Cuz because that's the best you gettin' Cuz."

This guy is gonna "Cuz" me to death. "Yeah yeah, no problem man, that's a done deal. Lemme get one!"

Junior smacks a new pack in my hand to get me started. I'll be up smoking all night. No way I'm lying down for a little shuteye with twenty who the fuck knows who moving freely about the room. Like I said, it is a classroom-sized space, but unlike school, bars cover the windows. Not safety bars so you won't fall out but big thick jail bars to keep you in. I can see Main Street through the glass, life going on like normal for everyone but me and all these happy idiots. My dentist's office is right down the road, like a block away. On my next visit, I'll have to let them know I did a little time right across the street, they'll be so impressed.

I see through the window some birds on a wire and think of summer mornings years ago, me and Billy would park down by the Hudson Terrace restaurant along the river and watch the sunrise after another night of driving drunk and chasing girls. We'd sit on the hood of my Olds drinking Bud long necks, using a slingshot to fire pebbles at the morning choir of birds on the telephone lines. Boys will be boys.

Billy man, so sad what happened to us. I thought we would be best friends forever, I loved that kid. Now I'm sitting in jail for something we did together, while he's off doing whatever amazingly impressive shit he does these days. It doesn't seem fair. Ain't life a bitch.

Sunday morning I am informed by a guard that somebody has filled my commissary account, so I now have the wherewithal to stock up on some butts and snacks. I am already in debt to Junior, three packs of Reds, plus nine Slim Jims, basically all I've eaten since I got here. It reminds me of a math test from years gone by; *if Cuz borrowed one pack of smokes and three beef jerky from Junior and had to return three times the amount borrowed, how much would Cuz owe Junior?*

I fill out a req, check off his stuff, and plenty for me too. One more day here in the joint, but better safe than sorry, so why not splurge? "Thank you so much!" I euphorically tell the guard, grabbing my bag of goodies. Ripping open a box of Chocodiles, I cram one in my mouth. Ravenous, I sit on my slab and stuff the rest of them in my face like a starving bum. This place is really bringing out the best in me.

CHAPTER 5

I CHAIN-SMOKE ALL THE WAY TO MONDAY MORNING AND MY SHOW-
down at the county courthouse, a majestic pillared relic that is connected
to this dirty, moss-covered jail. The most beautiful building in the city with
a hairy wart on its face.

A guard escorts me into the courtroom with handcuffs on, and of
course, my family is right there in the peanut gallery, staring at me as I enter.
The fucking shame I feel, regardless of how petty the crime, this shame that
fills my body is like molten lava in my veins. Everyone in my family has a
strange look on their face. They are all seeing something they cannot process, and it is leaving them in dumbfounded paralysis.

Ma often tells me that it's always darkest before the dawn. When you're
dealing with something bad, always remember that this is just a moment
in time, it will pass, and you will prosper again. I'm paraphrasing here but
trust me, she always has the words I need to hear. Even when, like now, she
can't say a thing. Mom prepared me for this.

I had spoken with my sister yesterday on the phone and she said that
Dad was working on getting me a good lawyer for court, but as they say in
Sara's Italian family, he came up with *ugotz* on judgment day. Because this
is such a low-level criminal case, it is deemed by my father that a public
defender can handle the matter. Let's hope he's right.

My case is called. I'm not nervous, although hearing "The people of the state of New York versus Bryan Grayhill" does sound a little ominous; that's a lot of people against me. But this isn't a big deal, I tell myself. Yes, I pulled a fire alarm, and it was four years ago. They sent me up the river for the weekend, I've learned my lesson, should be case closed. My parents and siblings brought a stack of letters that they presented to the court on my behalf, written by my bosses, my teachers, priests, and family pets, attesting to my otherworldly attributes and accomplishments. The Judge, perched gloriously high above us peasants, grazes over the paperwork with little interest, then calls me to my feet. Old as dirt with a mop of white hair, Your Honor isn't happy to see me. He is not happy ever, is my guess.

"Mr. Grayhill, you clearly have no regard for the law and no respect for this court, your parents, or yourself. This malarkey (yes, he said it!) does not sit well with me, not in the least."

Take it back down to DEFCON 1, Matthew, this is not starting out well.

"The recommendation of your Probation officer (this is all *her* fault!) is to release you this morning with time served, however in light of your callous disregard for authority, I'm going to go out on my own here. You will be remanded back to the county jail for the duration of the week and then released Friday afternoon. You will also be required to perform 200 hours of community service upon release."

Anything else you old fart?

"Bail is not possible," His Majesty continues, "as this case will be closed on Friday. The file will be sealed under youthful offender status, a gift from me. This will allow you the opportunity to learn your lesson and not be tarnished further by this matter moving forward."

The cranky old fucker smashes down the gavel, his words became my reality, and that's that. Yes, you do the crime you do the time, I get it, but this is nutso. I'm really spending the rest of the week in jail? Hey, good call on not getting a real lawyer, Dad. This public defender schmuck said nothing more than required by the court, I was doomed from the start. The fucking Shaggy DA could have put up a better defense for me.

My loudest thanks and FU goes to the probation officer Faith Macalroy. She's probably only a couple of years older than me and is in way over her head. One person was crying in the courthouse after the Judge threw the book at me, and it was her. My immaturity allowed me to place all the blame on her, how could she do this to me? She should have at least called me with a warning.

In the end, I did have a disregard for the law, the Judge was right on with that. Thank God they never caught me for the really bad shit I did...

I leave the courtroom with a sullen nod to my family. That's all I can offer as my hands are again cuffed behind my back. There is nothing to say anyway, the die has been cast. Back to the rectory; pray for me. Returning to the jail, I gear myself up for the next several nights. I'm ready, this doesn't scare me.

I'm not an overly emotional person by nature, don't get too high or low. I once had a girlfriend who equated my emotions to "a piece of dead wood floating down the river." I've gotten "Hello? McFly? Anybody in there McFly?" on more than one occasion due to my lack of emotion. It just takes a lot to move the needle for me. I'm not "dead inside," as I've been accused of, just naturally stoic; it runs in my family. We take life as it comes and figure it out as we go with some sarcasm and a wry sense of humor.

This whole experience should be a wake-up call for me, I definitely know that, and certainly plan on trying harder to make better decisions in the future, especially regarding the laws of the land. When push comes to shove, we'll see how I do.

Back to the rectory, I figure Junior will be surprised to see me. "Later Cuz, thanks for the memories," I told him upon departing for my hearing this morning, supremely confident my life in the Big House was over. Turns out Junior is the one no longer around, having been transferred or otherwise removed during my absence. He is in on a drug charge, like most of the guys here, and isn't getting sprung anytime soon. We hardly knew ya, Junior. This leaves me as the only white guy in the room. Nobody cares.

It's after "lights out" and my bunk mates, or fellow criminals, whatever you want to call them, are sleeping. I get up and step around their bodies, navigating through the mattresses on my tippy toes and quietly going to the door. I'm wearing a gun belt and in the holster, there is a bottle of Canola Oil. I swing open the door and surprise the half-conscious guard with a flying kick to the face, knocking out some teeth. He instinctively goes to pick them up, but then lets them lie and begins to chase me. I start running while shooting the Canola on the floor, then glance back to see the guard go head over heels, landing face down on the checkered tiles.

"Stop, Grayhill! What are you doing?" he bumbles through several missing teeth, lying helplessly on the floor. "You only have three days left, don't do this to yourself."

Ambling back to the fallen guard, I kneel and put my mouth next to his ear. "I can't do the time, Man. Sara's waiting for me Dude, she's not going to wait much longer. I didn't even do anything, why am I even in this place?"

Still facing the floor, the guard is drooling blood and begins laughing manically. "You heard the judge, Grayhill; you're full of malarkey, that's why you're in here." He finally looks up at me as I reach for his keys, and I see it's Mr. Timin from school, his smiling mouth glistening with spit and blood.

"Oh man Timin, you're a fuckin' mess," I remark with disgust. "Are you gonna call the coppers on me again, you little Baby?"

With that, huge tears start shooting out of his eyes like a cartoon and he cries, "Whaaa, whaaa." He's suddenly wearing a big man's diaper with a long pin in it. "You're such a bully! Such a … such a meanie!" he whines in a baby voice.

"Wow man, I'm sorry Timin, I'm sorry. I take it all back, all of it! It was just a prank!" I declare, and now I'm crying those big Baby Huey tears too, really wailing.

Timin stands up. He's magically back in his usual suit and tie, his teeth are Chicklet white, hair perfectly coiffed. Slowly he rears back and then punches me in the mouth so hard that his bloody fist, embedded with my teeth, comes out through the back of my head. This jolts me awake from the nightmare, both of my hands frantically touching my face and head, feeling for the blood and brain matter oozing out.

I'm pissed at myself for falling asleep in the first place but man, what was that damn dream about? Nobody's moving in the room and I consider trying to fall asleep again so I can get back to it. Instead, I light up a butt and think about it. I guess on the inside, I'm feeling bad in some way. Bad for Timin, bad for my Dad, even bad for Faith Macalroy. I've been feeling sorry for myself but maybe I should be worried about those I'm adversely affecting. Am I still dreaming, thinking like this? "Fuck them," I whisper under my breath.

CHAPTER 6

THE NEXT COUPLE OF DAYS PASS BY PRETTY UNEVENTFULLY. Nobody gives a rat's ass about anything but themselves in this room, I'm 100% ignored, which is of course fine by me. I took a shower Wednesday afternoon and was obsessed with not dropping the soap, another prison movie no-no. We all know what happens when you drop the soap! I ran into a guy from high school in the shower area, Keith Miller, which was briefly mortifying for me until I realized he was also in jail, so we were in the same boat. If anyone in school had marked us down for "Most likely to be incarcerated," you won.

"Grayhill," he addressed me as he walked by like we were in gym class instead of the slammer.

"Sup," I nodded casually, and that was that.

Meals are served on plastic trays, which we jailbirds eat while sitting on our little mattresses, like kindergartners at milk time. Thursday night, dinner was a shit sandwich that looked like someone regurgitated it from lunch directly onto my bun. I should have called the front desk and requested that Whopper! As always, I didn't eat their food, sticking with my Hostess treats instead. After mealtime, things change.

"Grayhill, gather your shit and come with me," charges the mustache guard from the day one cavity search, of which I've enjoyed several more since. I don't value anything in the world enough to hide it up my ass, but they won't take my word for it. I grab everything as instructed. My present life is all in one brown bag and consists solely of junk food and smoking materials. Junior taught me how to roll my own, reminding me of the Lucky Strikes with no filter that my Grandpa smoked when I was a kid.

"Where are we going?"

"Upstairs to block A. You're getting a big boy bed tonight in a real cell, and a new best friend," the guard informs me in a foreboding tone.

"Oh, uh, that's not necessary. I'm leaving tomorrow if somebody else wants to take my place. This doesn't seem fair." I watch television, my good sir, I know my rights!

"Not my call. This is what's happening, Grayhill, you don't have a fucking choice."

We climb up a flight of metal stairs, and now this jail thing is on. I am going behind bars, big thick bars, and this feels so much more dangerous than my time in the rectory. We stop at a row of cells, maybe five little lock-ups, all with the doors open, and then one main door to lock in all five. It's like stalls inside a barn. A little community of perps and it looks like I'll be having maybe ten new friends, not just one.

It's so dark. The walls are dark, the floor is dark and the lighting is dark. I can only make out silhouettes of the others as I walk past their cells. What the fuck? Is this a test of some sort on my last night, to see if I can make it in the big time? Did Timin call in a favor to get me up here?

"Lay low, nobody will bother you, Grayhill. Take the first cell right here," Mustache advises with surprising compassion as he clanks the barn door shut.

I put my paper bag on the bed. Looking at the sorry mattress, I think of the old broad from the burger commercial who cries out, "Where's the beef?" The cell area consists of that tiny mattress on a metal plank and a stainless steel sink with a toilet jutting out of the bottom. I should have reserved a suite.

One more long night to go. As I sit down and start to roll a cigarette, I notice there is a TV on the other side of the bars, within reach for us monkeys to change the channel and whatnot. Nobody is watching, at least not that I can see. Sally Jesse Raphael is on the black-and-white screen, squawking with some politician types on stage. I mosey on up to the TV, reach through the bars, and change the dial a couple of clicks until hitting "I Love Lucy," and then turn it up a pinch.

"Do. Not. Touch. This mother fuckin' TV again," some dude suddenly threatens in my ear from behind. His smoky breath breezes across my face and the menacing tone of his voice tells me it's time to brace myself, something is about to go down. Looks like it's time to brawl, but as I clench my fist for a fight that would probably end with me being taken to the morgue, a third party emerges from the dark.

"Back it down Cuz," a familiar voice demands of my tormentor. "This is my guy, he's good people!"

The smoke-breathing monster disappears without a word as I count my blessings.

"Junior! I'm so happy to see you, man, thanks Cuz! I thought you were gone," I said, giving him a man hug for saving my ass.

"Okay okay, easy on the hugs, Cuz. That's not a good look up here in the Zoo," he replies. "Give me a couple of smokes, we'll call it even."

"Yeah, sure thing Junior. Welcome to my little hellhole," I say to him happily as he sits on the stainless toilet in the cell and lights up the smoke I just rolled. "Damn Bro, I was sad to see you were gone. I figured you got sprung out of this joint."

"Na Cuz they threw me up here in the Zoo so they could watch me like a monkey in a cage they always shuffling guys out of the rectory don't like us to get too comfy down there these fucking guards," he babbles on, as discombobulated as ever. "Why you here Cuz you said you was rolling out on Monday," he finishes.

"Long story, Bro. It didn't work out like I thought it would."

"Never do Cuz, it never do. I got a month to go in the can," he continues, "then Junior's heading west, I'll go all the way to Hawaii if I can Cuz, that's where I need to be. My brother's out there in the military so that's where I'm heading next so I can work on my tan, been on the inside too long," he grins, showing me his chalky white arms.

A guard clanks the bars with his nightstick and says sternly "Back in your hole, Hippie."

I keep talking as Junior rises, telling him, "Hey, it's nice to dream. I hope it happens for you, Cuz. By the way, I am officially and positively getting out tomorrow, so thanks again for keeping me in one piece. I owe you, Cuz!"

"No problem, Rookie. Give 'em hell out there, maybe I'll see you out west one day," he says with a salute, tossing his butt in the toilet. "Fuck the Rock!"

"Fuck the Rock!" I shout back with my fist in the air, "Fuck it, Cuz!"

For the rest of the night, I smoke more than sleep. Hanging off the puny bed, my mind drifts to Sara and thinking about how I will explain to her my week of radio silence. Eventually, my thoughts arrive on our heavy petting and make-out session, at which time I even give brief consideration to a little yanky my wanky, but smartly decide better of it. The atmosphere isn't quite right, to say the least, and I do have some pride. Hope springs eternal has a whole other meaning tonight; tomorrow is my day to get sprung.

Friday morning, finally. The sun barely penetrates through the tiny jail windows as I eat a Twinkie for breakfast in my fancy new cell before being moved back downstairs again. I escaped block A unscathed, thanks to Junior. These guys are not doing hard time in the county jail, so any misstep will fuck things up good for them. They are not looking for more trouble; everyone just wants out.

I'm moved back to the holding area where I entered almost a week ago, and will now wait here for my brother to come pick me up. It has all been arranged, though when it happens exactly, I don't know. Nobody tells me anything around here.

I wonder how the past week of being MIA will be received by my friends. I'm sure nobody is too worried if they even noticed. It doesn't matter to me, except for Sara. My Sara experience was on simmer and getting ready to heat up when this little legal interruption hit. I'm sure she's confused, if she even still cares, about my being incommunicado for a week.

I finally see my brother enter the door and walk up to the front desk guard, who is behind the partition with the Burger King microphone. Finally, it's time to wake up from this nightmare. Ed sees me, purses his lips, and nods his head imperceptibly in my direction.

"How can I help you, Sir?" the guard asks Ed. He is not the same one that offered me a shit sandwich upon my arrival but I nonetheless have my fingers crossed that my brother wouldn't make the same mistake I did.

Ed plays it straight, of course. Unlike me, he's no dummy, saying only, "I'm picking up my brother, Bryan Grayhill. He's right there," pointing in my direction.

The husky guard struggles to his feet as if his underwear is made of cement. "Wow, you two look like twins," he smiles at Ed jovially. "It's like I'm looking at a Xerox copy. You handsome fellas should be on a soap opera or something."

"Yeah, we get that a lot, the twin thing. I'm a year older," Ed informs him in monotone, not looking to engage.

"Couple of good-looking fellas," he reiterates happily, easily the nicest prison guard ever. "Hey Tony, open up for Grayhill," he directs to my old friend Mustache.

"Let's do it," Tony says to me, as the lock to freedom clanks open with a turn of his key. I've already changed out of my orange inmate duds and am back into the dirty civvies (short for civilians, thank you TV) that I was wearing last Saturday. It was with great hesitation that I re-applied the droopy drawers that I was wearing a week ago. They were especially ripe after marinating in their own stench for several days inside a manila envelope. I have no possessions to collect other than my clothes, having left behind my remaining commissary booty in the cell upstairs. I figured it would make one of the guys happy, or maybe it causes somebody to get murdered. I don't really give a fuck.

Ed's car is right outside on the hill, parked exactly where the police cruiser dropped me off. I take in a deep breath of the great outdoors as we approach his ride, a very sweet Chrysler Laser that he proudly purchased all on his own. He sticks in the key and unlocks my side first, like the gentleman he usually is not. Ed opens the door and I notice there's a fluffy pillow on my seat.

Wow, a little jaunt in the slammer and I'm getting the kid-glove treatment. I sit on the pillow and say to Ed, "Let's get the fuck out of here man, no need to be so chivalrous. What's with the pillow?"

"I thought maybe your ass was sore from all the bangin' you took this week," Ed grins, and we share a laugh at that.

It's going to take me a lot of mental processing to calculate the effects this week behind bars has had, but right now I feel good, no worse for wear. In reality, this episode left a scar of shame across my psyche that will never not be there. You don't get paraded in front of your family with handcuffs on and then sit in jail for a week without some residual damage.

"Push in the lighter, Asshole," I tell him as Ed smokes his tires onto Main Street, leaving my strange trip behind. Matthew, take it back to DEFCON 5.

CHAPTER 7

O N THE WAY HOME, MY BROTHER STOPS AT TURIELLO'S PIZZA place in downtown Rockland; from one joint to another. We've been going here multiple times a week since moving from the Bronx in 1972. Ed and I used to walk here when we were in elementary school, little kids roaming the streets day and night, without fear, back when a dollar was enough for a slice and a fountain soda. There's another pizza place on the far side of town, but nobody I know goes there. Turiello's is king.

Ed is older than me by just one year but considerably wiser. He's always been the family's shooting star, while I'm the firecracker that blows your fingers off. Ed was born a scholar and cruised to a college degree. Conversely, I stunk up school with a bad attitude and minimum effort. We are a case study of how two people raised in the same environment could be so different in every possible way. Ed and I have very little in common but still, share an unbreakable brotherly bond. He is as funny as anyone I know, and our ball-busting is all in good fun. We've never come to blows, like so many other brothers.

He orders a couple of heroes for us to split, Chicken Parm and a Meatball. I grab two bottles of chocolate Yoo-hoo without asking Ed (we always drink Yoo-hoo) and plop down at a table across from the counter, while he pays. I'm a convict, my pockets are empty.

"I'll add this to the thirty bucks I put into your jail account, Dickface," he says, sitting across from me in a red vinyl-covered chair while stuffing the change into his Velcro wallet. "Anyway, tell me all about it. I'm dying to know the details."

We clink the glass bottles together and both sing out "Yoo-hoo," like the nerds in the commercial.

"Wash, rinse, repeat. The same exact shit happened every single day," I start, as we both light up and Ed pulls the tin ashtray between us. "Except for the last night, which was by far the worst, because they sent me up to the real cells and some angry fucker almost murdered me when I touched the TV. But being in the place didn't bother me much. The bullshit reason that I was even in there is what kills me. How do you get thrown in jail for something so stupid?"

"Yeah, at the end of court Monday, after they took you away, we all went outside the courthouse and were like, shocked really, just standing around trying to tell Mom it would all work out. That probation lady Grace or whatever her name is came over all apologetic and crying. Mom was pretty chill with her."

"It's Faith, and wait till I see her, I won't be chill on her at all," I say righteously. "Listen to this shit," I start. "One time I showed up in her office for probation and my hand was pocked with a bunch of little burn marks I got from working the sauté station at work. So this Faith chick sees the burns scabs and asks me if I have AIDS! I mean, you can't fix dumb, man. She fucked me over good."

"Whatever Dude, you need to calm down before you end up right back in the slammer. Shit's over now," he says, as a silver pizza plate with our sandwiches is put up on the counter.

"Eh, you guys all set," the owner Nico alerts us in a thick Italian accent. His lips are all but invisible under a bushy black mustache, which I jealously admire. Yes, this is our pizza place.

Finally home, Ed pulls up the driveway of our ancient house, a three-story behemoth straight out of the Addams family, hidden at the end of a dead-end street in South Rockland. I look for a yellow ribbon, tied around the old oak tree, as the Tony Orlando song plays in my head. Alas, no ribbon, but there is a little sign on the door, "Welcome home, Bryan." So humiliating. I wonder if Junior still gets a sign when he comes home.

My Mom and sister Lauren are waiting in the foyer as we walk in. Being all together is like looking through a kaleidoscope, us kids are carbon copies of our beautiful Mom, each with dark brown hair and a light Irish skin tone. Lauren has recently moved to an apartment in town, so this is a special trip for her. My mother bought this house without help over ten years ago, finally giving her three children a place to call home, after shuffling from apartment to apartment for the entirety of our young lives. This is our Shang-gri-la, and as with most of the good things in our lives, we have my mother to thank for it. Mom is the first to greet me upon entering the house, and I get a long hug with a few extra pats on my back as the familiar scent of her perfume envelops me.

"Yeah yeah, I know, the black sheep has returned. Thanks for the welcome party guys."

"Glad you're home, Bry," my sister greets me. "I'll keep the sign in storage for next time," she jokes.

"Laugh it up, Fuckers. Get it all out of your system, I'll give you a free pass for today."

"You mean like a get out of jail free card?" my mother quips. Hardee har har. Even Mom's a comedian.

"Whatever, Guys. Who knows the time?" I ask nobody in particular.

"Time for you to fly free, my brother," Ed chimes in with his own stupid jail joke while flapping imaginary wings.

My sister announces, "Okay family, I have to run. It is Friday night after all. Unlike the rest of you, I have a life."

I walk outside with Lauren, wanting to ask her what she knows about Sara. "Hey, I wanted to mention, Sara Addeo was asking about you a couple weeks ago, I saw her at Billy's kegger. Said she knows you from hanging out with her sister Tara at their house when you guys were in high school."

"Yeah, Sara was around back then, always with that smart-ass creep Chris Garvey. I never said anything to Tara but that kid used to stare at my tits all the time, even if Sara was sitting right next to him. What a skeeze," Lauren recalls. "And all they did was fight."

"That sounds like a fun relationship," I reply. "What's the point?"

"I don't know, Bry, what's your fuckin point? Why you asking about her?"

"We've been talking, that's all. She's pretty cool," I answer.

"Okay, well good luck with that," she says dismissively, adding a skeptical glare as well. "From what I heard the boy toy is still around. I just had drinks with Tara a few weeks ago, and you can't ever say I told you this or I will fucking kill you dead, but her sister said that Sara has some issues about being alone, something about their Dad when he was little, like he was an orphan or something, I don't know. Anyway, they've been trying to get her away from this kid Chris and she just keeps going back. So in summary, sucks for you, Dingleberry! Why don't you try the little sister instead?"

"What a great idea, why didn't I think of that?" I reply facetiously. "Well, I don't know about any boyfriend. She seemed pretty single the other night when we were playing a little game of tonsil hockey together."

"And we're done." Lauren swings an about-face and walks off.

"I'm just kidding around," I say, knocking on the window of her car but she ignores me and drives off.

My Mom and brother are conversing inside the door as I re-enter the house. "Okay, Jerks, think of something funny and maybe I'll laugh. I'm grabbing a shower and getting on with my life."

And that's it, I am back home like I'd never left. I go upstairs to the solitude of my room, pick up the phone, and call Sara. I'm a little nervous but hopeful the chemistry we shared during our previous conversations is still alive. She answers on the first ring. "Hello?"

"Hey Sara, it's me."

"Who's me?" she replies playfully. "Sounds like Bryan Grayhill, but I think he's dead because I've been trying to call him for a week and nobody knows where he ran off to."

I can tell she's happy to hear from me, which is a big relief. "Uh-huh, I'm sure it seems that way. Sorry about that. Let's get together tonight and I'll explain it all when I see you."

"Aww, I can't tonight, I already have plans. My college roommate is here for the day, but tomorrow is good for me. Is everything okay, Bry?"

"Yup, I'm good. Tomorrow works for me." Unless I get thrown back in the clink.

"Okay, I'll call you when I get up, Big Guy. We can get to the bottom of your mystery disappearance. You're not calling from the Bermuda Triangle right now, are you?"

"Nope, right here in good old Rockland," I reply, finishing off my cig and dropping it in a Diet Coke can already stuffed with other floating, stinky butts. "I'll be eagerly awaiting your call," I add with some sarcasm.

"You better be, Grayhill. Don't disappear on me again! Have a good night."

"You too. Don't do anything I wouldn't do," I say like a spaz.

I'm relieved; everything with Sara seems as good as I could have hoped for. Maybe things are about to start going my way for a change. This past week has me all wound up and I need to get out of the house for a while. "Ma, I'm going for a drive," I scream up the stairs.

"Okay Honey, be careful," Mom replies.

"Don't get arrested again, Asshole," Ed shouts.

"Try to get a life while I'm gone," I yell back while shutting the front door and leaving it unlocked, as always.

My '69 Olds is parked on the lawn off the left side of the driveway, out of everyone's way, since it's been sitting dormant for a week. Pulling open the dented car door, it makes a loud bang while disengaging from the front fender, as if the metal is being hit with a hammer. To say this thing is a shitbox would be putting it nicely. I fire her up and hear the Yankee game coming from the radio. I don't even know who they're playing, don't care either. The announcers are talking up Roberto Kelly, the next great center fielder, they say. I switch it off and rummage through my cassettes, not sure what I'm looking for, but I'll know when I see it. "Hell yes," I say in triumph, finding Springsteen's "Born to Run." Everyone is listening to the Boss's latest these days, "Born in the USA", but thanks to my sister I know his really good stuff came out a decade earlier. I hit fast forward because I'm close to the end, flip over the tape, and the harmonica on "Thunder Road" eases through the speakers.

Rolling off the lawn, I head to the Tappan Zee bridge, a three-mile span that crosses the Hudson River to Westchester County. Our street runs parallel to the water, the span only a stone's throw away.

One minute later I'm doing 75 in the left lane at the mouth of the bridge. I jump in on the song and sing along with Bruce ... "*Show a little faith, there's magic in the night, you ain't a beauty, but hey, you're all right,*" I shout, then throw a Red between my lips and push in the lighter.

I switch between singing and smoking for the next couple of hours as I also alternate thinking about what was and what will be. I follow the Deegan south past Yonkers raceway, to the Van Cortland Park exit in the Bronx, then make a U-turn back on the highway heading north and go right past the apartment house I was born in 20-something years ago. As I pass Van Cortland again, now on my left, I wonder what would have been if my Mom stayed in this neighborhood and we grew up here. Like so many of the Bronx Irish, our family escaped the "Boogie Down" for the suburbs as soon as we were able. I probably would have ended up in jail or something if we stayed.

I exit off the Deegan onto the Saw Mill Parkway in Elmsford. The Saw Mill is a bendy two-lane raceway with lots of trees and I fly around the curves doing at least 80, having the road all to myself and knowing it like the back of my hand. The Cutlass may not look great, but it still has some life left in the engine. I'm oblivious to where I'm going, just following the music. Billy Squire's "Everybody Wants You" blasts from the radio as I speed up the parkway with my brights on.

I'm looking forward to tomorrow. I'll be waking up in my own bed, after what will surely be the best night of sleep I've had in my entire life. I plan to rake the yard in the morning for my Mom as a surprise, to give her a little reminder that I can be a productive member of society, not that she has any doubts. Nobody believes in me more than my mother, no matter how much I screw up. Sara is also tomorrow; big day.

I'm not really thinking about the whole jail thing too much, just glad to be out. My eyes are getting heavy as I exit at Pleasantville then turn around in the Friendly's parking lot and get right back on the Saw Mill going south, the same as I did down in the Bronx an hour ago.

Eyes fluttering with exhaustion, the car now feels as big as a cruise ship, and I can barely keep it from drifting off towards the shoulder. Music pumping, windows open, I'm struggling to stay awake.

Finally pulling up our driveway a few minutes later, relieved to have made it without crashing, I kill the engine and toss my keys on the floor by the pedals. I shoulder bump the car door open and head to the house, taking two last pulls from my smoke and flicking the butt onto the asphalt.

It's nice to be free again. As I reach for the door handle, I'm thankful. The future is mine, again.

I brush my teeth and am immediately out like a light. No raping ass pirates to worry about tonight.

CHAPTER 8

WOKE UP SATURDAY AT TWO P.M., MY WEEK OF NO SLEEP IN THE Big House finally catching up with me. Thankfully I never mentioned to Mom that I was going to be working on the leaves today so she won't be disappointed that I didn't get around to it. I noticed when getting up to pee earlier, my red digital clock reading 9:55 at the time, that it was blazing hot for a September morning. I'm now soaked in sweat as I light my first butt of the day and drop the match in a soda can next to my bed.

After the smoke, it's straight to the shower. I make it a quick one to avoid the calf-high puddle of soapy water I'll soon be standing in, due to a drain that's been 90% clogged since the dawn of time. As an "adult," you'd think I would do something to alleviate a problem such as this, but instead, I simply ignore it and hurry through my shower. It never actually occurred to me that it would take less than five minutes to fix. I'll just slosh around in here for years and never attempt to solve the problem. This may be a pattern.

"Sara just called," Ed shouts through the door. "If you want to use the phone, do it now," he instructs me, "I need to make a call and I'll be on for a while."

"Okay, just give me a second to dry my ass." I hastily towel off then go to my room and call Sara back.

"Hello?" her Dad answers sternly.

"Hello Sir, is Sar—" I begin to ask.

"Hold on!"

"Who is it?" Sara asks in the background. Her Dad yells back, "*Come cazzo faccio a saperlo*?"

"Geez Dad, why do you have to be so rude," she complains to him before speaking into the phone. "Hello?"

"Sup Sara, it's Bryan. Checking in."

"Hi Bry," she says faintly, then loudly shouts "Dad hang up, I got it. Dad!" followed by the earthquake in my ear which is her father hanging up the phone. Serene quiet envelops the line, and then Sara continues. "Hey, sorry about that."

"Oh yeah, no problem. Thankfully I don't speak Italian."

"He's in a bad mood today. Don't worry, he wasn't talking about you."

"Good to know. So what's going on for tonight?" I ask.

"You're going to kill me," she starts, "but I forgot I made plans with Heather and those guys for later, she reminded me last night. We're going to the Crossing in Congers. You can totally meet me if you want to."

"Eh, maybe," I play it nonchalantly. "I'll see if Pat wants to go with me. I'm not really down to hang out with your grade all night, I'm not feeling that."

"Whatever you think, Bry, it'll be fun though, lots of people will be there," she goes on. Sara is the only one I want to see.

"Okay, on second thought count me in, sounds rad," I reply halfheartedly, figuring I'll take what I can get.

All of a sudden the sound of a phone being dialed comes across the line. Beep boop beep beep beep boop bop. "Ed, I'm on the phone, I'm on the phone!"

"I told you to hurry up. Let's go!" he screams back.

"Give me a second, Man," I reply, waiting to hear the click of him hanging up before giving Sara the okay to continue.

"Cool, I'll be there at 10. Heather is picking me up so maybe you can drive me home like last time?" she asks in a flirty tone.

"Your wish is my command, Queen Sara. See you later," I sign off, then shout to Ed. "It's all yours!"

After my brother finishes with the phone, I call Pat and he is cool to meet me at the bar around 10. He lives 15 minutes from the Crossing and will walk over after the Met game.

"Sara Addeo, huh?" Patty Funk questions me. "You're really swinging for the fences with this one. I heard she gets around my man. Easy as Sunday morning."

"That doesn't even make sense, Asshole." I snap back.

"Don't get pissed at me. All I know is she has a lot of experience driving a stick," he giggles.

"Yeah man, you're hilarious. Nobody knows how to drive a stick better than you, Funk. Clean up tonight, try not to be such a smelly pig and maybe some heifer will pop your fat cherry," I half joke in an annoyed tone.

Arriving to the bar promptly at ten, I park right against a fence adjacent to some railroad tracks. It's called the Crossing for a reason, long freight trains pass by only 75 feet away. The gang's all here. Through a thick blue haze of cigarette smoke, I see the Funk yapping it up with some guys from the class of '83 he played football with, over by the pinball machine in the corner. The place is pretty small, all dark woods and neon beer signs, music I don't recognize blaring throughout.

"What's up, Palooka?" I greet Pat while simultaneously nodding at his boys.

"Doing well Gay-Hill, doing well," he smirks while motioning with his head toward the bar. "Your lady awaits."

"Thanks, Funky Brewster. You working on a little 'stache there, Patty?" I ask, noticing some random dark stubs struggling to grow above his lip. "You're really trying everything to hold on to that cherry as long as you can."

Patty strokes his new whiskers in admiration, then starts rapping. "Ladies love me, girls adore me, even the ones—"

I walk off mid-verse. Sara is with the aforementioned Heather and some other friends, all of whom are a couple of years older than me. It doesn't matter, they are invisible, it's Sara or bust tonight. When she sees me, Sara runs over and jumps in my arms, not caring who is watching, and lays one on me for the whole place to see. Her showy greeting is a relief, I wasn't sure if she was going to be standoffish because of my disappearance, or because I am a couple of years younger than her, and also her friends are all here, looking on with interest. She has the most amazingly beautiful white teeth, her smile so bright it could be a picture hanging in a dentist's office.

"I am so happy to see you! I missed you!" she tells me gleefully, grabbing my hands.

"Yeah, me too. I was starting to think I was never going to see you again after Billy's kegger."

She holds one finger up, smiles, and says "Well first, you didn't call me for like a week straight for whatever freaking reason, and second," she continues while popping another finger in the air, "I had some stuff of my own to take care of."

"Okay great, we both took care of some shit. Now we can get down to business."

"Seriously though, Bry, where have you been? It was weird, I was getting worried."

"I was in jail all week," I reply with a grin.

"Haha, that's a good one. Me too," Sara laughs.

"Let's talk about last week next week, how does that sound?"

"I don't even give a fuck honestly, I'm just glad you're here now, Bry Guy!" she smiles.

Wow, I went from the Big House to the Penthouse in one night. Inmate of the year right here. We hang out at the Crossing for a few beers and then head back to the chess tables by her apartment.

The rest of the night is a carbon copy of the last time we were together. We smoke (mostly me), drink (mostly me again), and fool around a little, right out in the open on this hot September night. No jackass cops show up this time to shoo us away. I came clean about the week prior, telling her "I shit you not, I was in jail last week. It was all having to do with that asshole Timin at the school from a couple of years ago. I'm so stupid."

"Oh yeah, Cara told me about that when I was away at college. She said they made a big deal about it back then."

"Yeah, well four years later, it's finally dead. This is the last chapter, besides community service, which I have to do at 8 o'clock this morning," I frown.

"So crazy. That's the last place I thought you were. Jesus, I can't believe you were actually in jail."

"Well don't judge me on it. I'm not as white trash as I sound."

"Like I give a shit!" she glows. "With lips like these," stroking my lips with her index finger, "and an ass like this," she purrs, taking a chunk in her hand, "you're good with me, Grayhill."

I finally walk Sara to her door and we stand there kissing for another few minutes, the dim porch light not slowing us down. "One more thing before you go," she says, with the finger up again. "Like I said in the bar, I had some stuff of my own to take care of, that's why I couldn't hang out before. You know I went out with Chris Garvey on and off for a long time and even some since I got back from college—"

"I've never heard of him," (not true), "but if this guy is still around then by all means, don't let me get in the way."

"Chill out, Big Guy, that's not what I'm saying. I had to tell him it's over before exploring this thing with you. So I did, and it's over," she emphatically states.

"Okay, cool. Let's get it on!" I jokingly sing as if I'm Marvin Gaye, feeling so relieved Sara mentioned that her old boyfriend is out of the picture now. We share another make-out session before I finally drive off as the sky lightens with morning.

Bleary-eyed a few hours later with my head spinning from just being so damn tired, I skid to a halt in the gravel parking lot of the address given to me for community service. It is 7:55 and I've had no more than two hours of sleep. Thank God for my atomic alarm clock. I am one block north of the county jail at a little work trailer in the middle of a vacant lot. I shut off the Olds, push down the lock on the passenger side, and get out of the car. The front fender makes its loud pop, announcing my arrival to the group of degenerates who are standing around shooting the shit, waiting to work.

At eight o'clock sharp, a tough-looking Army type marches out of the trailer to address the motley crew in his command. There are about 15 or so guys on this detail, from the very rough-looking to others that seem quite out of place. Burglars and Bankers, I'd say I fit somewhere in the middle. "Listen up," yells Crew Cut, wearing a tan police uniform with a gold sheriff star on the chest. "If this is your first rodeo, then find a guy that's been here before and get the gist from him."

Three minutes later we're all jammed into a little yellow bus, on our way to who knows where. When I was in school they called this the Short bus, the connotation being that the kids on here were a little short on smarts. Ironic because here I am riding blindly down the road with these criminals. Turns out I'm no genius either.

When I was little, my mother drove the retard bus, as it was also known, and I used to ride with her from time to time. Memories from back then are few and far between, but I still recall being amazed that the little bus had a big handle for the door like a regular-sized bus, and I proudly swung those doors open at each stop, pretending I was in charge. I also remember singing "Me and Julio Down by the Schoolyard" with my Mom on the mini-bus, as she drove and I sat in the seat behind her. The reminiscing is diverting my attention away from this present misery.

My seatmate elbows me back into reality. "Yo, I'm Tommy," he announces, his curly black hair suffering from a severe case of bedhead. "We're going to the leaf pile today, I can tell. I've been there for the last two weeks. It's a disgusting pile of wet leaves, from all over the whole county, one big mountain. We just have to climb up and push them down."

"Okay, thanks, Tommy. Sounds like a great morning," I say facetiously. Community service is raking wet leaves? I pictured reading to the elderly or teaching sports to children, not doing the community garbage work.

Well, this heap is indescribable, and the stench is enough to convince me that my rake will hit a dead body any second. It's such a unique and ghastly odor, I don't think I'll ever forget it as long as I live. We spent four hours in this radioactive garbage dump.

On the bus ride back to our meeting spot, I am ready to pass out from the stink, but it doesn't seem to bother anyone else. The group is rambunctious, most of the guys hooting and hollering. Being in trouble is fun! I don't get it, this is misery, but to each his own. I'll be keeping to myself, thank you.

Arriving back at the cars, I get a blanket from my trunk and spread it across the front seat to keep it from stinking. The irony is not lost on me that last night I had the most beautiful girl in town sitting right here on this seat and a few hours later, here I am wet and dirty after three hours of forced labor. I'm going to have to find a way to compartmentalize this demeaning work and not let it bring me down. Next time I'll daydream of Sara and try to block out the reality that I'm just another loser on the chain gang.

CHAPTER 9

'VE BEEN BACK TO WORK AT FREDDIE'S FOR A MONTH NOW, NO harm no foul. The jail thing is way back in my rear-view mirror like it never happened. Freddie's is a big restaurant in Tarrytown, New York. It's a popular spot for casual food and drinks, as well as a fun place to work.

"Dirty Box, add on two Chinese chicken, three all day," I yell to the salad man Jake, who someone affectionately nicknamed that because he smells like a musty attic.

"Gimme an all day," Jake whines back while littering his station with lettuce and everything else he touches as we tornado through a hectic lunch.

"Three Chinese Chicken, two Beef Taco, one Chicken Taco, and three Club, one no tomato," I shout.

Dirty Box is in the weeds, someone's going to need to jump on with him. I'm working the "window" for lunch today, which means I organize checks as they come in, call them out to the line cooks, garnish with fries or whatever is required and make sure the tables go out complete. I'm running the show, if lunch goes down the tubes, it's on me.

"How long on table 45?" asks the expediter, a manager who pulls the plates from the window and then calls for runners to send them out.

"Two minutes," I blindly reply, because two minutes is what we always say, even on a well-done burger that's not even hit the grill yet. Just keep the line of tickets moving, keep talking to the other cooks and lunch will be over in a blink, which it is.

Every restaurant has an employee section and after the lunch rush, I'm devouring a bacon cheeseburger upstairs at table 81. Meanwhile, the "Dubs" seated around me smoke and bitch about the kitchen, customers, and whatever else is bothering them. Dubs is slang for waiter/waitress; restaurants use their own language for everything. In all of the places I've worked at, usually, most of the staff gets along amazingly well. Drugs and alcohol are the glue that keeps the team together. Hooking up with a co-worker happens all the time, and who's doing who is always the talk of the employee section. Everyone is around my age, so this is like the college partying scene I never had.

I began my employment here a year ago as a busboy and have now done practically every job in the place except bartender. I've been working in restaurants since I was fourteen years old. My first job was as a dishwasher, paid cash under the table, no working papers required. The business has always come easy to me and is full of fun people, most of them hot girls.

The servers at Freddie's can easily be mistaken for clowns as they sit around in their vertically striped red and white uniform shirts, looking like referees for the circus. Some dubs also wear suspenders with buttons stuck all over them, like "Nano nano," and "Cowabunga," basically advertising their virginity.

I stub out a smoke in some ketchup on my plate and rise. I'm switching to the front of the house tonight and will be waiting tables. My strategy is to make the high hourly rate in the kitchen during the day and move out on the floor for the cash at night. I'm the only two-way player on the team. Not to toot my own horn but I'm easily the best at both. I run circles around the other dubs and work every station on the line faster and cleaner than almost anyone else. I'm humble to boot.

With one last table camping in my section at the end of the night, a busboy hands me a note written on a folded-up cocktail napkin that reads "Hey Hot Stuff, come find me at the bar," with a big red lip print at the bottom. I smile and stuff it in my pocket.

I've been expecting Sara to come in tonight. She's a server at a bar across town, which makes me insanely jealous because I know what goes down in this business. We've been spending all of our free time together over the last four weeks and can't get enough of each other.

Sara is dressed in her work clothes, the typical black and white worn by most hospitality staff. The only place you can wear a Freddie's shirt is Freddie's. "Hey, Babe!" I smile at Sara and jump the two steps up to the bar. "How was it?" I ask, swooping in for a kiss.

"Hi, Handsome," Sara whispers, leaning over for another quick peck. "It was good, same as usual. Hundred bucks, first out, no complaints," she answers while taking a sip of her current favorite wine, Sutter Home White Zin.

I point out to Sara my last customers, sitting among a bunch of empty tables. "There's some campers left in my section, I dropped that check an hour ago," I complain. "Let me go clear everything but the tablecloth, see if they get the hint, and leave."

Sara looks at the two guys I'm talking about and grabs the back of my shirt as I begin to walk away. "Bry, those two fuckers are the guys that ditched out last week and stuck me with a $25 check," she exclaims, rising to confront them.

"Wait, are you sure?" I ask her.

"No doubt, one hundred percent."

"Stay here, I'll take care of it."

I walk over to the table the two are sitting at, pull out a chair, and sit down with them. They are a couple of average-looking white guys, about my age. "Hey Fellas," I began as I push the bill across the table, "what's taking so long to pay this? You guys have been sitting here for like an hour. Don't even fucking think about pulling the dine and dash on me."

"Dude, you can't talk to us like that!" Bozo number one, wearing a Mets hat (of course), declares. "There's no law against taking our time."

"I make the law tonight, you Little Fuck. I know you guys skipped out on your bill at The Beer Tap last week, too," I challenge them, as they look at each other with a knowing glance. "So you're going to pay this bill right now in front of me, with a nice tip for my time."

Met hat throws two twenties on the tip tray as they both rise to leave. "Here's your money, Bro, but I don't know anything about the other one at the Beer Tap. You got that mixed up," he informs me.

I block their path. "Oh, I'm sorry, I got it mixed up? Tell you what, I'll pay your tab from last week at The Tap, you don't have to worry about that anymore. Instead, I'm going to knock the shit out of you and your stupid friend, right here and right now. I'll give you a twenty-five-dollar tune-up, how's that sound, Mr. Met?"

They are toast. Tweedledum throws two more twenties on the table and Mets hat promises, "We'll see you again, Tough Guy," as they begin to walk out.

"For your sake, you better hope you don't. Stay the fuck out of here, and The Tap also. Tell your punk friends too." I snatch the money and bring it up to Sara, who has been watching the entire episode. "They said sorry," I lie. "It was an oversight on their part."

"Yeah right, what bullshit. But thanks for getting it, you're awesome. That was a real turn-on, Grayhill!"

"I'm glad you liked it. You can show me your appreciation when we get home," I smirk.

CHAPTER 10

NOTHING IS MORE EXCITING THAN NEW LOVE. THE FIRST THING you do in the morning after opening your eyes is think of that special person, and you're still smiling when your head hits the pillow at the end of the day, more in love than you were when you woke up.

Sara and I were parked in my car last week hanging out, fogging up the windows, when the Spinners came on the radio. "*Could it be I'm Falling in Love, with You Baby?*" breezed through the speakers.

Sara leaned toward her window and wrote "*I love Bryan*" in the condensation on the glass, adding a big heart next to her declaration. This was a milestone moment.

"I'm totally falling in love with you," Sara declared. "I already do love you."

I didn't know until she said it, but I was right there with her. "I love you too, Baby. I'm having the time of my life."

After we leave Freddie's, I watch her headlights in my mirror as Sara follows behind and still can't believe she's even into me, much less *in love* with me! She has turned my life around one hundred percent for the better since we began spending time together, I feel like I won the lottery. Sara's giving me some self-worth, which was at an all-time low after my week in jail. I'm ready for whatever is next with her, I can't wait. This is what I want.

I fell asleep watching TV last night after Sara left. I realize this as my sister Lauren kicks my feet, which are hanging over the edge of the couch, and wakes me up.

"What the fuck, Man?" I lash out.

"Get up Bryno, I need to ask you something," she states casually, not caring that she's disturbed me.

"Ah jeez, what's the problem," I ask, lighting up a Marlboro. "Why are you bothering me? I thought we were rid of you around here," I finish in a playful tone.

"Move into my apartment," she blurts out. "I sleep at Jeff's most of the time so I'm hardly ever there and I know you wanna get out of here," she reasons, "not to mention I need a break on the rent."

"Well, what happens when he dumps you? Then I'll be stuck staring at your ugly face every night!"

She scoffs. "Worry about your own little love affair, Jeff and I are solid." Lauren and her new guy have only been together for a couple of months. He is the lead singer in a bar band that has a pretty good local following, mostly young ladies. It isn't the ideal job for a boyfriend and I wouldn't bet on the relationship lasting too long. He is actually pretty cool; I'm hoping he sticks around.

Isn't this ironic? Lauren's three years older than me. She used to padlock her room shut to keep me out, and now she's asking me to live with her.

"Okay, okay, slow your roll," I implore, "give me a second to wake up." I snort some smoke through my nose as I sit up and think about it for two more seconds. "Yes. I'll do it." It's a no-brainer, why the hell not? The most obvious reason to say yes is it gives Sara and me a place to shack up without having to look over our shoulders every five minutes.

"How long's the lease?" I inquire. "I don't want to be locked in on that shithole."

"You've never even seen it Jerk, how can you say that? I can easily find someone else if you think it's such a shithole." She continues on, "And its month to month, we split the $600 rent and a few bucks for utilities."

"Word up, that's a done deal. When can I move my stuff?" I ask.

"First of all," she starts, "you don't have any stuff. Second of all, it's already furnished. I rent it from Mr. Munson, my friend Kelly's Dad. His parents used to live there."

"Cool, some old folks died in my new bed. Looking forward to it," I joke. I really am looking forward to it, a lot. This is going to be great.

She scrawls down the address with some directions and instructs, "Meet me there tonight after work and I'll show you around the place. I won't be there for the weekend, so knock yourself out. Oh, and I need $300 on the 1st."

"Wait, that's in like a couple days Lau, gimme a break here, I haven't even woken up yet," I plead.

"Dude, you have a full-time job and no bills. Welcome to the real world! Put your money where your mouth is or I'll find somebody else."

The phone rings as I am about to confirm. I get up to answer, still joking around with Lauren. "Okay Boss man, Toby be good and pay da' rent. I be real good fo da' massa." I put the phone to my ear and give Lauren a thumbs up as she waves goodbye.

"Bry, it's Billy!" my former friend Billy Gorman yells into my ear before I even say anything.

"Hey Man, what's up?" I reply, wondering why he's calling out of the blue. We haven't spoken since his keg party and if it was up to me, that's the way it would've stayed.

"Dude, you are not going to believe where I am right now!" he shouts excitedly, "Take a guess."

I have no idea, and I couldn't care less. "You got me Bro, sounds like maybe at a payphone in Times Square?"

"No, not even close. I'm doing 80 right now on the Palisades Parkway! I'm talking on a fucking car phone, Dude! How does it sound?"

"Wow, that's insane! Who do you know that has a phone in their car? I've never even heard of that."

"I know right? It's my Uncle, he's like a millionaire stock guy. It's a big Lincoln with a sunroof, and the phone is right here on—"

Just like that, the connection ends, which is perfect timing for me. Now I don't have to make any false promises to get together. He was obviously calling to show off. Pretty cool though, I'll give him that.

CHAPTER 11

THE NEW APARTMENT IS WORKING OUT EVEN BETTER THAN I could have hoped. As promised, Lauren is never here, like I prayed she wouldn't be. Her boyfriend Jeff lives five minutes away, but I haven't seen her in weeks. Here's hoping one of his little groupie girls doesn't mess things up for me, I don't want Lauren showing up at my new place anytime soon. Sara and I are spending all of our free time together, and this is our home base.

When I was a sophomore in high school, a movie came out that changed my life in a couple of ways. "My Tutor" was the story of this rich kid whose parents got him a super-hot tutor to help him study for a big test. Along the way, she teaches him all about the birds and the bees, and the T's & A's as well. Relevant then because this guy was living my fantasy. Relevant now because Sara has become *my* tutor and she is giving me the sex education that I didn't know I was missing. Talk about clueless, I had no idea. Everything me and my friends know about sex we read in Penthouse Forum. Tonight I'm getting another free lesson.

"C'mon, Bry. I can't believe you never fucked anyone doggy style," Sara purrs, as she rolls over on all fours and sticks her ass up toward me. "Grab my hips and jam that thing in," she instructs. So I did. I'm not one to deny a lady's request.

After the most exciting minute of my life is over, Sara heads off to the bathroom. I jump up right behind her and follow, pressing my body against hers as she looks in the mirror. "Fuck man, that was amazing. Thanks, Baby. You make me feel so good," I whisper in her ear. "What did I ever do to deserve a girl like you?"

Yes indeed, life feels like a magic carpet ride these days. Our relationship was growing stronger by the minute and nothing was going to slow us down. At least that's the way it seemed.

It's the last weekend before Christmas, which will fall on Tuesday of next week. It's an exciting, joyful, festive, and chaotic time for all. Sara and I are rock solid. When she says goodbye to me, Sara sometimes tells me "I love you more than anybody loves anybody."

"I love you more today than yesterday," I'll sing back, "but not as much as tomorrow." And so it goes.

Tonight is Friday and we are both working. I'm on the line at Freddie's and will get out early, but Sara works the lounge late at The Tap and she won't be done until after midnight. We plan to meet back at the apartment afterward like we do every weekend. She has a key so she can get in anytime.

I get home a little after eleven and leave my ratty work sneakers by the front door; do that in the summer and they'll be crawling with ants in the morning. After stubbing out a butt, I climb to the second floor apartment, peel off my clothes, throw on some sweats, and plop down to watch some TV.

Sportscaster Warner Wolf is doing his shtick on channel 2, excitedly shouting his trademark lines "swish" and "let's go to the videotape." I'm half paying attention as I am not a fan of winter sports and don't care what the Knicks or Rangers are doing. I'm Yankees only.

Next thing I know it's five a.m. and the tube is buzzing with the black and white bullseye thingy, indicating that the broadcast day has ended. I light up a Red and try to gather myself. Sara is not here. What is happening? Well, there's nothing I can do at this hour to confirm if she's okay, or even where she's at. My only option is to drive across town and check her apartment complex. Surely she has a good reason for not being here. Damn, I wish the answering machine was working, although if Sara had called, I assume the ringing would have woken me up.

I pull into her parking lot ten minutes later and Sara's spot is empty, so I furiously cruise around like a psycho, looking for the little blue Ford she drives but it's nowhere to be found. The sun is up now as I angrily return to my place. I'm back home and of course, no Mustang waiting here either. I trudge upstairs and fall back on the couch again, hoping against hope that this whole thing didn't just go to shit, but feeling that it probably did.

I leave the phone on the coffee table, right in front of my face, in case Sara calls. It rings at 11 a.m. and practically startles me onto the floor. Up until this point, our relationship has been perfect, not a cross word has been spoken. That's about to change, in a big way.

"Hello," I croak through a fog of cigarette residue and exhaustion.

"Hey Bry, how was your night last night?" Sara asks as if she's lying right here next to me.

Play it cool, Brother, I remind myself. Never let 'em see you sweat. "Ah yeah, my night was good. Where were you, I expected you over here after your shift."

"No Bry, I told you I was going home last night after work, my auntie is here for the holidays and I wanted to hang out with her this morning," she tells me, convincingly enough.

"Oh cool beans, I must have missed that. Did you go straight home from work?" I calmly ask, then take my tone up a notch, "because when I drove past your place at like 5:30 this morning, your car was nowhere in sight. And you know we had plans last night, like every fuckin' night, so where the hell were you, Sara?" I am now losing my cool. Frankly, I'm surprised it took this long. "Please don't give me this bullshit story about your aunt, I'm not fucking retarded," I bellow.

"Whoa whoa whoa whoa whoa," she cautions. "Who the fuck do you think you are? Please don't tell me you think I'm lying about being home with my auntie."

"I know you're lying. Where was your car if you were home? Auntie Schmanty, Sara, the fucking jig is up. For all I know you were hanging out with your old boyfriend that you told me about. Did you give him a little Christmas gift to unwrap? You know I heard some shit about you being easy, I guess it was all true."

"Oh, you heard I'm easy, huh?" Sara asks, now fully pissed. "You don't know shit! Don't believe everything you hear, Bryan. I was with one guy in high school, one fucking guy!"

"My ass, one guy. That's hilarious," I scoff, then continue to press about her whereabouts last night. "Anyway, answer the question, where was your car?" So much for playing it cool. Words are flying out of my face faster than I can process the damage I'm doing.

"My sister Cara had my car last night, you Prick, I have no idea where she was. And for you to think I was with Chris, or anyone else, that's messed up too. You don't love me like I thought. Who even are you right now? *Puoi andare a farti fottere!!*"

Uh oh, she's breaking out the Italian. Did I jump the gun here? Could I be wrong? No, I wasn't. I *knew knew knew* she was up to something sneaky last night. With who or what and where I'm not sure, but something went down. Still, I need to take a deep breath and relax. Mom always told me to count to three before blurting out something that I would regret, and as usual, I didn't follow her advice. "I'm sorry for losing my shit there," I apologize. "I don't know what the fuck you did last night, but I know you messed this up because you were supposed to be here and instead found something better to do. I hope you had a good time! Have a Merry Christmas!" I shout sarcastically, then slam the phone back down in its cradle without letting her respond. When it starts to ring incessantly, I rip it out of the wall and throw it in the street, then let out a primal roar. "FUUUUUCKKKK!!!"

CHAPTER 12

I'M NOT WORKING TONIGHT, SO I GRAB A FEW THINGS AND GO TO my Mom's, in case Sara is planning on coming over to my apartment and pleading her case. She could just as easily be coming to tell me to fuck off, but either way, I want to avoid her. I'm still fuming over the whole situation and will likely wreck everything forever if I don't take some time to myself. Look at me, thinking things out!

I've been in limbo since the fight with Sara. It's the same feeling I had several months prior when I was sitting in the Rock on my first night, the uncertainty of it all leaving a similar pit in my stomach.

Sunday morning, I wake up at the crack for my community service crap. We've graduated from the leaf pile to spending the last several Sundays hammering tiles on the roof of somebody's mansion. It's probably the mayor's house, for all I know.

I pop the door of the Olds and head out, slowly rolling down my street and steering the wheel with my knee while lighting up a smoke. A piece of white paper is folded under my wiper, so I turn them on, swishing whatever it is up to the corner of the windshield so I can reach out and grab it. I stop the car and open the handwritten note. It says only "ti amo," which means nothing to me. I was kind of hoping this was something from Sara, and that may be, but for now, it shall remain a mystery.

After completing another morning of slave labor, I stop into my favorite deli in town on the way back and grab the Sunday staples; The Daily News, and a bacon, egg, and cheese on a roll. This deli is a family-owned place with the parents and kids working the counter. When Ed and I used to walk to town as youngsters, our Mom would tell us to get her cigarettes or whatever at this same deli, the "Bigots," she would call it. What did we know, we thought that was the name of the family that owned it. Wrong. That's not who they were, it's what they were. Ironic considering they would be out of business without money from the folks they slandered.

As I leave, a local bum approaches me. He's a fixture on the streets here in Rockland, well known for his shopping cart full of junk. "Lemme get a cigarette, Boss man?"

I take two out of the new pack, light them both, and hand him one. "Here you go, Pops."

Back at Mom's, I pull up the driveway and park at the top, intending to bring out the hose and wash my car, right after I wolf down my sandwich and check headlines in the Sunday paper. It's a mild enough day and also, the car has "*I love dick*" written in the trunk dirt, no doubt courtesy of Ed. I fill up a bucket with hot water at the kitchen sink and squeeze in a little Palmolive, then spray the car down.

Exhausted and heartsick, I aimlessly go through the motions as quickly as possible. I have an old Yankees beach towel in the trunk and grab it to wipe off any standing water. With the trunk lid open, I can see the wet driveway through the rotted quarter panels. This car is a rusty blue bucket of bolts that has ripped seats, a cracked windshield, and the steel in the belted radials popping through the bald surface of the front tires. Expectations are low, I only require it to start up and go. She didn't justify the wash, but I am killing time and thinking about my next move with Sara.

Mom's yellow VW Bug clickity clacks up the driveway, stopping right behind me. I'm not looking but there's no mistaking the sound of a Bug. She parks right on top of the hose and shouts out "Hi Honey!" loud enough for the whole neighborhood to hear, asking, "To what do I owe the pleasure?"

"Hey, Ma. I'm trying to wrap up the hose so please back up a little, you parked right on it."

She rolls back a foot and continues. "So nice to see you," she cries out, as enthusiastically as ever. "What are you up to?"

"I'm going to watch the Giants/Cowboys game with Ed," I lie, not wanting to share my business, although it might be fun to see him go nuts if Dallas loses. His epic meltdowns are a sight to behold.

"Is Sara coming over?"

So much for not sharing my business. "She's not, Ma. We got in a pretty gnarly argument Friday night and aren't exactly on speaking terms right now."

"Oh, Bryan," she starts in, "I'm so sorry Honey. Is there anything I can do to help?"

"No Ma, there's not. She didn't show up after work Friday and I wigged out."

"Oh Honey," she says, rubbing my back as I dry the hubcaps. "It will all work out."

"It won't work out Ma, 'cause she was with her old boyfriend and is lying about it. She said she wasn't but the more I think about it, I know in my gut it's true."

"Sounds like she's trying to sell you the dog, Honey," my mother tells me. I look at her quizzically, as if she's speaking a foreign language. "When I was a kid, that's what we said when someone told us a big lie; don't sell me a dog!"

"Good to know, Ma. It's practically the nineties so let's keep up with the times. She's full of shit, that's all you gotta say."

"Well fine, maybe she's full of shit, but my advice is to just give her a chance, you never know," she pleads. "I saw her here this morning, I heard a car and looked out. Maybe she wants to talk, Honey."

"Oh okay, then that explains this," I reply, screeching open my door to get the note I found on the windshield this morning. "I didn't know what this was."

"Aw, I love you, it says, "ti amo," I love you in Italian," my Mom informs me.

A flash of happiness hits me until I think of the big picture. "Yeah, right. She loves me, and she loves him too."

CHAPTER 13

I'M REALLY MISSING SARA SO MUCH. I JUST FEEL AWFUL AND empty, especially about going off the way I did and not even listening to her side. Maybe the whole Auntie thing is legit. Whether her story is bullshit or not, I need to let her tell it. I hop in the Cutlass and head back to my apartment, making a pit stop along the way at the A&P to grab some frozen pizza and Diet Coke for tonight. I'll call Sara when I get back to the apartment and see what's up.

I'm on the express line at the grocery store, 10 items or less. I always count everybody's stuff on the quick checkout line and of course will be the first one to confront anyone who exceeds the limit. The cashiers don't care, so somebody has to speak up for the rule followers. I'm the ultimate hypocrite who only cares about rules when I'm adversely affected by others not obeying them. I recognize the guy in front of me in line, he owns "*Frank and Beans*," the popular hot dog joint on Broadway, a couple of doors up from Turiello's Pizza. They have good food and a reputation for making everything fresh while you wait. Mr. Fresh Dog dumps several boxes of "Weenie-Licious" brand Corn Dogs on the conveyor. He looks at me sheepishly, knowing he's busted buying this frozen crap to sell as his own. Another liar, par for the course on this fucked up weekend. Don't worry Guy, I got bigger franks to fry.

It starts raining on my way home, just enough to ruin the car wash. I lug a brown bag full of junk food (less than ten items, of course) upstairs and throw it all in its respective spot, opening and closing the fridge door quickly to avoid the rotten smell trying to escape. I sit down on Lauren's bed to call Sara, necessary because the living room phone is out on the street somewhere, in pieces. All these barbaric behaviors have been passed down by the men in my family from generation to generation. When things don't go our way, we break shit.

"Hey, Sara," I mumble contritely as she answers the phone.

"Not Sara, Cara," replies her sister. "Phone!" she shouts out into the abyss.

"Hello," Sara picks up.

"It's me," I offer.

"What?" she snaps.

"I got your note." Pause. "I thought you wanted to talk."

"I do want to talk, obviously, and I want to put this all behind us. I also want you to apologize for being a savage the other day. You need to understand that I was not with Chris and haven't talked to him in a long time, it was a misunderstanding that you thought I was coming over that night. I promise you, Bry, swear on my life, I wasn't with him!"

"Okay Baby, if you say so. Yes, I'm sorry for getting so pissed. I still don't understand how you could have mixed up our being together Friday like we always are. That was the plan, we talked about it. I'll take your word on it for the sake of peace, but we need to talk more about it after the holidays. If you still want to be with me for Christmas, that is."

"Of course I do Bry, that's why I left you a note saying I love you this morning," she declares, finally letting her guard down a little.

"Yeah, thanks for that. I don't speak Italian by the way. Comprende?" I laugh.

"That's Spanish, you Idiot," she replies, laughing too.

"For your future reference, *no hablo nada.* Also, what was that Italian you threw at me the other day on the phone?" I ask.

She repeats it in a question. "*Puoi andare a farti fottere?*"

"Yeah, that sounds like the one."

"You can go fuck yourself!" she replies with a hard tone, to emphasize she meant it.

Eddie Murphy did a bit in his stand-up act where his wife caught him walking out of another woman's house as she was driving by. When he comes home an hour later, his wife says "What the fuck Eddie, you cheatin' Mother F'r, I just seen you with another woman. What do you have to say for yourself?"

"Wasn't me," he responded without hesitation.

"What the fuck you mean it wasn't you, I saw you with my own two eyes!"

"Wasn't me," Eddie repeated calmly.

This is how I feel now, like Eddie's wife. I'm convinced something went down with Sara on Friday night, but there's nothing I can do right now. This has been the best two months of my life, and it's either accept her story or go on my way, and I'm not prepared to do that yet. I'll just do what I always do, ignore the elephant in the room and hope it goes away.

CHAPTER 14

"**Y**OU'RE LUCKY I FINALLY GOT YOUR NEW NUMBER FROM ED," Patty Funk begins as we drive south on 87 to Manhattan, "or you'd be watching this game on TV." I haven't seen him since our night out at the Crossing, back in the fall. I've been spending all of my time with Sara ever since.

"First of all, Dummy, I don't give a crap about the Rangers, so if I wasn't going to the game with you, the last thing I would be doing is wasting my time watching it on TV. Secondly, let your fingers do the walking. I've been in the phone book for months."

Sara and I made it through the holidays well enough, and once the awkwardness of our first big fight faded a bit, we were pretty much back to our old selves. Pretty much. Her story isn't changing so I have to take it for the truth. In reality, I'm just trying to block it out and move on.

I'm looking forward to hanging with Patty tonight, we are long overdue for some fun. It's a mild night for mid-January so I roll down the window halfway and push in the lighter, happy to be the co-pilot for a change instead of driving. WPLJ is playing The Pina Colada song on the radio as we fly down the highway. Funk is singing along, but he hilariously changes the words, crooning gleefully "If you like Penis Colossus, and Licking My Vein."

We speed by a cherry red Ford Mustang convertible crawling along in the right lane. "Patty, why'd you sell your Mustang? Sara has the same car as you, those things are going to be worth a lot of bread one day."

Funkster ignores my question and instead gets serious. "Listen Homey, I don't know what's up with you and her these days, and it's none of my business, but you are my boy so—"

"Spit it out Funk, what's your point?" I urge him along.

"Dude, her old boyfriend Chris Garvey lives right down the street from me."

How do I not know this crucial piece of information? "AND?"

"And her blue Mustang was in his driveway around Christmas, I saw it when I got home one night and it was still there in the morning when I woke up."

"Ahhhh, why didn't you tell me? That seems pretty fucking relevant, don't you agree?" I shout.

"Right, I didn't realize it until you just mentioned she had a Stang, then it came back to me," he continues. "So you had no idea?"

"Oh yeah, I knew. I told her it's no problem if she wants to go over there and bone him anytime the urge hits," I reply sarcastically. "Of course I didn't know! I suspected it and knew it in my gut. That fucking little liar!" I punch the dash in anger, so mad at myself for going along with her bullshit.

We continue the drive to Madison Square Garden, the "World's Most Famous Arena." I am steaming the rest of the ride. How can this be? I felt so in sync with Sara, yet she was off on her own taking care of business with this other guy, according to Pat. The excitement of mid-town Manhattan and the buzz around the Garden usually gets me hyped. New York City is like no place else in the world, but tonight I keep my head down and sulk as we walk along the crowded streets, feeling zero excitement.

I smoke and drink my way through the game, obviously preoccupied with the bomb Funk dropped on me earlier. The Rangers got whipped as usual but there were several bloody brawls to help pass the time, both on the ice and in the stands. The game ends at 9:45 and we shuffle along with the exiting crowds down the stairs and out to 34th Street.

"How about we get a beer? Let's chill in Gotham for a while and let the crowd thin a little," I suggest.

"That's fine Dude, no rush," Pat agrees. "There's a Freddie's across the street if you want to go there."

"Asshole, I work at a Freddie's, in case you didn't know. Do you want to go empty some garbage cans, garbage man?" I bust on him.

It's "Rubbish Ambassador," he jokes, referring to his surprisingly high paying job.

We find a little hole in the wall a block away, packed with Ranger fans wearing their Davidson and Duguay jerseys like they just played in the game. They're talking about the team in the We and the I, like "We gotta get better on the power play," or, "I would have scored on that pass." Okay, macho men. Trust me, the Rangers don't give a fuck about you.

"Bro, I got some bad news," Pat tugs on my sleeve. "Chris Garvey and his boys are at the end of the bar, they must have been at the game, too. Check him out, his name is on the back of his jersey. Stay low, he is not to be fucked with."

I peek over Patty's shoulder. Good looking dude, average size, not too intimidating. Garvey is with some friends and I recognize one of them from Little League. Tommy or Bobby, something like that, if I remember correctly. "What's the big deal?" I shrug. "Shit man, I don't even know the guy, never said two words to him, why would he have a problem with me?"

"Ah, because you're fucking his girl, that's why. Word is he ain't happy about it," Pat continues.

"Who's word? What are you talking about, Patty?"

"I hear things, man, gossip around the neighborhood. I haven't talked to you in a while but I heard Chris is pissed about losing Sara, and like I said, he's a bad mother fucker. He boxes at the YMCA, so I suggest you steer clear."

"He boxes at the Y? Whoop-de-fuckin-do, is that supposed to scare me?" I ask dismissively.

"Please just trust me, he'll wipe the floor with you, Gay-hill."

I'm usually not one to shy away from a throw down but it doesn't sound like Patty's messing around. "Say no more, I'm sold. I don't see how that little dude is gonna kick my ass but I'll take your word for it." We chug our beers and then head for the door, seemingly having dodged a bullet, for now. Sounds like it's only going to be a matter of time before I meet Chris Garvey face-to-face.

I pay for the garage since Funk drove. "What are the chances we run into this fucking dude right after I mention him to you," Patty remarks while we stand around waiting for the car to arrive from the recesses of the garage.

"Murphy's law. Story of my life," I gripe, handing the attendant a couple of bucks and jumping in the car. Patty makes a right out of the lot and goes west toward the Hudson. An already bad night is about to get so much worse.

Approaching a traffic light around 55th Street as we drive up the West Side Highway on our way out of the city, I fire up a cig and then hand the lighter to Funk. He shows no signs of stopping as the light turns red, suddenly screeching his Pontiac to a halt in the middle of the intersection.

"Sorry, I was trying to light my smoke," Pat explains regarding the hard stop as he throws it in reserve and backs up a few feet. A car lighter burns bright for one cig, but if you wait too long, you have to suck as if your life depends on it to get another one going. He pushes it back in to heat up again. As we wait for the light to change, the car behind us taps our bumper. A second later, as the traffic light turns green, they do it again. Hard this time, giving us a real jolt.

"What the fuck is this," Pat shouts, putting the car in park so he can get out and see what's up with this asshole. He opens his door and is immediately jumped by at least two guys on the street. Everybody is yelling and cursing, it's all white noise.

"Hang in there Patty," I scream, hopping out to join the scrum. As soon as my feet hit the street, I'm knocked on my ass by somebody lying in wait. It's an ambush! I'm a big guy and Patty is enormous but we are outnumbered here, a bad situation is developing. My face rests on the blacktop as I wonder what's coming next. Time is now standing still, yet it feels like this has been going on forever.

"Hey Bryan, allow me to introduce myself," the shadow standing above me says, moving in closer so I can see his face. Ahh, now I get it, this is the infamous Chris Garvey. I guess someone saw us in the bar after all. "I'm the guy who's been leaving you sloppy seconds. You can have Sara now for all I care Pencil Dick, but you're making me look real bad with my boys, and that's not gonna fly. Robby noticed you in the bar back there and I just wanted to say hello."

"I'm sensing a little sarcasm," I reply deliriously, getting to my knees and considering my options. Seeing him up close, maybe I can still take him, but that thought vanishes as Garvey suddenly picks me up like a feather and throws two shots. It's like Batman is hitting me, he fires a quick left (WHAM!!) that immediately blows my eye up, then a right (POW!!) that's probably broken my nose, blood flowing everywhere. He tosses me back in the car like a bag of trash. Okay, I can't take him.

"This is what happens when you fuck with me," he says definitively. "And if you tell anyone who did this to you I'll rip out your tongue next time. Don't make me look bad again, Fuck Face."

"You got it, Kemosabe," I reply sleepily, little stars circling my head like in a cartoon. I'm laughing to keep from crying, still in shock over what just happened here. Shooting him a bloody, broken grin, I ask, "Does this mean we aren't going to be friends?"

Garvey gives me the bird and saunters off with Robby (aka Tommy or Bobby from Little League) and his crew, having successfully fired his warning shot. It could have actually been a lot worse. I've gotten into some scraps before but never took a beating like this. As they screech away, Patty sits in the street licking his wounds, then he finally crawls back into the car and just stares at me.

"Bro, I know. I'm sorry, Man," I apologize to Pat, blood bubbling from my nose. "Holy shit, that was crazy. He kept saying I was making him look bad with his boys, whatever the fuck that means."

"Yeah Dude, that means he wanted Sara but you stole her. Now you know what happens when you stick your pole where it don't belong," Pat says exhaustively, trying to catch his breath.

"Sorry, Patty," I apologize, my head pounding. "That's the last thing I expected. Sara said she was done with this guy; I didn't mean to steal shit. Anyway, you look pretty good Dude, you handled your business out there."

Pat pulls the car over to the side of the highway so we can get our shit together. "Yeah, well you didn't. Looks like Chris Garvey is your new Daddy."

"Oh yeah, no doubt." I stick my thumb in my mouth and start sucking it like a baby, then Patty and I share a tired laugh. My still-lit cigarette is on the floor, burning a hole in the carpet. I pick it up and puff it back to life, taking a long drag before passing it over. Pat wipes my blood off and takes a pull.

"You need to do some boxing at the Y," he laughs, "or get a bodyguard."

"That's what I got you for, Patty! Nice job by the way," I say facetiously. "Let's roll out, Funk. Somebody's got some explaining to do."

My face isn't the only thing that was broken tonight. Now I have to deal with Sara.

CHAPTER 15

AGAINST THE ODDS, MY SISTER AND HER BOYFRIEND JEFF ARE still going strong, so strong Lauren told me she's moving in with him and is not going to continue our little deal on the apartment after May. Looks like I'll need to get a roommate or move back to my Mom's for a while.

I haven't seen Sis in weeks but today is her birthday so I give her a call and the answering machine picks up, always preferable to a live voice. The recorded message is an awkward little skit they put together: *"Hi this is Jeff! Hi this is Lauren! Leave us a message, and don't make it boring!"*

I'm compelled to come back with my own embarrassing ditty: *"Happy Birthday Lauren, it's your brother, Bryan, your message is wack, trust me I'm not lying."* Pleased with myself, I hang up the phone on this chilly, damp afternoon, the last day of April 1989.

It's been a few months since I broke it off with Sara and damn, I miss my tutor. After the brawl with Chris, I disappeared on her again, this time to recover from the fight and to steel myself for a confrontation. Sara finally copped to the fact that she was at Chris Garvey's house on that fateful Friday before Christmas. After getting drunk at the Crossing, she claimed her friends brought her to Chris', dropped her car there, and then Sara said she woke up the next day on his couch, but nothing happened between them. Combine that bullshit story with the royal beat-down Chris bestowed upon me, and the writing was on the wall; it was time for me to move on. I wanted to believe her, but it was all too much and the trust was gone. We haven't spoken since, and I've longed for her every day we've been apart. Last night I dialed every digit in her phone number but the last before pausing and then hanging up. I'm really fighting it.

My community service stint ended a few weeks ago, so I went to a Sunday game at the ballpark in early April and I'm going back again today. Yankee Stadium is my happy place, as familiar to me as my family and hometown. There is nothing like going to a game, walking out of the tunnel into the light of the field, seeing the lush green grass, and hearing the crack of the bat. I have so many deeply personal memories of this place, yet share them with millions of others who are watching the team they also love just as much. We all think of the "House that Ruth built" as our own. The best thing for me is I will watch intently for three hours and not worry about anything in the world outside of this park. If there's one thing I can rely on in life, something I can always count on, it's that Yankee Stadium will always be right here for me.

I buy a five-dollar nose-bleed seat at the ticket window. My ducat is ripped in half at the turnstiles and I head through the tunnels to the area under the net behind home plate. I flash an usher my ticket along with a ten-dollar bill for his taking and now I'm sitting five rows off the field with a smoke and a beer at first pitch. The Yanks score four in the first and thump the putrid White Sox to even their record at 12-12 on the young season. In baseball and life, Spring to me is all about the possibilities of what's to come.

The game is over in two and a half hours, time to hightail it out of here. I stand in the tunnel and watch the last couple of outs then run through mostly empty corridors before the exiting crowds hit. Back out on the Bronx streets, I order up a dog from the Sabrett cart and then head up some stairs to the long plexiglass passageway, which empties into the parking lots on the far end. Some old dude robotically plays *"Take Me Out to the Ballgame"* on the recorder, which reverberates from one side of the tube to the other. It makes me think of the song "*Hot Cross Buns*," which will now be stuck in my head for the rest of the day.

My car is jamming up the ramp to the Deegan in a heartbeat thanks to a primo parking spot that cost me an extra five bucks. I tune my radio to 770 WABC and listen to the new announcer John Sterling wrap up the game and play the highlights. This guy is good on the mike, hopefully, he sticks around. Sterling takes a break to announce its "Miller Time," and then continues, "If you've got the time, we've got the beer."

Seeing as it's a beautiful late afternoon and I have no plans tonight, or ever, I decide to stop in on my Dad and his happy little life. My father recently moved to Dobbs Ferry and has a lovely house right on the Hudson River. I live on the west bank of the river, and Dad is on the east. With a pair of binoculars, his place can be seen across the water from my bedroom window. We are separated by only the river, but it feels like an Ocean.

I have no memory of my Dad ever living with us. He's been coming and going like a fart in the wind my whole life. He isn't the worst; he certainly isn't the best. Mom housed us kids, fed us, protected us, and nurtured us. Dad showed up from time to time, with no rhyme or reason, and entertained us with a ball game, amusement park, circus, fireworks, or whatever. He swooped in like Superman in his fancy company car, and we always had fun. If we didn't see him for a week, or a month, or even six, nobody noticed. We took what we could get, and didn't want for more. Lauren was three years older than me and she had no interest in Dad by the time she turned 15. It was always me and Ed, waiting around for him to show up. He could easily be two or three hours late to pick us up for a sleepover, yet every time, we were ready when he said to be, naively expecting things would be different. We never learned. Mom promised us that when we have kids of our own, these times would help us to know what *not* to do as a father. Some would call my relationship with him complicated, but I find it very simple. As little kids, we worshiped our tall and handsome Dad, but as young adults, his deficiencies as a father have come into focus. It's best for us to have no expectations, and therefore we are never disappointed. He's living in his own world and we, his older children, are a peripheral part of his life, as he is to ours.

Dad isn't home. "He took the boys to Little League at the elementary school. He's the coach, you know," his young wife Rita, all gussied up in a hot pink tracksuit, informs me as we stand on opposite sides of the screen door. No invitation inside seems forthcoming. They have twin sons, five years old now. Everyone in the family really adores the boys, who certainly don't deserve anything but our love. They have Dad full time and if that's going to be a good thing for them, God bless; we don't want it.

"No, he never mentioned it, I had no idea he's the coach," I shrug. My Dad doesn't know jack shit about baseball, so that team is gonna suck.

"I'll tell him you came by," Rita says, clearly wanting me to go away. She doesn't give a fuck about Dad's first three kids, and we most definitely don't give a fuck about her.

"Yeah thanks, please do that. Let him know," I reply while backing away from the closing door. Catch you next time, Coach.

CHAPTER 16

THE SUN IS GOING DOWN AS I PULL INTO MY DRIVEWAY AND lookee lookee here! Sara is sitting on the hood of her '67 Mustang, parked in the spot next to mine. As she climbs off and we lock eyes, I try to suppress the glee I am feeling. Having achingly missed Sara, seeing her unplanned is so euphoric and powerful for me. I can't contain my happiness as a huge smile takes over my face, and before a word is spoken, I'm working through in my head all the scenarios this meeting can possibly offer. Keep your cool here, Grayhill. I park my car and strut my way over to her, hoping she's thinking the same thing I'm thinking.

"Bry," is all Sara says through those gorgeous teeth.

"Hi Baby," I smile back as I take her hand and make a beeline up the stairs to my bedroom, not speaking a word or even turning around to look at her the entire way. We both strip in unison, then I sit down on the bed, and Sara climbs aboard.

"Fuck me," she breathes into my ear, then whispers "I missed you, Bry," as I feel her tears dripping down my body. When you love something that gets taken away and is replaced by longing and sadness, it's such a gift if you can get it back, even for a second. The feel of her, the smell, the taste, the sound. This is mine, I want this. These shared moments with Sara are my best, I love myself when I'm being loved by her. Sara had made me evolve and grow when we were together, it's a me that I'd never known before. They say love is fleeting, but I want to stay in this moment forever.

"I think you're the most handsome man in the world," Sara compliments me as we lie naked on top of the bed covers, her hand stroking my face. We have spent the last several hours together but haven't done much talking. "I never stopped thinking about you for a minute this whole time. You've been haunting me."

"Aww Sara, I know, I know, it's been killing me too. Thank God the Yankee season started," I crack.

"You Jerk!" she laughs, giving me a little love tap on my ass.

"I'm kidding, I'm kidding," I promise. "I've thought about you 24-7."

"So what have you been up to these past few months?" she inquires, likely her roundabout way to ask if I was with any other girls.

"Nothing at all. Work, home, and now Yankees."

"Me too, except for the Yankees." Sara quietly stares up at the ceiling for a minute, then turns to me. "I want it back. I want what we had, and more," she implores.

"I do too Sara, I never wanted to stop, but honestly I'm not sure if we can get it back. There are too many skeletons in your closet." Actually, I'm not worried about the dead, I'm worried about the living. As much as I love this girl, I still don't trust her with the old flame right around the corner. Why *wouldn't* Chris be trying to get her back?

"There's no more skeletons. What's it going to take? I only want to be with you, Bry!"

"Ah man, I don't know, Baby. As long as that Garvey kid is around, I'm not going to be cool with it." Apparently, Sara is still not aware that I've met Chris (If you want to call his fist in my face having met him), but that is certainly adding to my apprehension. I'm not looking to be his punching bag again.

"C'mon Bry, I'll do anything," she pleads, "I just want to be with you! Nobody can make me happy the way you can, I've realized that over the last few months. I'll do anything you want," she declares again.

"Move to Hawaii," I blurt out facetiously. "If we're alone, halfway around the world, maybe then I'll have you all to myself."

"Let's do it," Sara smiles and then rolls over without saying another word, backing up against me in the bed as we both fall asleep.

I woke in a panic at nine the next morning, for two reasons. I was supposed to be at work 15 minutes ago, but my alarm clock didn't go off, instead, its red digits are blinking, indicating a power outage overnight. The biggest reason for my angst is the crazy proposition I made last night about moving to Hawaii with Sara if she really wants to be with me. I don't even know where the hell Hawaii is! It must have been on my brain after hearing Junior talk about it back at the jail, so I just threw it out there. Maybe she'll forget I even mentioned it.

From the second I uttered the words we both realized that getting away from here together is the only option we have if this relationship is ever going to work. Of course, at the time I was just being a wise-ass, randomly picking a place. I didn't mean it, but after a night to sleep on it, why the hell not? I have nothing keeping me in New York except Sara, so if she's in, I'm in. Even if she's out, I'm still in. New York has been nothing but a nightmare for me, so why not get out of Dodge? She knows, deep down, though I'm sure she will never admit it, that whatever she once had with Chris needs time and distance to kill it once and for all.

I call in sick to work, fake cough and everything. Sara is already up and watching TV. Tammy Faye Baker, whose face looks like a sad clown, is letting go of her emotions on the Today show. I brush my teeth and we share a good morning kiss.

"This is a nice change," I remark of her sitting here on my couch, curled up in the corner.

"What's wrong, are you sick?" I heard you on the phone with work."

I'm walking back from the kitchen with a Diet Coke in one hand, Entenmann's chocolate-covered doughnut in the other, and a lit cig hanging out of my mouth. "I'm fine, but I overslept and decided to take advantage of the fact that my favorite person is sitting here," I smile while leaning in for another kiss. "Did you notice your toothbrush is still in the bathroom?"

"Aww, I did. You never gave up on me," Sara says through a grin. "So are we going through with this insane plan to move?" she asks, having not forgotten about my suggestion.

"After the year I've had, it's time for me to go somewhere; anywhere but here. There's no way we can work things out here in Rockland, so the question is, are you really willing to do it? What's up with you and Chris these days?" I ask her. "Is he going to care what you're doing?" And by care, I mean is he going to jack me up again?

"Last I heard, he left until the end of the summer, I don't even know where. I haven't spoken to him in a while."

"If you say so," I reply skeptically. I'm sure I'll be getting down with Chris again someday, it seems inevitable. "So you want to move?"

"Don't threaten me with a good time, Grayhill. Where you go, I go!" she answers emphatically.

"Then call me Bryan the Hawaiian from now on. Surf's up!" I holler, jumping on the couch and balancing on an imaginary surfboard. I happily sing my version of the theme song from Hawaii 5-0. "*Dah dah dant dah dah dah. Dant da dant da dah.*" That and the Brady Bunch episode with the haunted tiki encapsulate just about all I know of Hawaii.

I finish the song and then get quiet for a second, all of a sudden deep in thought. Is Sara Addeo, the untouchable Sara Addeo from high school, actually sitting on my couch right now telling me that she wants to be with me, and only me? Start a life? "Sara, I get it, we're fucking around here, but is this seriously something you want to do? I can be a grade A fuck up, and if we move off somewhere, I'll be the only person you have to rely on."

"I think it's the perfect time for it, Bry," Sara replies confidently. "And I don't think you're a fuck up. You've always treated me amazingly and we will be together, relying on each other, and helping each other. Just don't get thrown in jail again, that won't be good," she remarks.

"For the record, no more jail jokes, or even references please," I instruct, the subject still a sore spot for me. "Anyway, if you want to do this, we should go for it. If nothing else, we'll have a story to tell for the rest of our lives."

"I'm 100% in, Bry guy!" she assures me, holding out her hand to shake on it. "100%!"

"We'll see what your parents think. I'm sure your Dad won't be too happy," I warn.

"Nah, he's not that bad. I've been gone the last four years for school, they're used to me being away."

Sara and I pull ourselves together and then go to the library. Moving to Hawaii will now become our singular focus. I've been coming to the Rockland Library since I was in kindergarten. As a child, I remember sitting mesmerized in the kid's room downstairs, watching movies like "The Red Balloon," which was about a boy who accidentally let go of his balloon and followed it all over creation. He really loved *that* balloon!

Today I'm all grown up (depending on who you ask) and here to find out where in the hell Hawaii is. We work the Dewey Decimal System and eventually find the reference books. Sara knows it's somewhere to the west, but we are equally stunned to learn how far.

"Sara, this says it's like seven hours past California. Jesus, I thought it was part of the United States."

"Well it's a state, but it's not part of the states. It's in the middle of the ocean," she explains.

"No shit Sherlock," I laugh, pointing to the map we are both looking at. "I thought it was connected."

"This is totally rad, going to a mysterious place nobody's ever been to."

"The Brady's have been there," I grin. "Alice too."

"You know what I mean, Numskull. Nobody we know in real life."

The librarian overhears us and offers a helpful recommendation. "May I suggest you get the Frommer's guide if you are planning a vacation to Hawaii. It's easily the most useful reference for travelers," she informs us.

"Oh, thanks so much," Sara replies happily as she jots the name down with the little golf pencil they have in the scrap paper box.

"Actually, we're moving there," I declare enthusiastically.

"I see. How wonderful," the librarian comments, with zero enthusiasm. "I hope everything works out."

Of course it will, lady. What could go wrong?

CHAPTER 17

TODAY IS MAY 1ST. TIME TO CALL MY SISTER LAUREN AND LET HER know I'm moving out of the apartment too. "Tell your landlord Mr. Whatever his name is that we will be out by June first," I succinctly tell her answering machine, having no extra time to leave another rhyme. I don't share my plans to vacate New York altogether, and for now will just say that I can't afford the place without her.

After Lauren, I tell my Mom I'll be coming back to the house in June. She is ecstatic, of course. "Oh Honey, that's wonderful, I can't wait," she glows as usual.

"It's not for long, I just need to save a little money."

"As long as it takes, Honey. I'll always be here for you if you need me."

Sara and I figure that it will take at least three thousand dollars in cash to find a place and get settled after landing in Hawaii. We need plane tickets as well and I have no idea how much that will set us back. Our goal is to leave around the end of August, as long as we can save up the money. Working in restaurants will give us the chance to put away a lot of cash and we agree to let nothing get in the way of our goal. Since all we'll be doing is working for the next few months, Sara suggests maybe we can do it together. "Why don't you see if you can get me a job at Freddie's?" she asks.

"Yeah, why not," I reply agreeably, but in my head, I know that idea would be the death of me. While I had previously told Sara that she has too many skeletons in her closet, Freddie's is my graveyard, and I don't need any of my past transgressions buried there messing up our already fragile union.

I know the kitchen manager for Freddie's in Bergen, New Jersey, and decide to give him a call, see if he can help. He worked in the Tarrytown location with me back when I first started cooking last year.

"Kitchen, Chip speaking," my guy answers.

"Eh, Vinny Gumbotz, it's Bryan from Tarrytown Freddie's," I greet him, using my best Bronx dialect. "How you doin'?"

Chip has jet-black hair greased back and a heavy Bronx accent, he may as well be straight out of the mob, so I tease him that he looks like a gangster. I usually call him a goofy mafia nickname, like "Tommy Salami," or "Charlie Ten Toes," always making up something stupid.

Chip laughs as he recognizes my unique greeting. "Oh, look who it is, Mr. New York! What's going on? Did you open up your restaurant yet?"

"Not yet my man, but you'll be the first to know. I'm saving the head dishwasher job for you! Hey seriously Chip, me and my girl are looking to save up some fast money for a vacation," I fib, "at the end of the summer. I'm hoping you can hook us up with some shifts. You know I can do front or back of the house. Sara needs training and menu knowledge but she's a great server, and a hustler, too," I emphasize.

"Sounds good my man, let me poke around and see what we can come up with for you guys. It's a perfect time to ask, kids here live in the weeds, we could definitely use some stars," Chip responds. "I'll get back to you, Brother!"

A week later, Sara and I are set up. I had told her that there were no jobs available in Tarrytown but they needed help in Bergen, and she didn't question it. I easily transfer from one Freddie's to the other and Sara is trained and making money in less than a week. We came and left work as a couple, nobody knew us, and we aren't trying to know anyone else. Work, make the money, leave. Come back the next day and do it again.

It's time to tell my family about our master plan. I moved to LA on a whim a few years ago so it won't be a major surprise to them that I'm on the run again. It's the where, and with whom, that will get a reaction, and I'm pretty sure it's not going to be a positive one.

"Dude, do you know how fucking far away Hawaii is?" Ed starts in on me after I tell him the news. "And you're going with Sara Addeo, of all people? Man come on, are you so pussy whipped that you have to follow it all the way to China or wherever?" he blasts me.

Jesus, I'm moving almost to China? That does sound far. "It was my idea, Douche bag. Not all of us shack up with the first girl we get a hand job from like you did."

"It's your funeral," Ed cautions. "Don't say I didn't warn you when it goes to shit."

And so went the reactions of just about everybody I told our news to.

Lauren: "Oh my God, you are so dumb. Why go fuck things up over there when you can fuck everything up for free right here?"

Patty Funk: "Sara's a babe but this looks a little desperate on your part."

Dad: "Please don't ask me for money to fund this disaster."

Mom, always in my corner no matter how poor the decision, is the only one that shows some support. If her children make a bad choice, she will always pick us up and encourage us that everything is going to be alright in the end, then share some words of wisdom to help us avoid a similar outcome in the future. She would never say "I told you so."

"Bravo to you guys," she lauded us. "Don't go all willy-nilly without a plan. Save some money first, and when you're ready, I say why not? When I was your age I already had a little one and two more on the way. Life is for living. It's going to be a great adventure, Honey!" Hers is the only approval I need, which is a good thing because it's the only approval I got.

I went to Walden Books in the mall and bought Frommer's Guidebook to Honolulu, Waikiki, and Oahu, which the librarian had suggested to us. Sara and I are meeting at five o'clock at Turiello's to work on our plan. She made me promise not to look at the book without her and is already sitting at a front table, smiling as I walk in. Such a beauty, Sara is treated as royalty here like she's the queen of Italy. The last time we were here, she was speaking in Italian about where on the boot her family was from with the men behind the counter, who were all paying rapt attention.

After greeting each other with a big hug and a long kiss, we sit down hip to hip on the same side of the table as the pizza guys look on enviously. That's right boys, this paisan is all mine!

"Without further ado, may I present to you the Frommer's Guidebook," I state to Sara in an uppity cadence, placing the book in front of her.

"Without further ado?" she teases with a smirk while opening up the book. "Nobody says that, Weirdo."

"Well, I say it." She cracks it open and we start scanning the pages. "Lot of maps," I remark, "so that's good. I can't pronounce any of these street names, man." I pick one randomly. "K-A-L-U-A-N-U-I Street, I spell out. Kaluunewee maybe? I have no idea."

"It doesn't matter," Sara tells me. "What we really need this for is the hotel listings. I'll go through them and find one that we can afford."

"It has to be close to the city," I remind her. "Let's find Freddie's and use it as a home base since that's the only place we know for sure we need to go."

"Okay, let me just flip to the restaurant section." Sara licks her thumb as she turns the pages. "Oh, this street is easy to pronounce. Freddie's is 950 Ward Avenue." She turns a few more pages and finds a map.

"Right there," I say upon her finding the page, "and all the hotels are down here," my finger sliding across to the other side. It looks close enough to me.

"This book is definitely helpful to have, but it's really for people planning a vacation," Sara decides.

"True, but how else could we find a hotel without these listings? Maybe go to the library and use the phone book. They have them from every state, but no details like this guide."

"Yeah, I'm glad you got it," she says, putting the book into a big bag on her shoulder and standing up. "I gotta go, dinner with my family, remember? Time for me to tell them the plan. Without further ado!" she mocks me playfully.

"Oh yeah, okay. I'll walk you out," I reply, then turn to the counter guys, all three wearing tight white t-shirts, one dirtier than the next. "Nicky, let me get a chicken parm hero. I'll be right back."

He gives me a thumbs up as we head for the door and then yells loudly to the back, "One chic parm hero!"

"I could have done that, Paisan!" I laugh, and we exchange smiles. I walk her out and then return to scarf down my sandwich, with a slice of pepperoni and a Yoo-hoo, of course.

Later that night, Sara called to let me know that she told her parents of our plan and her father wants to "have a discussion" with me.

"He's not going to pull any of his Hong Kong Phooey shit, is he?" I ask uneasily.

"Only if he doesn't like your answers."

Well, that's not very comforting. "Will you be there to translate, and also to keep him from murdering me?"

"Bry, my Dad speaks perfect English, he just uses Italian around the house. You don't need a translator, there's nothing to worry about. Come to dinner here this Sunday, everything will be fine."

"Okay, I'm sure it'll all work out. I'll do what the Godfather does; I'm gonna make him an offer he can't refuse," I laugh menacingly.

At my mother's suggestion, I drove down to Arthur Avenue in the Bronx and got some fresh cannoli's for my discussion with Sara's father. Arthur Avenue is the Mecca for Italians, and a cannoli is just the door opener that I need. I couldn't attend dinner on short notice because of work but arranged to meet with Mr. Addeo at his home before heading to Freddie's. Just us, mano a mano!

"Buonasera," Sara's Dad begins upon opening the door to their spacious condo. "Nice to finally meet you!"

"Bryan, Sir. Nice to meet you as well," I smile, extending a nervous hand to shake.

"Call me Angelo," he says affably, calming my nerves. Even with his mostly bald head and wispy comb-over, Angelo is a handsome man, tall and fit. He exudes confidence in himself and is nothing like the grouchy curmudgeon I'd imagined. I'm offered a seat on the couch, which is covered in clear vinyl. If there was a question as to whether Angelo was first-generation Italian, the couch cover answered it a resounding *yes*. "What can I get you to drink, Bryan?"

"Water is fine, please," I answer, and Angelo fills a couple of glasses from the faucet, ice cubes popping.

I sit with the white bakery box on my lap, its red and white string authenticating the freshness found within. Wearing tennis shorts, my legs immediately grip onto the sticky couch cover and render me immobile. Sara's Dad puts down two glasses on the coffee table and sits across from me.

"Thank you, Angelo. Cheers!" I say, holding up my glass and saluting him in the same fashion I had toasted his daughter around a beer keg the night we hooked up. "I brought fresh cannoli's from Arthur Avenue," I tell him, offering the box.

He takes it with a smile. "Bribing me with baked goods from the old neighborhood, that's a smooth move, Buddy," he laughs. Sara calls me buddy sometimes, usually when she's mad. "By the way, it's *cannoli*, just so you know. Even if there's more than one, you never say I got some *cannoli's*. Just wanted to mention that. It's like moose, you understand?" he asks rhetorically. Angelo continues on, his weird grammar lesson apparently complete. "Yes sir, I grew up right off the Avenue on Belmont, this smell takes me back," he remarks, prying open the corner of the box for a whiff. "I appreciate it." Angelo spends some time reminiscing about the old days, then he finishes with the big question. "So what are your intentions with my daughter?"

So much for easy breezy small talk, it's time to step up to the plate. "Well, ah, Angelo," I begin, rubbing my hands together unconsciously, "I care so much about Sara and we have been talking about traveling and going on an adventure together, and we figure Hawaii would be an amazing experience. We both have the time, and I have a job available there, so we thought why not? Pending your approval, of course. We will plan it out and be very well prepared before leaving." I went with this line of bullshit, instead of listing all the things Sara and I are running away from.

"I see," he responds, then we have a long, uncomfortable stare-down. What's the verdict, Angelo? He finally continues, his gregarious tone now subdued. "Understand I will hold you responsible for Sara. This is serious, nothing is more important to me than my daughters," he starts, all business now. "In karate, we say *spirit first, technique second*; now that you have this vision, stay focused and execute it successfully."

"I will protect her with my life, Sir. Even if we get attacked by a pack of mooses," I smile at him, rolling the dice on a dumb joke. He doesn't get mad, but he doesn't laugh either. Like most of my jokes, I'm the only one who thinks it's funny.

We continue our discussion, speaking of my family, my job, and our plans for Hawaii. I'm sneaking a few peeks at the clock behind him, my need to be at work a ready-made excuse to get going shortly. It was a very comfortable conversation, I found Angelo mostly nicer than nice, he even invited me to learn some karate before we leave.

"Our dojo is called "*Lightning Karate*." It's downtown, across from the post office. Stop by sometime."

"Yes Sir, I'd love that." I know he can be very intense, I've heard him on the phone, but besides the few minutes of serious conversation, and the grammar lesson on cannoli, this visit was a piece of cake.

Thankfully I've gotten him on a good day, as he has with me.

Peeling my legs off the vinyl, I stand and we exchange good wishes, even sharing a man hug. If our visit today was a picture, it would be of blue skies, puffy clouds, and sunshine. Here's hoping I never see the lightning or hear the thunder.

CHAPTER 18

BIRDS CHIRPING, MOWERS MOWING, SUN SHINING. IT'S A PERfect spring morning, especially because I'm waking up with the love of my young life beside me. Sara's wearing a tattered old Reggie t-shirt from my drawer, it says Jackson on the back with the number 44. Talk about sexy!

"Morning, Bry," she kisses me before scooting up to the top of the bed for a look out the open window.

I shimmy next to her and flick a fat bumble bee off the other side of the screen. "Perfect day. Smell that freshly cut grass!"

"Gorgeous. I love the spring!" Sara agrees, pointing outside at some little girls playing basketball in their driveway. "That was me when I was a little kid, always outside hooping it up with my sisters."

"Hooping it up? Sounds serious," I remark.

"All-county my last two years of high school, Buddy Boy. I'll take you down anytime."

"Thanks for the offer, I'm going to pass. I suck at basketball; therefore, I hate it."

Sara raises an eyebrow. "What a shame. You're wasting that height, Big Guy."

"Yeah, I'm a waster, what can I say? I do the bare minimum, that's my M.O. Sorry I'm not a super popular, over-achieving star like you," I bite back, immediately spoiling the good juju this beautiful day is providing.

"Bry, are you being serious right now? What did I do to make you get so defensive? Sounds like someone's got self-esteem issues, but don't take it out on me!"

I pause before continuing. "Sorry, you're right. I'm edgy, still leery about Chris. I just want to get the fuck out of here with you. I know he's a lot of things I'm not (an ass-kicking psychopath, for starters), and that intimidates me."

"He is a lot of things you're not, Bry," Sara speaks softly to me, "and that's a good thing. You're everything to me now and that's not changing. Stop worrying about it."

We look out the window in silence for a while, watching the neighborhood flower with activity.

Sara turns to me. "We got a good thing going, Grayhill. Don't sabotage it for no reason. I love you, more than anybody loves anybody!" She kisses me, then gets up, gathers her stuff, hits the bathroom, and then drives off. I watch from the window as her car fades away, wondering where she'll roam from here.

It's the last day of May and we have to get all of our stuff out of the apartment. Lauren is scrubbing the tub, along with the rest of the bathroom, even though she hasn't taken a shower here in months. "I don't want everyone saying I'm the pig because you can't clean up after yourself so it's obviously up to me to scrub this disaster of a bathroom," she lays into me. "I hope Sara's ready to be your maid." My sister is on the warpath; I need to keep my distance.

Withdrawing to my room and a mountain of dirty clothes, I start stuffing them in garbage bags, shoes and sneaks in garbage bags, everything in garbage bags. I tie them up and throw the bags out of the second-floor window, right next to where my car is parked. Could you be any lazier, I think to myself. You have no class, man. Who does shit like this? Well, I do, I'm doing it right now. Guess who else does it? My Dad, of course.

While I'm tossing my life, crammed in trash bags, two floors down onto the driveway, I recall him once angrily stuffing our Christmas tree out the window of our apartment when we were little, just like the Grinch. It may even be my first memory of my father. Certainly, it was the first of many memories I have of Dad blowing his top. Just as Nathans is famous for hot dogs, Grayhills are famous for bad tempers.

As I continue to heave the stuffed plastic bags out the window, it reminds me of another garbage bag story from when we were kids, living in the apartments on Gedney Street. One of those days Ed and I were sitting in the lobby forever, waiting on Dad to pick us up for a weekend at his fancy house, where he had just moved at the time with his equally fancy young wife. He finally rolled up like Boss Hogg in his humongous red Cadillac Eldorado and double-parked in front of the building, blocking traffic. The king had finally arrived! This guy is the reason I make my own rules and do what I want because I've been watching him do it all my life. Ed and I walked out with our brown paper bags, Dad unlocked the trunk and we tossed them in. His first words spoken to us, after weeks or possibly months of not seeing his two boys, are not "Hey guys, sorry I'm late, I've got a big weekend planned," or, "I've missed you so much!" No, what he said was "What's with the grocery bags? You look like a couple of fucking Puerto Ricans from the Bronx." We didn't even know what that meant at the time, but the comment, and the tone, have always stuck with me. Maybe I do have some Daddy issues after all.

Speaking of Daddy issues, Lauren is done with the bathroom and is now walking through the bedrooms doing a final tidy-up. She hasn't said two words to me all day.

"Lau, why you being so quiet?"

"I'm fine, nothing to say is all," she snaps back, obviously not fine.

"I know this is about me and Sara, what's your problem with us? I love her, this is a good thing."

"Oh really, do you? I think you're mixing up finally getting laid on the regular with being in love, Bry. I have news for you little brother, sex is not love. You were just in fucking jail, like seriously, I don't get what you guys are thinking, moving so far! What's the rush, you guys just met. You're like a dumb puppy following her around. Who's going to help you when you get thrown in jail out there?"

"Who fucking helped me here, Lauren?" I shoot back. "Have a little faith. Jesus!" My sister has always been watching over me and it would make me feel better to have her blessing on my relationship with Sara, but that won't come easy. "Fuck your opinion, Lauren. I know she loves me too, and this was my idea to move. I need a change of scenery. Trust me on this," I plead.

"I'm just telling you, she's on the rebound, Bryan. She doesn't love who you are, she loves who you're not! It's a classic move. Believe me, I'm a girl, I know what she's doing," Lauren insists. "It may not be on purpose, but I don't want her using you. That girl's got fucking issues."

"She's not using me, that's not what's happening here. Thanks for your concern but I'm not worried."

"Okay, well I am. Good luck, Bry, do what you want, not my business. Anyway, clean that kitchen like your life depends on it," she threatens, "because it does. Lock the door and leave your key under the mat," she further orders me, while lighting up a long Virginia Slims 100.

"That's pretty smart, you smoking those super long cigs," I chide her. "If you like to smoke, it's a no-brainer. You get like five more drags."

"Yeah I'm smart like that, what can I say? Clean the damn fridge," she demands, and just like that, Lauren marches off and our little cohabitation has come to an end.

I stand in front of the refrigerator, psyching myself up to open the door and begin cleaning. I will not be surprised when I open it if Zuul, the demonic fridge dweller from the Ghostbusters movie, jumps out and attacks me, that's how badly this thing needs cleaning.

I finally go for it, yellow rubber gloves protecting me from the dangers that lie within. Tossing out some ancient hamburger meat that's dark and rotten, I hold my nose and remove it from the drawer, thankful it's so spoiled that even the putrid smell has mostly died. I remember when we were little kids my Mom used to roll raw chopped meat into little balls, salt them up, and then we would pop them in our mouths like candy. Nobody will be popping down this shoe leather.

Next out is a slimy head of Iceberg, my resolution for eating healthier going into the garbage with it. Sara's in great shape and eats mostly good things. I had visions of myself joining her on the fitness train but, alas, it wasn't meant to be.

Looking in this fridge is like standing in front of the mirror for me, it's a reflection of my personality. Lots of good intentions and ideas, but most were not followed through on and were left unfinished.

"Don't be so hard on yourself, Bryan," I speak out loud to no one. "It's a little rotten meat, not your fucking life."

CHAPTER 19

TWO DAYS TO GO. SARA AND I HAVE WORKED OUR ASSES OFF ALL summer, managing to bank almost four thousand bucks for the trip. The move, actually. Our one-way tickets, JFK airport to Honolulu, arrived in the mail last week. Sara has been spending most of her time these last few days with her family, or so she says. Yup, that lingering Chris doubt will always be there for me, or at least until we get on the plane. Then it's au revoir to that pain in my ass. I'm constantly looking over my shoulder for another ambush but it's been all quiet since the bloody beat down in Manhattan; maybe he really has moved on.

"I'm hungry, Bry, do you have any food in this place?" Sara asks upon waking. Her sister Cara dropped her here at my Mom's house last night so she could borrow the Mustang, which will be hers to keep in a couple of days.

"Nothing good, I can promise you that. Let's run into town and grab something. I need some smokes anyway," I inform her, grabbing my keys and prompting her to get moving.

"Oh, you need cigarettes, no wonder you're raring to go," she teases while taking an imaginary puff with her toothbrush.

"I know you're being funny but if I don't get some cigs, I will smoke a toothbrush," I laugh at her while rifling through an ashtray of butts, looking for a candidate to hold me over until I get a fresh pack.

"Let's go, Smokey the Bear. Only you can prevent me from starving," Sara jokes as she heads down the stairs.

"Click, click, click," and a bunch of red lights on the dash is all I get from the Cutlass when I turn the key. "Fuck, this thing is dead," I growl, stating the obvious to Sara. "I don't know shit about cars so, um, it's about a fifteen-minute walk to town if you want to do that."

"Fine with me, Bry, I'll never say no to a little workout."

I stick out my tongue to show Sara that just the thought of walking into town exhausts me, but I need those smokes. "Alright, let's go. It's a beautiful day, why not take a stroll down memory lane?" It's been a while, but I've made this trek more times than I can count. In a car, on a bike, a skateboard, running, walking, in the rain, snow, and sunshine. "Okay, ready for a tour of my childhood?"

"I'm ready for some food is what I'm ready for."

"Well you get a free tour too, so let's roll." I find a nice butt in the Olds' ashtray and spark it up as we exit the car and begin the walk.

To get into town, all you do is go to the end of our street and make a right onto South Broadway, then walk a mile or so down the bucolic suburban sidewalks of South Rockland. Large and very old three and four-story homes with big porches and unique architecture provide plenty to look at as we move along.

On the corner of our street behind tall walls of shrubs is Adam Fudderman's house. Adam was a weird little kid with an Afro of curly red hair, tons of freckles, and big gopher choppers to top it all off. We called him Alfred; he was a dead ringer for the kid from Mad magazine.

"Boy named Alfred used to live here," I begin my narration to Sara. "Us neighborhood kids used to stand behind these bushes and throw snowballs at the cars coming down the hill," I say, pointing up the street. "Man, people used to freak out. One guy chased me all the way home and told my mother."

"Oh my god Bry, that's so dangerous, you were a bunch of degenerates. Your Mom must have been pissed."

"Nah, she didn't give a shit about stuff like that. I don't remember what happened but if anything she probably told the guy off."

"You've been trouble since way back when, Bry Guy."

"Not really, just stupid shit like that. Boys will be boys, what can I say? I also remember watching the '78 Bucky Dent playoff game at the Fudderman's. Me, Ed, Alfred, and his weird old Dad were glued to their little black & white Sony."

"I have no idea what you're talking about. Who is Bucky Fucking Dent?"

"Yeah exactly, that's what they call him now in Boston," I laugh. "It doesn't matter, he's just an old Yankee. I know you don't care but that was a pivotal moment in my life." Closing my eyes, I'm back in Alfred's living room, hearing Bill White shouting from the TV. "*Deep to left. Yastremski will not get it, it's a home run!*"

"Come back to me, Bry, I'm losing you. It's 1989."

"I'm just saying, there's nothing better than beating Boston. There are only three certainties in life Sara: death, taxes, and Boston will never beat the Yankees when it counts."

"Okay, I get it. Take a deep breath and relax before you pop a chubby. You're talking about a stupid game from when you were like ten years old."

"I know, but this is me, Sara, this is how I became the person you love," I joke, wrapping my arm around her tightly as we walk.

"Yes, Bry, you're a baseball Gaylord. Let's move on," she replies, having heard enough Yankee talk.

On down Broadway, we come to the overpass, which extends above the highway leading to, and from, the Tappan Zee bridge. There is a waist-high fence for clear viewing of the river.

"Speaking of my neighborhood boys, we used to spit Oreos on the windshields of the cars down there during morning traffic jams. Splat!" I finish, then hock a loogie over the side for demonstration.

"That's disgusting. If some little brat did that to me I'd have killed them."

"Oh yeah, they wanted to, trust me, but we were up here laughing, out of harm's way."

"And what would you do if some kid did that to you today? Probably murder them," Sara chastises me.

I give a dismissive wave. "Yeah, you're probably right, Baby, what can I say? That was then, this is now."

Holding hands, we kept walking and I kept talking.

"This is where I had my mug shot taken after the Timin thing," as we pass the police station. "I had my first cigarette on that trail back there," I continue, pointing behind some trees. "Me and my friend Jimmy used to make prank calls in there," gesturing to a big house.

Sara kept on listening, and she didn't like the picture I was painting. "I think it says something about your character that you did all this bad shit when you were a kid, Bry. Not for nothing but I hope you got it out of your system."

"Like I said Sara, that was then, this is now. Of course I've changed," I try to convince her, along with myself.

We walk the next few blocks in silence. Sara's had enough of my yarns and I'm sulking because she called me out. Finally at the Bigots Deli, we buy lunch and a pack of Reds. I give a couple to the bum outside the place, then we sit down on some grass at the corner of Cedar Hill to wait for the bus. "Out of gas, Bry?" Sara asks.

"I'm lazy, this is too much walking for me, let's just grab a ride. Sorry if I scared you with all my crazy stories, I'm definitely not like that anymore," I assure her.

"I get it, don't worry. As long as you treat me nice, I'm happy," she assures me.

"Okay, if you say so. You're not having any second thoughts about our trip, are you?"

Sara gives me a big smooch. "Absolutely not, Mr. Grayhill. It's perfect timing for us, I'm super excited."

"Thanks, Baby, me too. Can't wait."

The Red & Tan bus line lumbers down Broadway, and I give it a desperate wave, in case the driver intends to speed by this designated stop for some strange reason. We hop on the cool, empty bus and I tell the driver "Washington," which is a street like three minutes away.

Strolling to the back, we pick seats near the little exit doors. Our stop is already approaching so I pull the string above the window, creating a muffled little "ding" that alerts the driver to let us off. It's more like an unsatisfying half a ding, leaving the cord puller unsure if it has even been heard. I've seen many riders pull several times as the lonely little bell provides no assurance that it will stop.

The bus squeaks to a halt, my measly ding a success, and I scream out "Thanks!" as we bop down two stairs and push open the small exit doors, which swing out. Departing the bus feels akin to entering an old western saloon where you barge through the chest-high wooden doors. "Whiskey, Partner," I request of my imaginary bartender as I step onto the curb.

We trudge up the driveway, home at last. "Get used to it, Bry, we're going to be doing a lot of walking in Hawaii I bet."

"Yes, don't remind me."

"Are you going to miss it here?"

"Not for one minute." The old neighborhood won't miss me when I'm gone, and I won't miss being here, either. I impersonate Arnold in my awful Terminator voice while giving a wave goodbye to the neighborhood. "Hasta la vista, baby!"

For what seems like the millionth time today, Sara just rolls her eyes as I carry on.

CHAPTER 20

ROLL OUT OF BED EARLY ON WEDNESDAY MORNING, AROUND 10 a.m. Tomorrow is the day, and I'm feeling the excitement of something big coming. I light a smoke and drop the match in a soda can, listening for the satisfying sizzle that comes when it hits the liquid left at the bottom. Time to pull out my suitcase set from under the bed, some very basic luggage I bought a few years ago at Kmart. It's nothing fancy, but a big upgrade from the brown bag days; my Dad would surely approve. There's a big suitcase with a couple of smaller ones inside.

The large suitcase handle still has the tag from my most recent flight, LaGuardia to LAX. When I left California a couple of years ago, I didn't fly back to New York, I drove. A cross-country trip squeezed into a tiny Chevy Chevette, a car not made for comfort.

"Oh my, Honey, are you sure you want to drive across the whole country?" my Mom asked at the time. "Where will you stay along the way? You could get lost and nobody's going to know where you are. What if you get caught in one of those big dust storms they have out west?" she worried.

"Ma, give me a break. A dust storm? I've got a better chance of seeing Christie Brinkley on the highway in a red Ferrari than getting caught in a dust storm, don't worry about me. I went to the Triple-A office and met with a guy who mapped the whole thing out, he even gave me some places to stay along the way. I'm leaving LA and taking one highway all the way to the East Coast, then 95 north to home. It's going to take like three days."

"Okay Honey, it'll all work out, I'm sure. It will be a great adventure for you."

The whole boring, uneventful, and lonely trip took less than two and a half days. I drove that poor Chevette into the ground, on the last leg going for 15 hours straight. I was over this adventure.

My time in LA pretty much sucked. I didn't grow as a person, didn't have any real friends, and spent most of the time longing to be back in New York, where I had been so miserable (mostly due to the Canola fiasco) that I'd decided to come to California in the first place. I guess if there is one thing I learned, it's that your issues and problems always go with you, they don't stay behind. I'll have to take a second look before I leave for Hawaii and make sure my latest problem, Chris Garvey, isn't hiding in my luggage.

After packing, I stand in the shower contemplating my life. I'm happy. Tomorrow I'm moving to Hawaii with a girl I love. We have some money and I've got a job at Freddie's in Honolulu waiting for me. What we don't have is a place to live or any friends (unless Junior made it out there!), not to mention knowledge of the city we are moving to and who knows what else we are going to face. But I'm in love, feeling equally loved in return, and not having any second thoughts about the move, no matter what my sister thinks. I don't have the foresight to worry about the what-ifs, and like I said, I'm happy today. Besides Marlboro Reds, the thinking "It'll all work out," was also passed down by my mother. It would probably benefit me, and Sara as well, if I broadened my scope and look a little further into the future. Adults should do that.

I said goodbye to my Mom last night with a homemade dinner and this morning my Dad is coming to take me for a farewell breakfast in town. I can't remember the last time I saw him. He picks me up in his latest Caddy (he was only half an hour late today, which is best-case scenario) and we take the short trip down Broadway to The Strawberry Place, an ancient greasy spoon that serves the best breakfast around. The restaurant has a cozy feel to it, with people of all sorts sharing the small space without complaint. Rockland has a funky hippie vibe to it like everyone is still on some groovy pill from the 60's that mellows them out. That's what the crowd in here gives off to me this morning. We take a seat at the counter, instead of waiting thirty minutes for a table.

"So this is the big day," my Dad begins as we look over the menus. The way he said it, the tone sounds condescending, like he's mocking me.

"Nope," I answer curtly. "Tomorrow is."

"This is great, I'm so proud of you," he continues, and this time it feels genuine. I was being a little paranoid when judging his tone a moment before. "You've come a long way since last year, my boy."

Of course, he is referring to my week in jail, which will always be a line of demarcation in my life. "Thanks, Dad, I appreciate it. I'm trying."

Our breakfast is delivered and my Dad meticulously begins preparing his food for consumption. We both got a stack of pancakes and some well-done bacon. "Very well done bacon. Very, very, crisp," my father had instructed the server when ordering, as he has previously at every breakfast in the history of his life. Syrup and butter are generously applied, and then my Dad cuts his entire plate of pancakes into little squares before having a bite. Meanwhile, I cut my flapjacks using a fork as I eat and am done with my food before he even begins eating his. The waiter came by to clear my plate and I order another stack so I don't have to sit here with nothing to do, just staring at my Dad not eating.

"This joint reminds me of a place in Riverdale we used to go to when everyone was still just babies. You would be covered in food, just a fucking disaster, and your brother would be looking on like you were crazy. Even as babies, you guys were so different. Lauren was so patient with the two of you."

On and on, Dad just keeps talking, all the while his next bite of pancake hangs off his fork for minutes at a time, going up and down with his hand gestures. My insides churn while I watch syrup and butter glisten from his fingers and drip down his arm, but it doesn't seem to bother him. It's like watching a kid happily playing while their diaper's full of shit. Can't they smell that?

Dad continues to regale our morning with old-time stories that make the otherwise arduous process of watching him eat breakfast semi-bearable, before finally turning his attention to me. I feel inner peace as he opens a wet nap to begin cleaning himself up. "So what are you hoping to get out of this move, Bry? You've had a tough couple of years and seem to be turning things around since you met this woman. What's your goal?"

"I don't really have any goals set, Dad. Just getting to Hawaii is my goal, I haven't thought about what I want to accomplish once we're there."

"Well, you should think about it. Plan it out in your head and visualize it. Make sure you keep on this upward trend. Figure out where you want to be in six months, Bry. What do you think?"

"Shit man, I don't know. I love Sara, I want to be with her. She makes me happy and gives me confidence. I'm feeling really good about us; we'll be a good team out there. In six months, I just want to still be happy."

"Well that sounds great Son, I'm glad it's going so well with her. Just remember, it only takes a second for a storm to come through and change everything in a relationship. Work on your own foundation because sometimes the only one you can count on is you. Keep it in the back of your mind, don't forget to take care of yourself, and stay on this upward trend."

This is a big-time speech, the likes of which I've never received from my Dad. "Okay Pop, I'll do my best. Thanks for the words of wisdom," I tell him, happy to have my father acting all fatherly. What took you so long, Dad?

As we return to the car, he gives me an envelope and instructs me not to open it until we find an apartment in Hawaii. "If you open this before you find a place, what's inside will self-destruct in thirty seconds," Dad says with a sly grin as if he were a TV spy. "Love you, Boy. Take care of yourself out there Bryan."

"Love you too, Pop."

Thankfully, we end on this good note before my big move.

I grab the phone to call Sara and say goodnight after a long day of packing and cleaning up. I put the receiver to my ear and hear her say hello before I even start to punch the digits.

"Baby, I was just calling you!"

She laughs. "Well, I called you first, Bry guy! I guess we're on the same wavelength. I'm already in bed, just want tomorrow to get here already."

"Me too, can't wait to get out of here with you. I'm so tired, I'll be asleep the second we hang up."

"Okay, then I'll let you go, love you. Don't forget to look for me in your dreams tonight, I'll be the girl searching for you. Come find me!"

"I'll find you, Baby! Love you so much."

I hang up, close my eyes and begin searching for Sara.

CHAPTER 21

"**F**UCKIN' YANKEES ARE 14 GAMES BACK WITH A MONTH TO GO," Ed complains as he takes two smokes out of the classic red and white Marlboro box. We are standing next to his car, waiting for Sara to get here. It's time to go to the airport.

"I honestly haven't paid attention since they traded Rickey," I reply as he lights the two butts and hands one to me. "They need to fire Dent and bring Billy back again," I proclaim, but only half-heartedly.

"You alright man?" Ed asks, changing the subject. "This is a big deal; you don't have to be all Johnny Bravo. I'd be shitting my pants. You ready to do this or what?" he asks.

"Too late to turn back now," I shrug with a smile. "I got new batteries in my Walkman, some fresh mixed tapes, a few Baseball Digests for when I'm not sleeping, and a couple packs of ciggy butts. They have two or three movies during the flight, too."

"I'm not asking about the plane, Numb Nuts, I mean are you worried about living out there and shit?"

"Not at all Dude, I'm psyched for it. My job is all set up at Freddie's and from what I can tell by the stuff at the library, rent is way cheaper there than it is here, so maybe we'll be living large, at least that's what I'm hoping."

"If you say so, Man. I hope it's as easy as you're making it sound. I'll be rooting for you dummies. Hey, before I forget, make sure you call Mom a lot, she doesn't care about the long-distance bills and is not as cool about this as she's letting on," he finishes.

Sara and the blue Mustang finally appear from around the curve, her sister Cara at the wheel. The car pulls to a stop in front of us, Sara all smiles in the passenger seat.

"Grab her crap and let's go," Ed instructs, "you have to be there at least half an hour before take-off."

And just like that, we are off on this insane undertaking to a destination that we may as well have picked out of a hat. Not for a vacation, we're staying and not planning on coming back. Yeah Ed, maybe I am going to shit my pants after all!

Following a layover in San Francisco and then a long delay before take-off, we are finally moments away from touching down in Honolulu. The no smoking sign dings, followed by an announcement from a stewardess that there's no more smoking, just in case we didn't see the sign or hear the ding. I snuff out my millionth smoke of the flight and I'm ready to land.

Sara is in the window seat and I'm next to her, both of us looking down on the blue water with excitement. I'm surprised to see Pearl Harbor right below us as the plane speeds over it. I know what Pearl Harbor looks like from the pictures in our history books but I must have missed it in the Frommer's Guide and embarrassingly I didn't know it was here in Honolulu.

"Oh my God, there's Pearl Harbor," I announce excitedly to Sara. "Look, there's Pearl Harbor!"

"Relax Bryan, yes I see it's fucking Pearl Harbor," she growls back.

"Whoa whoa whoa excuse me. I didn't want you to miss it." Jeez, where the fuck did that come from?

The stewardesses pass out some forms to sign before landing, asking if we are bringing things like fruits, vegetables, bugs, flowers, or pets into the

Hawaiian Islands. Seems like Sara has a bug up her ass, but I don't mention it on the form. What's up with the bad attitude? It's weird timing since we are finally about to land and start a new life together, something we have been planning for months.

"Love you so much, Baby," I hug Sara, taking the high road and leaning in for a kiss. "So glad we are doing this together."

"Me too Bry, me too," she assures me with a smile, "Sorry I snapped. I just need to get to the hotel and you know, decompose for a few."

Say what? Come again? "I think you mean decompress, unless you're planning on killing yourself."

"Yeah, that's what I meant," she confirms, and we both laugh. Sara is smart, way smarter than me. That just came out wrong.

As we walk off the plane, we get "lai'd." Beautiful floral wreaths are hung around our necks by an equally stunning Hula girl, looking fresh from a Luau with bare feet and a grass skirt.

"Aloha, welcome to "Ha-why-E," our hula girl glows melodically.

"Thank you!" we happily reply.

"Mahalo! In Hawaii, mahalo means thank you."

"Okay, well thank you again," I quip, then point a finger before saying "mahalo" with a wink. I can be a total cheeseball sometimes.

We walk along with all the tourists headed to baggage claim, an aura of excitement in the air. Of course, all these folks have a return ticket home, but Sara and I are about to get working on a list of urgent tasks, not relax on the beach for a week.

The taxi line is thankfully right outside of the baggage area, which makes perfect sense. The New York airports make you walk forever, lugging your shit around. We have five big bags in total. When you're packing for forever, you can't really overdo it. I somehow figure out how to carry three of the suitcases while Sara handles the other two. We slowly shuffle out through sliding doors as the perfect tropical air envelopes us, palm trees and other exotic plants swaying in the breeze.

A long line of orange taxis wait next to the curb and as each one pulls up, the driver gets out to open the trunk and toss the bags in. After a short wait, it's our turn. Luckily our guy is driving a Chevy Caprice with enough space to easily handle our luggage. The well-tanned, fit driver, wearing a floral patterned shirt, slams the trunk lid down and jumps in the car.

"Where we going, Braddah?" he asks when we are settled in the back. "Lemme guess, Waikiki?"

"Ah, yes," Sara speaks up. "I have the address right here," she continues, reading from the Frommers. "151 Uluniu Ave," she sounds out as best she can.

Me being the typical New Yorker, I'm on high alert. "How much?" I ask aggressively.

He pulls down the meter and happily replies, "I dunno, Braddah, let's wait and see, maybe we gonna' hit some traffic."

How can there be heavy traffic on an island, I think to myself, but then ten minutes later we are in bumper-to-bumper gridlock comparable to Times Square at rush hour. Why wouldn't there be traffic in Hawaii? It doesn't matter, we are enamored with the sights and our excitement is bubbling over. "Wow Bry, I didn't realize it's so built up here! It's really like a pretty big city," Sara declares.

"Totally," I agree. "It doesn't even feel real yet. We're surrounded by beautiful mountains in the middle of the Pacific. This is like a postcard. Rockland is such a toilet bowl compared to out here."

I asked the cabbie a couple of questions when we first got going but he didn't seem too keen to chat us up so I just left him alone to drive. Fifteen minutes later his meter is at forty bucks. I suspect he probably has the tourist rate and one for the locals. We are most likely getting screwed, but I'm not going to start our journey off by razzing this guy over a few dollars. "How much longer?" I wonder out loud; the Frommers said it's a 15-minute ride.

"Hang Loose Brah, it's just round da' corna," he informs me. Obviously, the people from Hawaii have some kind of weird dialect or made-up language. We park curbside at a crappy-looking little hotel/ motel called "The Mariner." Sara had called and reserved a room after seeing it in the guide. Whoever took pictures for the book should be given an award because this place is pure shit compared to the photos. Sara and I are hoping to find an apartment right away and need to be out of this place in a couple of days at most, we don't have the money for an extended stay. Our suitcases single file on the sidewalk, I generously hand my "braddah" a fifty.

"Mahalo!" he smiles while handing over his card. "Call me when you ready go home, Brah."

That's going to be a while, but no need to share the plan with this guy. "Mahalo," I reply, like a touristy dork.

CHAPTER 22

AFTER A QUICK TOUR OF THE MUSTY-SMELLING LITTLE ROOM, which is heavy on shells and floral decor, we make collect calls home to report our safe arrival. The conversations are quick, good wishes and luck are exchanged, with a promise to talk again in a few days.

Sara sacks out immediately, so I grab the rainbow key chain and head out to explore a little. A blond guy at the front desk wearing a tacky shirt with fish designs on it tells me to make a right out of the front door, walk two blocks and I'll be in the heart of Waikiki.

"Got it, thanks. By the way, Bro, our room smells like shit, we may need to upgrade."

He cups his mouth as if telling me a secret. "The whole place smells like that, don't take it personally."

I nod my head in acceptance, then light up a smoke and head out. I'm at the ocean before I get down to the filter, at which time the realization hits me that I have not eaten for hours and am starving.

On the beachfront, there's a fast food type joint called "The Big Kahuna." I don't know what a kahuna is, but I'll take two. After buying a bacon cheeseburger and some fries, I go back outside and sit on a cement wall, setting it all out to have a little picnic for myself and enjoy some people watching.

It's twilight, tourists are leaving the beach and slowly migrating back to their fancy hotels along the strip. I wonder while watching the procession, why does everyone on vacation always look so miserable? Like this is so tough, being in Hawaii doing nothing but eating and sleeping for a week.

Anyway, some vacationers are across the street from me, looking like a herd of cattle as they wait for the traffic light to change so they can cross. The "walk" sign illuminates and everyone starts trudging straight toward me, sandals shuffling in unison. When they get to my side of the street, people mostly peel off to the left, and some to the right. At the tail end of the group is a big guy, tall and fat with long curly black hair, he's covered in tribal tattoos. The man doesn't go left or right. He heads straight at me and sits down on the wall.

"I love Big K fries, Braddah," he begins in the local tone I heard earlier from the cabbie, then he picks up a fry and dangles it out of his mouth like a cigarette.

Now I've seen it all. "Dude, what the fuck are you doing, my man."

"This my fuckin' spot, Haole Boy, and that makes these my fries, Braddah," he reports factually.

"What am I on Candid Camera here? You can't be serious?" I ask him.

"Dead serious, Brah." He goes on, asking "How about I give you one deal? You buy dem fries back from me, for twenty dolla, or I buss ya head wide open like one coconut, Haole Boy? How you like it?"

First of all, what the fuck language is this weirdo speaking? I look around and of course, nobody is paying attention to us, why would they be? I see no cops, no lifeguards or Guardian Angels, nobody that can help me not get fucked up here by this guy. Where is Curtis Sliwa when I need him? Trouble just follows me, man, that I already know, but this is supposed to be a new beginning. For fucks sake, I've been in Hawaii less than two hours.

Well, I don't think I can take this guy, he's like a sumo wrestler on crack. What I do know is that I can sure as shit outrun his fat ass. Damn, I should have

arate lessons when Angelo had offered. If we were in New York
taked be willing to risk a beating and go toe to toe with this bully. A
r'ack eyes don't scare me but now is not the time. Instead, I will run.
kay Dude, you wanna shake me down for a twenty spot, that's cool,"
standing up as I feign reaching my hand in a pocket for the money,
st, try my burger, Asshole!" I smack the food right in his fat face and
ake off running through the throngs of tourists. After a clean getaway
to the hotel I sit down on a bench in front and wonder if Hawaii really
is the tropical paradise I had envisioned.

"Patty, this burger blew up in his face like there was an M-80 inside it.
Oh man, this dude was so pissed," I say inside my head, wishing that my friend
was sitting next to me. Unfortunately, Sara is all I have on this day. I know one
person on this side of the world, and the last thing she wants to hear is that I just
punched someone in the face with my dinner. Walking up to the front desk of
the Mariner, still panting and sweating, I ask Fish Shirt, "What's a haole boy?"

"We are, Sir," he frowns. "White people from the mainland, the locals
call us haole," he sighs. "Better get used to it."

As I lie in bed trying to fall asleep that night, I can't stop thinking about
my confrontation with the hamburger thief. This temper of mine is a disease
that's been running through the Grayhill bloodlines for generations, and
I've got it worse than all of us. So far I haven't hurt anybody, but if I don't get
this under control, something bad will happen. I'm not even talking about
fighting, just impulsive acts that twitch out of my body. Whether it's smashing
and breaking things, throwing phones out the window, or even kicking down
doors, I've embarrassed myself more times than I can count. It happens so
quickly, I usually don't even see it coming. I need one of those turkey poppers
implanted in my arm, so I know when I'm cooked and ready to blow.

On the other hand, I've pulled over on the side of the road to push a
stranger in a wheelchair across the street, changed tires for people stuck on
the highway, picked up hitchhikers many times, and even given money to

strangers. Jekyll and Hyde, that's me. You never know what you're get, or should I say who. What I do know is I need to figure this out, it's too late.

Sara wakes up and snuggles next to me. "I'm all messed up from time change, my body doesn't know what to do," she yawns. "What are you still doing up?"

"Same thing I guess."

"What's wrong, Bry?"

Don't mention the fight today, I remind myself. "What's like the worst trait handed down to you from your parents, do you think?"

"That's a weird question, why are you asking?"

"I'm just thinking how when I get all pissed off and lose my shit, sometimes I get mad at my Dad. I hold him more responsible than myself because I learned to act like that from watching him."

Sara thinks about it for a second. "I hate to tell you but at this age, you're responsible for your actions, nobody else. You know right from wrong and have to learn from your mistakes."

"I know, you're right. I gotta figure it out. What about you and your family?" I ask.

"My parents are really solid, Bry, I've never had any big issues with them. My Dad is stern, he can even be scary like you've heard on the phone, but he's always been super supportive of me and my sisters. He didn't lecture me or shelter us when we were growing up, he was trusting and let us do our thing, and if he felt we were pushing it too far, he let us know. He was always watching, but he wasn't a jerk about it. Believe it or not, karate taught us a lot of discipline, which is good, cause my parents were gone a lot for work. It wasn't all hugs and kisses, but my house was peaceful."

"I'm happy for you, must be nice. Whatever your parents did, it worked. You turned out perfect," I smile, and roll over for some sleep. Sara inches closer and wraps an arm around me. She knows it's what I need.

CHAPTER 23

"**Y**OU SHOULD BE A MODEL," I TELL SARA AS WE LIE IN BED THE next morning, our first full day as Hawaiians. "Cindy Crawford doesn't hold a candle to you, and this body that I get to worship every day! How did I get to be so lucky?" I ask.

"Give me a break, Stud. I know you fooled around with half the school before we hooked up. Thanks to me, you finally know how to do it right," she cracks.

"Because I have you as my tutor," I agree. "Why don't you come over here and show me how you ride the bologna pony."

"Jesus Bryan, you always have to ruin it," she chastises me, "and it's more like a Vienna sausage."

"So is that a no?"

She scrunches her face in mock disgust. "Big time no," she replies, parading off naked to the shower.

Looks like I'll be riding the pony by myself this morning.

"Make yourself useful and go get us a newspaper," she calls out, "and some food, please. Chop chop!"

I do as instructed and head out for the paper, treading cautiously through the streets of Waikiki, on alert for that fat tubalard from the Big Kahuna. I find a little shop across from the ocean that has everything we need. Pasty tourists stock up on sunscreen and snacks for the beach as I snag the last copy of a local rag, the Honolulu Advertiser, and two cans of Diet Coke.

A McDonald's is on the corner and I get at the end of a long line for some breakfast. Who goes on vacation to Hawaii and eats McDonald's? No wonder everyone here looks miserable; all these tourists are doing exactly the same shit they were doing last week back home. I'm on official business this morning, getting a paper and finding an apartment, my eating Mickey D's is justified.

"Do you have to be smoking?" some fatty boombalatty Mama inquires of me as we wait in line to order.

"Do you really need another Egg McFatso sandwich?" I almost blurted out. Day two, confrontation two, and it's still early. I'm letting this one go. I flash her a screw-you smile and crush the butt under my shoe. See, I'm growing as a person.

Back at the hotel room, I spread out the goodies on a tiny table by the window and call out to Sara. "We got three kinds of McMuffins to choose from: Sausage, classic with ham, or... wait for it...Spam!"

"I'll have the classic," Sara shouts back from the bathroom.

"Well, classic signifies something was once good. I should have just said, "Regular.""

"Okay, I'll take regular."

"Did I mention I also have a Spam McMuffin?" I stress, tilting my head sideways quizzically as she enters the room.

Sara pulls up a chair and sits, unwraps a sandwich, and takes a big bite. "I'll pass on the Spam," she mumbles through a mouthful of food, "That sounds nasty. Crack open the paper and let's get a look at those classifieds, Bry."

We peruse the listings for a one-bedroom apartment and find several possible options. This ratty hotel is going to cost us $40 a day, which will add up quickly, so finding a place is priority number one. We circle the apartments that interest us and begin calling. After a couple of rejections and leaving messages for a few others, we finally hit on something with potential.

The phone is answered by a young boy who explains that his grandparents do not speak English very well. Through their grandson, we agree to meet at noon. Sara maps it out and I show the address to Fish Shirt at the front desk, who tells me it's a thirty-minute walk, meaning we have to leave now.

Like Sara had predicted, this would be the first of a lot of walking we, especially I, will be doing over the coming months. Following our map out of Waikiki, we go over a tiny walkway bridge and then past a huge mall and park. Continuing on, we pass a concert venue, and then what do you know, the Freddie's I will soon be working at is across the street from the arena. Next, we see the statue of "King Kamehameha," a placard reading he was the first king of Hawaii. His royal highness is wearing no pants and only a tiny cloth covers his family jewels. "This guy looks like he's waiting on line to get into Studio 54," I laugh to Sara. We continue through a sloppy area full of smut shops and undesirables that is labeled Hotel Street on the map, and then a couple of blocks later we arrive at the specified address.

Our prospective landlords greet us in front of the West Shore Tower, a tall thin building sparkling with brown tinted glass, at least forty stories high, easily the tallest building in this section of Oahu. What section it is, I have no idea. Mr. and Mrs. Tung are the elderly folks who have the apartment for rent. Greeting us with hellos and bows, they invite us to "come, come," as they walk to the main entrance. We follow them into the elevator and Mr. Tung presses the 16th floor, where everyone exits the lift and walks down a short, windowless hallway.

The apartment door opens into bright sunlight. A small galley kitchen is straight ahead, with bar seating between the kitchen and the living room. A hallway on the left leads to a bathroom and small bedroom, its balcony leading back into the living room. Oh yeah, and there are floor-to-ceiling windows that have an amazing mountain view. I'm in love. We'll take it!

"You have jobs?" Mrs. Tung asks, bringing me back to reality. It would have been helpful if their grandson, who had answered our phone call, was here to interpret, but unfortunately, he's nowhere to be found.

"Yes."

"You have money?"

"Yes. How much?" I ask.

Mrs. Tung points to the $600 on the paper and says rapidly "This. One, two, three, four," she taps the paper with her old wrinkly finger, four times.

$600 is the monthly nut listed in the classifieds, so I guess she wants first, last, and two months' security. "We can give cash for one, two, three. No four, too much," I plead in some sort of weird accent, trying to emulate her dialect. It's human nature, like yelling at a person that's hard of hearing.

"Okay, okay, okay," agrees Mrs. Tung, still speaking fast. "You give cash." She may not speak much English, but like everybody, she speaks cash. "Free electric," she finishes, "we include."

And it's that easy. No credit check, no references, no delays, no lease, or even a real conversation. We fork over the dough and take the keys. Sara and I just need to go back to the Mariner and get our suitcases, having solved our number one challenge, less than twenty-four hours after arriving. As we head back, I picture our cash savings in my head as a four-piece money pie, and after this, we are down a couple of slices.

CHAPTER 24

AFTER WE LEAVE THE TUNGS, SARA AND I ENJOY THE WALK BACK to Waikiki. Finding an apartment is what we have been most anxious about. Everyone back home said we were crazy, coming out here with no place to live.

"Bry, no offense but this place is the same rent as your shitty apartment in Central Rockland," Sara states anxiously. "It seems too good to be true."

Whenever anyone starts with "no offense," it's a guarantee they're about to offend you. "Why was my place shitty? We knew apartments were cheaper out here. Let's not look a gift horse in the mouth, Baby," I implore as we walk past King Kamehameha again, from the other side of the street this time. His bronzed ass is mostly covered by a cape, thankfully.

"I'm totally stoked, don't get me wrong. It just happened so quickly, I hope it's as great as it seems," she finishes.

"Another thing that's happening quickly is our money's disappearing, so I need to get into Freddie's and on the work schedule as soon as possible."

We had checked out of our room at the Mariner before leaving this morning and told them to hold our luggage behind the front desk, just in case we ended up taking the apartment. If it didn't work out, they assured us we can check back in tonight, as they have plenty of vacancies (probably because it's the crappiest hotel in town). Instead of rushing to bring our stuff over to the empty new apartment, Sara and I decide to enjoy the rest of the afternoon sightseeing in Waikiki.

As we stroll through the bustling shopping district by the beach, I notice a sign reading "Kalakaua Avenue," and think to myself Main Street would have been a much easier name choice. At Sara's request, we stop in to browse at several of the high-end stores that line the Ave. Shoppers in these big-time stores are predominantly Japanese (I think), and they look like they came ready to buy, with multiple bags hanging off their arms. Sara and I are walking around without two nickels to rub together, but it doesn't matter. We have each other, and a fancy apartment too! This day could not have gone better so far. As my seventh-grade hero Hannibal said on the A-team, "*I love it when a plan comes together.*"

"Love you, Cookie," I whisper into Sara's ear, as she looks admiringly at a shelf full of Gucci purses. "So lucky to be here with you," I continue, snuggling up from behind and kissing her ear.

"I'm the lucky one, Bry," Sara coos, giving me a hug before returning the expensive bag she was admiring back to the shelf. We walk back to the Mariner a little after six and collect our luggage from Fish Shirt, who appears to work 24-7.

"How about calling a cab for me, Haole Boy?" I smile at him.

"My pleasure, Homey," he replies while extending a hand to me for a high-five.

Sara looks at us like we're aliens. "What are you guys talking about?"

I wave her off. "It's nothing, I'll tell you later." Getting in the taxi, I take one last look around, searching for my sumo nemesis. "Sayonara sucker," I say to myself, jumping in and shutting the door.

We give the cab driver our new address at the fancy high-rise and ask him if there are any grocery stores nearby. He informs us that Foodland is a block away on the "Mauka" side of the towers. Sensing my confusion, he clarifies. "The mountain, Brah," and follows that with "towards the mountain and highway."

We have a lot to learn, man, a whole lot. "Let's drop off our luggage, unpack the sleeping bags, and then walk to the store," Sara says, "we can stock the fridge a little."

We lug our suitcases up to 1601 and I slip the key into the lock. "Would it be gay if I carried you over the threshold?" I ask her before opening the door.

"Totally. Just unlock it, Dork."

Sara walks in before me and feels around for a light switch as I bring in the first of the bags and set them down in the dark living room. She finds the kitchen light and flicks it on, then screams while simultaneously darting out of the apartment, cursing incoherently as she pounds the elevator buttons.

What the holy hell! Looking in the kitchen, everything seems in order to me. The white countertops and newer appliances are freshly cleaned. What am I missing here? I go out into the hallway and Sara is in tears, still pressing the elevator buttons frantically. "Sara, what's happening?" I ask. "What are you getting all freaky deaky about?"

"Oh my God Bryan, you didn't see that?" she practically shouts.

"See what? There's nothing to see."

Her face wears a look of total disgust. "When I turned on the light, no less than 10,000 cockroaches were scurrying all over the kitchen. I'm telling you, I couldn't even see the white counter," she cries. "That place is beyond infested; I'm never going back in there. I fucking told you it was too good to be true!"

Ah hell, it's always something, I think, shaking my head. "Okay, relax, it's over. Let's get the bags and we'll head back to the Mariner for the night. I'll call the Tungs and take care of this," I say, hugging her.

The lights are still on as I go back to get the suitcases I'd brought in earlier. Not a creature is in sight, but according to Sara, they are here somewhere, hiding out until the place goes dark again. I leave the light on as if this will solve the problem, and lock the door. As we board the elevator, I picture in my head another hunk of our money pie being eaten tonight by the upcoming cab ride and hotel. The thought has me briefly consider walking to Waikiki with all the luggage; that's how cheap I am. So much for camping out in our new apartment. Hopefully, this will still work itself out, I know that's what my Mom would say.

I hate it when a plan falls apart.

CHAPTER 25

I CALLED THE TUNGS LAST NIGHT WHEN WE GOT BACK TO THE Mariner. Thankfully, their grandson answered the phone and easily translated the roach problem to his grandparents. He told us they have a "guy for the bugs" and would call to get it taken care of right away. The apartment will be exterminated, cleaned, and ready by tonight.

My eyes open this morning to Sara propped up against the headboard, Walkman on, and tears rolling down her cheeks. This can't be good. "Hey, what's wrong?" I ask, thinking of all the scenarios it may be, while also selfishly wondering why my day needs to start off like this. "Hey," I tap her arm, "what's up?"

She takes off the headphones and replies, "Sorry, couldn't hear you. I'm fine."

"Oh, I see. You seem fine," I answer sarcastically, "just having the usual morning cry, I guess."

She gives me a tiny smile. "I'm just emotional, Bry. I'm getting my period soon and those roaches last night freaked me out. I'm thinking about us too," she finishes.

"Ahh damn, Baby, I thought we were going better than ever. What are you talking about?"

She grabs my hands. "No, no, we are, we are. I love the way you are taking care of me and doing everything. I'm thinking all good things about us."

"But?" I ask.

"No buts. I'm so happy with us and that's my happy feelings and then I switch over to thinking about those roaches and that's my bad feelings, and it's all just making me anxious in a positive and then negative way, so I'm trying to get a handle on all the good and the—"

"ZZZZZZZZZZ." I loll my head back and pretend I'm snoring, a not-so-subtle hint that she's gone on too long. This can go either way, but thankfully she laughs, instead of cursing me out. I'm catching her emotional roller coaster coming down the happy track.

"I'm feeling really good about us too."

"Okay, everything's okay, I'm fine. Just had myself a moment there," Sara declares. "I'm getting in the shower, and then we can talk about the apartment."

Sara calls out from the bathroom and asks me if I can wash her back. But of course, milady. Not too long ago a shower meant don't drop the soap or I might get raped. This really is paradise.

After thorough washing, I dress and sit at the table by the window. Looking out upon a canal, I see joggers and walkers share a path alongside the water as kayaks paddle by in the background, everyone looking fit and ready to face the day. We all have our daily routines, mine is just not as healthy. I light up a cigarette and begin reading the two-day-old box scores from yesterday's paper, as Sara goes through her hair and makeup ritual in the bathroom.

I read about the Yanks beating the Angels in a meaningless game at the stadium. Mattingly had four hits to raise his average above .300 and "Neon Deion" Sanders, the flashy rookie, went hitless and probably looked like an idiot while doing it, that gaudy dollar sign medallion hanging from his neck. So much for the classy Yankees of the Maris and even Munson days. These young guys are an embarrassment.

Sara strides out of the bathroom looking like a trillion bucks, sitting down next to me at the table. I'm rocking floppy shorts, a t-shirt, and a Yankee hat on backward, not to mention a cig hanging out of my mouth. Time to step up my game here pretty soon, but Sara doesn't seem to mind my lazy attire.

"Thanks for the wash, Bry guy," she grins. "So what's the plan for the apartment? Do you really think they can kill all those nasty ass roaches in one day, or ever, for that matter?"

"Maybe they know an all-star exterminator. Hopefully, he's the Bo Jackson of pest killing," I reply with a shrug. "We should go see how it looks, at least."

"Agreed. What time did they say it would be safe to get back in there?"

"Five o'clock."

"Five it is."

A radio is on for background noise, the Rolling Stones are singing "Start Me Up." Sara turns it up full blast and starts mouthing the song, doing a spot on Mick Jagger impersonation. Dancing with hands on hips, head bobbing like a chicken, and sticking her lips out, she is hilarious and spot on. So funny, and she knows it. We laugh our asses off.

"You crack me up, I love you so much. You're my everything," I tell her.

Sara takes a silly bow. "And I love you more than anybody loves anybody, Baby."

The apartment is immaculate when we return. No indication is present of even one roach having been there the night before, much less the thousands Sara claimed she saw, but we give it a serious once-over anyway. I don't see how it could be possible but it seems free of all the pests. She still has some heebie-jeebies, especially when I jokingly swat at her hair and yell "roach." We agree to give it a go, signifying our acceptance with a thumbs up to the landlords, which I follow with a bow to say thank you, for some reason.

After the Tungs leave, Sara looks over at me like I'm crazy, a little grin on her face. "What's with the bowing, Weirdo? If you're trying to offend them, I'm sure it worked."

"What can I say, got caught up in the moment I guess. Trying to be respectful is all."

"Don't try so hard next time," she shakes her head, "and can the Chinese accent."

"Gotcha," I say, having heard enough of her critique. "Let's enjoy the moment, okay? Welcome to our new apartment."

We officially move in, which takes 30 seconds because we only have our suitcases. Sara and I own absolutely nothing. Not a fork or a knife, not a stick of furniture, unfortunately, no bed, nada. We know the plan is to start at zero but it's a little more intimidating now that we are standing in our barren new home. It looks like we just finished moving out, not moving in.

We stay with our plan from the night before and head off to the grocery store for some food and supplies. Walking hand in hand to Foodland, I say "We have one day to get things a little set up at the apartment, and then I have to get into Freddie's and try to get some shifts, toot sweet."

"Speak English," she scolds me. "What the fuck is a toot sweet?"

"Oh my God, like, sorry," I answer, in my best Valley girl voice. "Let me, like, say it in your language. It means, like, super dee duper fast."

"Okay whatever, Mr. Big Words. I need to find a job too, and I'm also actually hoping to hit the beach this week before I start looking."

"The beach is for tourists, Baby. Let's worry about paying the bills first," I reply, unnecessarily curt. She picks up on my tone immediately, and I realize I'm about to get a mouthful.

"I know all about the bills, Buddy. Don't fucking tell me what I can and cannot do." Note to self: do not poke this bear.

We find the grocery store easily enough and fill our cart with the basics, getting some plastic cutlery, paper plates, chips, paper towels, toilet paper, soap, stuff like that to get us going. Dinner for me is going to be an old favorite, Totino's frozen pepperoni pizza rolls, Diet Coke, and cigarettes. Meanwhile, Sara put together something at the salad bar. Already I see a pattern developing with our choices.

The paltry haul at Foodland costs us almost $75, another chunk of money pie gobbled up. The prices are astronomical here. I did receive a five-finger discount on two cases of Diet Coke which I "forgot" to remove from the bottom of the shopping cart when unloading at the register.

"Do we have everything?" I ask on the walk home.

"It's only one night," Sara reasons, "We won't die if we forgot something."

"Unless the roaches eat us," I smirk.

After dinner, we roll out our sleeping bags in the bedroom. A normal person would have watched some TV before bed, but of course, we don't have one. This may be the first day in my life I haven't watched television. I don't know how the hell they lived in the olden days without one.

"Things are totally good," I say encouragingly to Sara as we lie there, trying to gauge how she is feeling. "We can one hundred percent do this. Hey, do you realize if this building was in Manhattan, the rent would be like five thousand bucks or something?"

"I know, for sure. We have to get a camera and take some pictures. Nobody is going to believe this is where we live. This crazy idea to move out here might just work out, after all, Mr. Grayhill."

"Who knows, maybe you'll be Mrs. Grayhill one day?" I tease Sara.

"If you play your cards right, maybe I will."

This is the perfect segue for us to consummate the day with some S-E-X, but Sara got her little friend this afternoon, so we won't be fooling around tonight. I would totally do it but she's not into that, the thought disgusts her.

Sara closes her eyes and is out quickly, leaving me alone in my sleeping bag, looking up at the night sky, like a lonely Boy Scout. The big difference is unlike a Boy Scout, who is well known for rubbing two sticks together vigorously, I'll only be rubbing one.

The deed complete, I'm fulfilled and ready for sleep. Laying on the floor of our empty apartment, we have nothing, but as my tired eyes look out upon the stars, I couldn't possibly want for more.

CHAPTER 26

SARA WOKE ME UP THE NEXT MORNING IN A PANIC. MY FIRST thought is that it must be roach-related.

"Bry, get up, get up," she shakes me. "I've been awake for hours, waiting to talk."

"Yeah yeah yeah okay, give me a second, Baby," I croak. My back is stiff and achy from sleeping on the floor. "What's on your mind?" I ask.

"What's on my mind is how are we going to buy stuff to make this place even halfway decent? We need absolutely everything Bry, and we don't have a pot to piss in!"

"A pot to piss in?" I question her. "Who are you, my grandfather?"

"Whatever Mr. Toot Sweet, my Dad says it all the time, who cares? I'm worried about the money, that's the point!"

"Okay, okay," I say, wiping the sleep out of my eyes. "Just relax, I'll take care of it. Can't we just wake up a little more mellow yellow and give it a few before we jump right into these serious conversations?" I ask.

"I know, I'm sorry," she cringes, "I'm just super wound up I guess, and I have to get it out."

"It's okay, I just don't worry that much. You should try to take it as it comes. Worrying doesn't help." Meanwhile, I've been stressing about our money pie every time we cut into it. "Listen, I have a surprise that will make you happy. I've been holding out on you," I grin.

"Oh, you have, have you?"

"My Dad was feeling generous and even though he told me not to ask for anything, he ponied up his Sears credit card and told me we could dent it for five hundred bucks!"

I opened the envelope last night. The card came with a note from Dad reading, "I love you, Bry! Let us know if you need anything else." Aww, thanks, Dad! My Scrooge of a father is turning over a new leaf.

Sara lit up. "That is awesome, so awesome. Your Dad came through big time!"

"He really did. Let's make a list of what to get and then hit it hard. Maybe I'll buy some Tough Skins for work," I joke, referring to Sears' brand of nerdy jeans.

The main thing we need is a bed, also a phone, and a phone book. We may as well have just dropped in here by parachute and don't know a thing about this place besides the basics in the Frommer's guide. People on vacation don't care where the phone company is.

"Time to find the library. We need to *edjumacate* ourselves on this place," I laugh, imitating a comedian we watched on TV (how I miss thee) not too long ago.

The news of the Sears card soothes Sara's worries for the moment. I can't wait to see what's on her mind tomorrow morning. Before heading to the shower, Sara brings me a can of Diet Coke from the fridge, while I stand against the rail of the lanai gazing down upon our new neighborhood. Why am I feeling guilty over stealing a couple of cases of soda from Foodland last night? Seems my conscience is trying to tell me something here, like don't fuck up this new situation with a stupid move like that. Didn't a week in the slammer teach you anything?

Lighting up a Red, I ruminate on this thought. I enjoy my first cigarette of the day like no other, pulling in deep drags of the sweet nicotine. Sure as I will light up this morning, I'll go to sleep tonight telling myself it's time to quit; that's the cycle. As I scrape the butt against the wall and flick it into orbit from the sixteenth floor, I resign myself to giving up on petty crimes like stealing soda. This is my intention, anyway.

Half an hour later, Sara asks a passerby in front of our building if they know of a library and she is directed to one only a few blocks from the tower. We walk in the pointed direction along city streets crowded with people who are clearly not tourists. Nobody is wearing bathing suits or flip-flops, like we saw in Waikiki. These folks are on the way to work or some other domestic task. Most everyone that's in this part of town is Asian, or Polynesian. We would learn in the coming weeks that our section of Honolulu is indeed known as "Chinatown."

In front of the library, an orange bus with writing that says "The Bus" in huge black letters on the sides, in case somebody is unsure what it is, chugs past us. I point it out to Sara. "Maybe we can find out how to get around on that thing."

"What a classy way to travel."

"Well, we can't take taxis all over the place unless you want to pay with something besides money," I smirk.

"Here we go again with the stupid sex jokes," Sara growls in admonishment, rolling her eyes. "If you want to give the cab driver a BJ, I support you."

Touché! Good one. "No, that's okay. I don't mind the walking."

Inside the library, we use a payphone and arrange for the installation of our very own line, which will be done tomorrow; very exciting! We get a bus map and directions to Sears, written down and then read aloud by a very encouraging librarian. "Catch the bus right outside the exit doors," she points down a short flight of stairs. "It will go three blocks and then turn left on Ala Moana Boulevard, which runs next to the park. The big mall will be on your left; you just can't miss it. Most of the people riding the bus will also get off there. Good luck, aloha," she signs off and waves goodbye.

"Mahalo," we reply, of course.

Following her instructions, we found the mall without a problem. After shopping, Sara and I ride the bus home with our selections made at Sears. We have two pillows and a set of sheets, one of those big round bamboo chairs with a circular cushion, as well as a box set of dishes, silverware, and a toaster, among other necessities. We pile everything in the chair and carry it together, like doctors holding a patient on a gurney. It's beyond embarrassing, even among the dregs of society that are riding on the bus with us.

A copy of Time magazine is on the seat next to me, with the headline "Drugs in the USA: Kids who sell Crack." It reminds me of my old friend Junior back in the Rock. I think a good thought for him, hopefully, my Cuz eventually finds the right path. I wonder if he ever made it out here like he had hoped.

Sara and I have a slow go but we make it home with all of the new stuff intact. Our home in progress, let's call it. We now have a mattress ordered, a chair, and some suitcases we can sit on in a pinch.

Our bed is delivered the next afternoon, right around the time the phone guy finishes doing his thing. Who knew the phone company charges $6.21 a month to rent you a phone? I didn't. We bought a Queen size mattress. No frame, box spring, or headboard. It's going to be sleeping on the floor, for now, that's all we can swing. Nonetheless, things are starting to happen, we are getting stuff done!

"Let's check the phone book for furniture stores, maybe we can find some used stuff or a thrift store like the ones back in Rockland," Sara suggests.

I'm out on the lanai smoking a butt, leaning on the railing. I watch a jet silently blasting through the perfect blue sky above, its exhaust leaving a thin cloud-like trail behind. Whoever is flying that thing, I'm impressed.

You made it, Brother! That would end in a ball of fire if I was the pilot. I'm a good bet to dent the car on a trip to the store, much less blast through the sky in a jet.

"Bry!" shouts Sara, ending my daydream. "We need more stuff!"

"There's a "Rent-a-Rama" a few blocks away. I can see it from here."

"Rent a what?"

I flick my butt 16 stories down, onto the top of the parking garage. I need an ashtray out here. If the landlords spoke any English, they'd probably ask me not to litter off the balcony. "Rent-a-Rama, Baby. They rent shit."

"Could you be a little more specific? What kind of shit?" she asks.

"Everything. TV, furniture. Anything and everything," I answer. "I knew people in LA who went there."

Faster than you can say "We probably just got screwed," Sara and I are walking out of Rent-a-Rama with an agreement to pay $75 a month for a little black and white TV, a wicker couch with pillows, one coffee table, two bar stools, and a cheap TV stand. Free delivery too! It seemed like a good idea at the time.

CHAPTER 27

WAKING UP ON A MATTRESS, AFTER HAVING SLEPT THE PREVIOUS night on the floor, it feels like we are royalty. I open my eyes and see Sara lying on her side staring at me, head propped in her hand. The sliding door is open and the temperature of the room is perfect, a Hawaiian mountain breeze cooling us.

"Do you believe in life after death?" Sara starts off the day with. So much for mellow yellow.

"You must be kidding? Please tell me you're joking," I reply, rolling my eyes but with a patient smile.

She's playing with my shaggy bedhead. "I'm serious, I really want to know! I want to be with you forever and I was just wondering if you have the same idea of forever that I do?"

"Oh, man, that's a tough one. It's such a deep question to start the day," I whine. "How about saying good morning first."

"Bry, please, play along! And good morning."

I close my eyes and start the snoring game again. "ZZZZZZZZ."

"Bryan, not funny. Answer me!" she shouts.

"Okay, okay, do I believe in life after death? I do. I mean, probably. I used to think once you die, that's it, your circuits are dead and you just rot away. I was watching some dumb nature show with my little brothers a couple years ago and I just thought about how amazing this world is, nature and all. If that can all be created somehow, then you can never say never. Maybe there is another level that your spirit goes to. What I do believe, for sure, is that this is some pretty heavy shit for the crack of dawn."

"You have to believe," she ignores me, "that we'll always be together, with our families, and our kids and—"

"Oh, we have kids in the future? Interesting."

"I want a lot of kids, four or five, and our spirits will all be together forever."

Standing up, I close out the conversation. "Let's get through the week first, Baby. Our journey to forever starts right now."

I kiss her and go to pee, then brush my teeth and head out on the lanai for my morning smoke. Gross on so many levels, guess I won't be quitting today. Back inside, I share one more thought on the life after death question, putting my arms around Sara's waist from behind as she brushes her teeth in the bathroom mirror. "Being here with you Baby, I'm the happiest I could ever be. I don't see how another life after this one could be anything but a bummer in comparison," I share with her, knowing I just scored some major points.

"Aww Bry, that's so sweet," Sara gushes. "That means everything to me."

She gives me a kiss, garnishing it with toothpaste. "Alright, enough with the mushy stuff, I have to get to Freddie's and see about some shifts today. I'm going to shower and go, it's time to get the money flowing in our direction," I tell her as she is now timidly inspecting the kitchen cabinets for her roach friends.

"Yeah, you should do that. Can you pick up a newspaper on your way back, so I can start looking too?"

"Will do," I answer, then jump in and out of the shower in a flash. Five minutes later and I'm kissing her goodbye. "I'll be back in a couple of hours. Love you!"

"Love you too, my man! Go get a job and bring home some bacon! Toot Sweet!" she jokes in a silly tone.

I make the walk to Freddie's in 20 minutes. It's on the route between the tower and Waikiki, right across from the Blaisdell Arena, which has Motley Crue on the marquee as the next concert (I'll pass, thanks). The lawn in front of the big arena is deep green and the size of a football field, with palm trees dotting the landscape. This is the scenery that you get from the windows of Freddie's in Honolulu. The one in New York has a view of their dumpster.

I got the name of the General Manager here, Paul LeBlue, from my man Vinny Gumbotz back in the New Jersey store. Paul is a white guy (a haole like me) from New Jersey who Vinny knows from some corporate training seminar or something. Maybe he'll be happy to see another east coaster and hook me up with some nice shifts.

I walk in at 10 am and interrupt a man moping the floor, asking him if Paul the manager is around. He disappears into the back without a word, and when he comes back, I am told Paul will be right up. This Freddie's looks exactly the same as all the others I've seen, except for the exquisite view. I sit down on a dark wooden bench, usually used by waiting customers, and think about my upcoming conversation with this guy. It will be my first meaningful interaction with an adult other than Sara since we got here. Our new landlords don't count, since they hardly speak English.

Turns out I have plenty of time to think, as Paul doesn't saunter out of his office for another thirty minutes. To make matters worse, before greeting me, he stops at a door-size mirror to tie his tie and fix his poofy black hair, a hideous tail braided down his back. "You look like a huge Douche bag, Paul," I feel like yelling out.

He finally meanders over, showing little interest in conversing. "Hey, how can I help you?"

I stand up and extend my hand, even though I really want to punch him in the fucking lip after having waited out here for over half an hour. He gives me a dead fish handshake with no eye contact, not a surprise. "Hi, I'm Bryan Grayhill. I'm hoping to pick up some shifts," I begin. "Chip Alexander, the KM in Bergen, New Jersey told me he met you at the last seminar in Dallas and said he was going to try to call you on my behalf," I finish.

"Oh okay, cool, that's so funny, Chip just called me yesterday," Paul informs me. "I told him I haven't seen you as of yet, and now here we are. He said you could do it all, pretty much a superstar back in Jersey."

Hey, maybe this guy isn't so bad after all. Who you calling superstar? "Yes, anything you need," I reply eagerly.

"No room for servers right now, but if you want to sub in, feel free to ask around. I can give you five or six shifts in the kitchen to start. Couple on salad station, or maybe sauté. What's your hourly rate in Jersey?"

"I was making $19.50 an hour when I left," I tell him honestly, knowing he can easily check and find out.

Paul laughs in my face. This guy is a fucking piece of work. My Mom would say he's *cruising for a bruising*. "Dude, I don't even make that here. Our pay scale is way lower than the mainland."

Not good news, but I don't flinch. "No problem. What can you pay me?"

"Best I can do for you is $10.50 an hour, and that's top dollar around here," he shrugs.

This is devastating news. Everything Sara and I are planning is budgeted on me bringing home at least what I was making back in New York. I should have checked this out beforehand, but as usual, I couldn't be bothered.

"Alright Paul, beggars can't be choosers. I need to work so please put me on. Do you mind if I hang my phone number next to the schedule, in case somebody wants coverage?"

"Yeah, of course. Give me that number too and I'll call when the schedule is ready," he says while handing me a piece of paper. "Fill out this application and bring it back with you next week."

"Got it. Thanks, Paul," I reply, as enthusiastically as possible considering the bad news he has just bestowed upon me. I exit through the front doors, out into the seemingly constant Hawaiian sunshine. Unfortunately, the new forecast for me is not nearly as bright.

"I'm home!" I call out while walking into the apartment thirty minutes later and tossing the newspaper down on the kitchen counter.

"How was it?" Sara asks, fresh from the shower with a towel around her body and another wrapped around her head. "Tell me in a minute, I'll be right out."

I drop down on the rented wicker couch and light up a smoke. My reflection stares back at me from the blank TV, which I'm too lazy to get up and turn on. This is no time for relaxing anyway, I need to figure out what to do about our lack of money.

"Do you have to be smoking on the new furniture?" Sara barks as soon as she reappears.

"I really don't give a fuck about this crap," I respond combatively, bothered by the sudden change in her tenor.

"Well you should, cause if you break it, you buy it."

I stare straight ahead, like nobody is in the room, letting silence voice my feelings. After a long pause, I ask her, "Is that all? Would you like to hear how it went now?"

"Yeah, I would. How'd it go, Darling?" she asks, like a wise ass.

"Not good, that's how. They don't have much for me at Freddie's. I can grab a few shifts in the back of the house but at only half my normal pay."

"Half your pay? Fuck that place then, you can get a better job. Let's hit the classifieds."

"I'm still going to pick up what I can there until I find something else," I tell her, "but I appreciate your support. Sorry I smoked on the couch," I say with a wink.

Sara changes the subject. "By the way, your Dad called after you left."

"Oh really, whoop de doo," I remark instinctively, having forgotten his nice gesture with the credit card. "What did he want?"

"Why are you always such a dick when it comes to your Dad? He helped us out with the furniture and he was actually really nice on the phone today. Why don't you give him a chance?" she asks.

"I've given him hundreds of chances. You have no idea what you're talking about Sara. You grew up with a Dad, I didn't."

She scoffs. "Oh boo-hoo, Bry. He showed more interest in me and us today on the phone than my father ever has, by far. Just because a Dad is in the house when you grow up doesn't mean he's present. You always say you did this, that, and the other thing with your Dad, which is awesome, and I don't think you realize he's trying. My father didn't do any of that shit with me. We did karate, that's it."

"He only tries when it's convenient for him," I plead.

"Okay, so he's not perfect, and neither are you. You guys need to stop pointing fingers and try harder. If you ask me, you two are making things way more difficult than they should be. You're just like your father!"

"Bullshit, I'm nothing like him. He is who he is and that's not changing. I am nothing like my father!" I insist again.

She shakes her head in disagreement. "Things between you could change. It takes two. While you're trying to improve yourself out here, work on things with your Dad, too."

"Who are you to talk Sara, you just said you hardly even talk to your Dad."

"That's a conversation for another day, Bry, my relationship with my Dad is fine. We're talking about you right now. Just promise me you'll give him a chance at some point. I know he means well even if he has a tough time showing it."

"Sure Sara, I promise I'll try. All right, enough with all this chitter-chatter. How about a little game of hide the salami before dinner?"

She laughs heartily. "If you have a salami you must have hidden it a long time ago because I've never seen it!"

I set myself up for that one.

CHAPTER 28

TODAY IS MY FIRST SHIFT AT FREDDIE'S HERE IN HAWAII. I'M working lunch on the salad station, which will be a piece of cake for me. The first day on the job is always a little weird; nobody likes being the new face. Reporting to work at ten am, I begin by checking the station's inventory, which should be plentiful with fresh greens and other ingredients. The previous night's crew should have done this, but they rarely did it well enough. I meet Paul again, the douchebag manager, near his office in the back of the kitchen, where he gives me a time card and I return to him my completed application. We walk to the stockroom and he gives me my "whites" for the shift. These are the ridiculous clothes you wear on a cooking line, they look like hospital scrubs, but white. Why they give cooks a white uniform, I'll never understand. We all look like Stevie Wonder finger-painted on us by the end of the day.

I change into the goofy pajamas and head to the line, where I stock the station and meet the fellas. The team consists of four guys (and the occasional lady, but not today) for lunch. One of us on the grill, one for fry, another for sauté, and me, your friendly neighborhood salad man. The boys are sitting around having a pow-wow, everybody shooting the shit and laughing it up. These dudes are all well-tanned and large, locals for sure, with tribal tattoos all over them. In the week or so that I've been here, the island seems divided among locals, Japanese, and then all the rest. I don't know the rules of the road yet but do know enough to understand that I am in the minority. Keeping it low-key, without too much enthusiasm, I introduce myself to them. They give me the once over, shake my hand, and ask "How'z it, Brah?" Everyone is nice enough, but nobody takes any interest in where I'm from or why I'm infiltrating their domain.

After our meeting, I return to my station at the end of the line. A tall skinny blond kid, with long straight hair, rounds the corner and punches the time clock next to me.

"Greetings, stranger in a strange land," he addresses me, taking off his shirt and replacing it with a striped Freddie's number. "How goes it, Brother? I'm TJ. And you are?"

"Hey man, what's up TJ?" I smile. "Bryan. Appreciate the intro."

"I get it, Bro, I do. Good to see another haole on the job," he stresses enthusiastically, tying a black server apron around his waist. "Where you from, Homey?"

"Me and my girl just moved here from New York about a week ago," I inform him.

He looks at me as if I just farted in his face. "You and your girl, huh? Excuse you, but have you not noticed the gnarly chicks out here, Dude? The last thing you need is some Betty jocking your every move," TJ chuckles, shaking his head in mock disappointment. "Anyway, let me bolt before Andrew Dice Gay snags me back here bullshitting. I'll holler at you later, Bry-man." Friendly guy. I aspire to one day be that nice.

No matter which Freddie's you work in, all of the ingredients and plates, most everything you touch and see, are the same. I make my way through a pretty slow lunch rush with no problems. After things slow down, I need to clean, restock, and prep for the next salad guy tonight. Everything dirty from my station needs to go to the dishwasher. I haven't yet met the guy working back here, they are in their own world behind a wall with a little window cut out to push the dirty dishes through. Whenever a dish guy wants to talk to someone, he peeks his head out. It reminds me of when I was a kid and the nosy old ladies in their housecoats would lean down to look out the open window of a Bronx walk-up apartment. I push the used containers through the cut-out and I instantly hear, "No Braddah, no way, take this shit out of here. This is my house!"

I look in to see who's yelling. It's an old fifty or so local dude, the guy is a brick shithouse. Tan, fit and losing his mind, this is no old hag from the Bronx. "Pardon me?" I ask, with an extra nice tone. I'm not exaggerating when I say this freak rushes out from behind the wall, grabs me by the throat, and throws me into the pot sink like a rag doll.

"Do you think I'm playing with you, Haole Boy?" he screams, veins bulging fire-engine red, like they could burst in my face at any second. I didn't utter a word in reply. I couldn't, he was squeezing my neck so hard, I was only able to gag and cough. I've never been so bum-rushed in my life, the guy jumping me for absolutely no reason. Skinny TJ saves my ass, getting between us and prying the bully's hands off of me, then talking the lunatic off the ledge before he committed homicide.

My new best friend and hero TJ takes me out back for a smoke, each drag lighting my throat on fire. That's where we are, sitting on a couple of milk crates, when Paul the manager came out and fired me.

"This just can't happen, Mr. Grayhill, much less on your first day," he begins.

I slosh up to my feet, pants dripping from being dunked in the sink. "Paul, I didn't utter one word to that guy. He attacked me out of the blue."

"Yeah, look at his fucking neck man, you can see the Chief's whole handprint!" TJ joins in.

"Shut it down, TJ!" Paul orders my savior. "Listen Grayhill, no matter what went on, we can't have it," he explains. "Chief's been on dish 15 years and never been a problem. He said it was you that was out of line and the other guys in the kitchen back him up on that."

"Well maybe his wife left him or his dog died this morning, but I didn't do a thing to him. The other guys are blatantly lying for him; you must know that!"

"All I know is you gotta go, Grayhill," he grins smugly. "It's not going to work out here for you."

So much for him being my fellow haole. "Paul, I'm begging you, I really need this job right now," I plead. "We just got here."

"Not my problem. I'll mail your check for today to the address on the application," he says before walking off. Then Paul has a second thought he wants to share and turns back to me. "Let me give you a little advice moving forward: try to fit in out here. Nobody likes a know-it-all all, especially one from the mainland."

Is this guy kidding me? Fucking rude little twerp is preaching on how to behave? "Okay Paul, I hear you, thanks for that advice. I'm very, very sorry for all of this," I counter, oozing insincerity. "One last thing before I go Paul, something I've wanted to ask since the very first second I laid eyes on you. Who did you blow to get this job? You're a disgrace man, firing me for what?" I finish. "Fuck you Paul, and fuck the fucking Chief with his stupid nickname. If he's the Chief, you're the Chief Dick Sucker! How about that, Asshole!" Now I'm finished. Classic Bryan.

He just stands there staring, letting me get it all out. "Hit the road," he says calmly, gesturing with his thumb like a hitchhiker. How do people stay so relaxed? I guess I'm not intimidating to this guy; more like a joke.

Sara is unsympathetic upon my return to the apartment. I am the boy who cried wolf, no way she's buying my story of innocence. "You need to take a chill pill, Bry," Sara fumes. "This tough guy act is getting played out."

I laugh purposefully, long and loud. "Did you hear me, Sara? I didn't do a thing! Some grandpa jacked me up because he was having a bad day."

"Right, right. I'm sure you didn't make one of your little comments to get him going," she snaps.

I'm alone on an island, I think to myself. "Sara, you're either with me or against me. Don't be against me, it's not going to end well if we aren't working together," I implore in a righteous tone.

"Stop it, Buddy, please. We have real problems we're dealing with here, don't give me some psycho-babble bullshit about us against the world. You need to start making some money. That's it!"

"Okay, well I've worked one more day than you so far, and bought all the fucking furniture, so who are you telling to make some money?" I retort lamely.

"Yeah, and you got fired because you can't control yourself," she admonishes me, "so get your shit together. How can you be such a chill guy most of the time, and then lose your mind over nothing? I don't get it," she yammers on.

I'm putting away some dishes from the drying rack as she continues carrying on listing my shortcomings. While reaching for a pan, I picture myself swinging around and smashing her right in the face with it, ala Bugs Bunny. Of course, I would never actually do it, but I'm beginning to understand how these things happen. Instead, I bang the pan down on top of the stove, creating a deafening crash.

"I'm going for a walk, Mommy, I'll try not to get into any more trouble." I storm out of the apartment, wishing I really was alone on this island.

CHAPTER 29

I SIT ON A KNEE-HIGH WALL OUTSIDE OUR BUILDING AND LIGHT A cig, now I'm the one having a moment. Cars stop and go at a traffic light, the drivers taking their transportation for granted as I jealously watch, wishing I had a mode of escape right now.

Quickly falling deep in thought, I know karma is catching up to me. No, I didn't instigate the Chief and truly was a totally innocent party to that insanity, but the karma gods have been keeping score and finally realized that I've been getting away with too much shit. What goes around comes around, that's what they say. Chief will get his too.

I need to control my impulses and stop saying whatever I want all the time and also quit feeling sorry for myself when something doesn't go my way. I'm conscious enough to be aware of my issues, but when I'm tested in a real situation, I revert back to unawareness. It's like I black out for a minute and then I'm stuck dealing with the consequences. I could have just run off when the sumo giant shook me down at the beach the other day, but of course, I had to smack him first. That's just one example of many. I give in to temptation, and sometimes I like it. I'll do better next time. Lighting up another smoke, I make a mental note to add quitting to the self-help list. Maybe tomorrow.

I sit alone on the wall for a while thinking, smoking, and listening to the music coming from a bar across the street, it's door wide open for my listening pleasure. The singing is remarkably horrible but nobody seems to care, it's a real party in there. I read the sign in the window advertising "Karaoke every day," with Chinese or Japanese writing below. I've never heard of it, definitely not for me, but to each their own. The energy of the place drifts out the door along with the music, and it feels good to be on the periphery of some happiness.

Outside the bar, a busboy stacks boxes of empty beer bottles in neat columns. As soon as the worker goes back inside the bar, a bum walks up to the cases and takes each bottle out one by one, checking the contents by holding it up to the street light and then drinking up whatever beer remains. Pretty industrious, my good man! I hope the high is worth it; he'll probably be shitting cigarette butts in the morning.

It's time to head upstairs, my self-loathing is over for now. Shit happens, I have to deal with it. Besides, it's been hours and my ass is falling asleep on this cement wall.

Back on 16, Sara is out cold, nestled in the big round chair. Lights beyond the windows twinkle in the night behind her. It's a perfect picture, too bad we don't have a camera. I kneel next to the chair and put my head on her lap, feeling remorse for the fight we just had. "I'm sorry, Baby," I whisper, stroking her arm up and down with my fingertips.

"Eeeehhhh," she moans like a tired monster, blowing up the tender moment. "Bed."

I pick her up easily and manage to navigate my way to the mattress without bopping her head into a wall, then gently lay Sara down and take her sweats off so she doesn't get too hot. We have only sheets on the bed, and I tuck her in. Nobody thought about a blanket and so far, it hasn't been needed.

"Goodnight, Sara." No response, not even a moan. One more smoke, my last because tomorrow I'm definitely quitting, then it's sleepy time for me as well. I stand at the bathroom sink and brush my teeth, too tall to see my face in the mirror. After a day like today, that's not a bad thing.

Sara is up and out of bed before I'm awake. Finally moving, I go take a piss and brush my teeth, then find her on the couch in the living room. She's on the phone and holding a finger up to shush me. "Thank you very much, Judy."

Sara rises and announces with glee that she has a job interview in an hour at Sears, our Sears, later this morning. "Full-time, Bry. This lady said as long as I can walk and chew gum at the same time, I'm in," she informs me, adding in a little happy dance and throwing me a hip-check. "Ce l-e-brate good times, come on!"

"Congrats! It sounds promising. You better get your ass moving, it's 9:15 already."

She replies in a baby voice. "Yeah, I have to be dare at eween. That's why Bry guy going to put Sara in a widdle taxi waxi after I put on my cloth-esy wouseys."

"Sure Baby, I'll get you a taxi," I laugh.

"Here," she says, back to normal and handing me the newspaper. "There's a boatload of restaurant jobs in there, I circled the good ones. Get on the horn."

Sara went off to her interview and a short time later, I was also dis-cussing potential employment. "Mike Miller, got it. Thank you. I'll see you at two," I confirm in my best grown-up voice.

The bar manager at a joint called, of all things, "Bryan's Parkplace," agreed to interview me for a bartender position that was in the paper. I jotted down the address and directions, then thanked him profusely for the opportunity; I'm going to meet him after the lunch rush today. Mike told me Bryan's is located upstairs in the Ward Center on Ala Moana, across from the park. I acted like I knew what he was talking about, but I'll find my way there. I picked up a colorful street map for a buck the other day and I've started to notice that everything is in the direction of Waikiki. Our apartment tower is at the edge of civilization, it seems.

I have plenty of time to walk to Bryan's and upon my arrival, promptly at two pm, Mike Miller is standing at the hostess stand, ready to chat. This interview is already going better than the last one I had at Freddie's.

My first impression of this place is *wow!* The dining room is laid out in front of ocean-facing floor-to-ceiling windows, and the bar is raised, off to the right side. Spotlights give the mirrors and bottles a sparkle. Beyond the bar is a huge outdoor dining patio, also with a beach view, of course.

"You must be Bryan?" Mike asks with a hearty smile. He has crazy curly blond hair, cut low to his head. It's all I can do to not stare, being so captivated by its curliness.

"Yes, hi! Mike, I'm guessing?" I ask, even though I'm pretty sure this is him.

"Guilty as charged," he lamely jokes, the frivolous comment briefly touching my jail nerve. As we shake hands, I imagine Mike seeing me in my orange INMATE outfit and saying "I'm sorry, the position has been filled." Thankfully, it's my little secret.

"Nice to meet you, Bryan. Fill out this application and I'll be back over to you in a few."

"Thank you," I reply, trying to calm my nerves as I take a chair at the table he pointed out for me.

Bryan's, "Home of the Dungeness Crab," I read in some kind of article framed on the wall. I don't know what "Dungeness" means, but it doesn't sound very tasty. On my application, I neglect to make mention of my three-hour career at Freddie's down the street. I'm pretty sure Paul won't be a very good reference.

Curly Q gives my application the once over while throwing in a few "Hmms," and "Ahhs," along the way. "Hmm," he whispers to himself, "New York." "Ahh," he exclaims next, "worked in California, too," and so on. "No experience behind the bar, I see," he continues, pointing out the bar, in case I'm confused.

"No Mike, that's true," I begin, "but I'm a quick study, I promise to catch on fast."

"Why do you think you would be an asset here at Bryan's?" Mike asks.

I feel ready for this question. "Well Mike, I may not know how to bar tend, per se," I start, hoping *per se* was used properly, "but I do know how to make every guest feel important. I serve my customers as I would like to be served. Again, I'm a quick learner, I'm neat, on time, responsible, and really care about pleasing people." I blow a little more smoke up his ass and the interview is over. We rise from the table and shake hands again. Curly Q informs me he will call later tonight with his decision.

"Sounds great Mike, much appreciated," I thank him, walking out the door with my fingers crossed. I'm feeling pretty positive about the interview. Now we wait.

Sara and I both return to the tower at around the same time. I am smoking outside, not on the couch, when she walks in.

"I'm in, Baby!" she crows as she makes her way out to join me. "10-6 Monday through Friday at the makeup counter. It's perfect, going to be easy peezy," she finishes.

"Awesome. How much?"

"Seven bucks an hour, plus I get a little commission on the sales."

"Great. I'm glad one of us is pulling their weight," I reply guiltily.

"Did you call the classifieds I circled?"

"Nah. I was flicking around on the TV and got sucked in on "The Price is Right," then I just couldn't get motivated," I lie.

"I know you're fucking kidding," she snaps.

I laugh. "Yes Babe, relax, totally kidding. I just got back from an interview for a bartending job, pretty close to the mall actually. The bar is named "Bryan's Parkplace," I shit you not. Crazy, right?"

"And what happened?" Sara asks, not acknowledging the irony of the name.

"Uh, the guy is going to call me, that's what happened. Tonight, he said. I doubt he'll pick me because I have no bar experience."

"That's the positive spirit," she remarks, again with the pissy tone.

"Didn't you just get a job?" I ask. "Aren't you all happy? Can the attitude, Toots, I'm pretty sure nobody wants to hear it. Does anyone want to hear this snappy fuckin' tone?" I ask around the empty apartment, digging my hole deeper with every word. "Anybody?"

"You're so hilarious, Bry, always know just the right thing to say. Call me Toots one more time, I dare you," she threatens. "Are you trying to never get laid again?"

"There's just no need to get all snappy and weird for no reason. Who needs it?" I ask rhetorically.

"Don't be such a sensitive baby, Bryan. Do I need to talk to you like a little toddler all the time? Does the big tough guy have a dirty diaper? Baby needs his ba-ba?" She goads me.

Jesus, this is all coming out of nowhere. Probably my fault, I'll surely be the one apologizing later, as usual.

The call from Mike at the bar came a couple of hours later. I am more nervous answering the phone than I was when riding in the back of a police car not too long ago.

"I want to officially offer you the job," Mike began, as I silently pump the air and gesticulate to Sara, who has been sitting alone on the couch writing letters. "Welcome to the team at Bryan's Parkplace."

"Wow, thanks so much, Mike!" I beam and am truly elated and so psyched to get this gig. "I will not let you down," I proclaim enthusiastically.

"I know you won't. Come in tomorrow night at six, Mike will start your training. Not me, another Mike. Wear black shoes, black pants, and an aloha shirt."

"Great, see you then. Thanks!" Looks like I need an aloha shirt, whatever that is.

CHAPTER 30

WAKE UP SATURDAY MORNING AND JUST STAY IN BED, ALTERNATing my eyes between the view of the mountains outside the window and the exquisiteness of Sara, asleep next to me. I've always thought a woman is at the height of her beauty when sleeping. It isn't because she's not talking, though that is a big plus. Something about the peacefulness captivates me. Eventually, I slip out of bed without disturbing Sara's angelic state.

I left a couple of strawberry Pop Tarts, unwrapped, out on the counter bar last night. This gives them the perfect texture for the morning, not too soft and with nice crunchy edges. As I grab my pastries and a can of Diet Coke from the fridge, I wonder to myself if the roaches came out last night and ran all over my breakfast. "What you don't know won't hurt you," I tell myself, gobbling them up.

"Hey, Bry," Sara whispers as she appears shortly after my meal, poking her head out from behind the bedroom door.

"Good morning, Sleepy Head," I tease. "Thanks for the action last night." She recedes into the bedroom without acknowledging my comment. After Mike called with the good news about the job, Sara and I buried the hatchet and made up. Totally made up.

"Baby, I need to get an Aloha shirt for work tonight," I shout in her direction, "whatever that is."

She mumbles something unintelligible from the bathroom while brushing her teeth.

"You don't give a shit?" I ask, trying to interpret what she said.

Sara rinses and spits. "No, I said it's a shirt! The flower shirt, the one that pretty much everyone living here wears."

"Oh, okay, got it. Can we go get a couple for work?"

"Yeah, let's take the bus to Waikiki. I want to get some T-shirts and stuff to send back home," she tells me.

"Hmm, maybe I'll do that too. Good idea."

A few hours later, Sara and I are walking down Kalakaua Street in Waikiki, the one parallel to the beach. We find an open marketplace called Duke's that has countless shops, selling anything and everything for the tourists. Sara picks out a few tchotchkes and t-shirts as well as a necklace for each of her sisters. I score a couple of aloha shirts for work, one with pineapples and another with palm trees. This is something I wouldn't be caught dead in back home. If the Funk could see me now!

As we walk back up Kalakaua to the bus stop, two kids about our age are walking toward us, ogling Sara big time. I'm used to men checking her out, but guy code says you turn away when you're caught looking, or you just might catch a beating. She's wearing tight white jeans and a bikini top, definitely worthy of a glance, but these clowns are flat out staring.

"What's up, Guys? Whatchu looking at? Mother Fuckers, why don't you take a picture it lasts longer," I start in on them, immediately dialed all the way up.

"Bryan, Bryan, Bryan! Forget it, let's go," Sara demands loudly.

"Yeah Bryan, let's go!" the guys laugh mockingly, snapping away at Sara with pretend cameras. "Stop Bryan, stop Bryan, you little Pussy," they go on, and then walk away laughing at my expense as Sara drags me down the street.

"Not a word," she demands as we trudge to the bus stop. "You're beyond ridiculous."

"Oh nice, that's what I get for defending your honor," I whine back at her.

"Please. You're defending your honor, not mine. I don't give a fuck about that. Guys have been looking me up and down since I was 10 years old. Men are pigs, and you're an angry pig!"

"Okay, gotcha. Let me be the first to say, my sincerest apologies to you," I offer, draping an arm around her and giving a big squeeze. I am being insincere but she doesn't pick up on it. "Love you so much, Baby."

"Love you, too," she answers automatically. "Please stop being mad at the world."

When we get back to the apartment, Sara takes my hand and leads me into the living room. "Have a seat, Big Guy," she starts, sitting down and patting the couch. Looks like I'm going to get lucky. Sara is about to gift me with a little action before I leave for my first night at the bar.

"Yes, Ma'am," I reply obediently, sitting down next to her with a goofy smile on my face.

She doesn't share my excitement. "It's not what you think it is, Stud. I'm not looking for an afternoon delight."

"Oh. Well, I don't mind if you are, it would be my pleasure to serve you," I grin hopefully in return.

"Bry, listen. When we decided to come to Hawaii, I told you that if you needed help being the man you want to be, I would be here for you. Remember, you wanted help to keep up the positive trend?"

"Yes, it's true," I agree with an eye roll, still disappointed in the direction our couch session is taking.

"Okay, well start with being accountable for your actions. Today was crazy with those guys, you need to have more control of yourself. What are you going to do if somebody looks at you wrong when you're at the new job tonight, jump over the bar and kick their ass?"

Depends on my mood, I think to myself. "No," is all I answer.

"We are here together Bry, nobody is taking me away from you. That's not something you have to worry about."

In my mind I picture Chris Garvey packing his boxing gloves into a suitcase, plane ticket in hand. "No, you're right."

"I need you and I'm counting on you. Did you ever watch Mr. Rogers as a kid? The next time you have that urge to lash out, ask yourself, what would Mr. Rogers do?" she instructs. "Just do that. Be Mr. Rogers."

A little extreme but I go along with it for harmony's sake. "Ha ha, hilarious. I'll do my best, and I'm sorry about today."

"Thanks, Bry, it's okay. I still love you," Sara grins.

"Love you too. Alright, time to get in the shower. Mr. Rogers needs to wash his balls," I joke, kissing Sara's head, still laughing at her silliness.

CHAPTER 31

I WALK INTO BRYAN'S FIVE MINUTES EARLY FOR MY SIX PM SHIFT. Never late for anything, I have my Dad to thank for that. All those wasted hours sitting around waiting for him have left a mark on me.

"Hey Bryan, nice Aloha shirt. Welcome aboard!" Mike greets me as we shake hands again and he escorts me to the bar area. "Let me introduce you to the younger, better-looking Mike," he promises. Better looking than you, Curly Q? You're not setting the bar very high there, mister! On cue, the infinitely better-looking Mike reaches across the bar to introduce himself with a handshake and head nod. He is around my age, with a muscular build and a pretty face.

"What's up my man, I'm Mike. How you doin?" he asks, in a tone that makes me think he actually cares how I'm doing.

"I'm good, I'm good. Bryan," I introduce myself with a smile. "Ready to go."

"Great, crawl under and we'll get started."

I squeeze through the tiny opening under the bar and we share another handshake, then Mike gives me a tour. He starts by opening all the fridges and describing the contents and their purpose. He goes on about the wine and liquor, glassware, menu, computer, and clean-up.

"Most of what we make is either a mai tai or a pina colada. It's all tourists at the bar, usually from the mainland or Australia. Australians don't tip and they smell too, so we don't waste much time on them. Apparently, they don't have time to wash their asses, too busy cooking shrimp on the barby, I guess. After 11, the other restaurant workers around town finish their shifts and come here. That's when we start making the real money. Hey, I gotta run to the head, be back in a second. Fake it if you don't know how to make it," he instructs before running off, leaving me on my own.

This bar is one of a kind. With three glass shelves of bottles running across the length of the back mirrors, and a glistening marble bar top, it looks straight out of the Taj Mahal. Soft blue light glows from a neon sign beside the register; 1 ¼ OZ SHOT. I decide right here and now that when I have my own place, this is what my bar will look like.

"Anything happen while I was gone?" Mike asks upon returning.

"No Sir, didn't move a muscle. So how long have you been working here?"

"Six months or so. I'm a student at UH, so this is perfect for my schedule."

"Okay, cool. Are you from here?"

"C'mon, Braddah," he mocks the locals. "Do I look Hawaiian to you? I'm from Boston."

"Really? I fucking hate Boston and everyone who lives there," I remark in a snarky tone, showing a slight grin to keep it playful. "When the best thing to ever come out of your city is baked beans, that's an embarrassment, man."

"You must be from New York. A Yankee fan, I take it? We hate you, too, trust me. Come up talking that shit in Fenway and you'll be eating a curb for dinner," he threatens, returning my sly grin.

"Well I don't want to fight, Bro, you seem like a cool guy. I'll let it slide for now," I laugh.

"Yeah, *I'll let it slide,* Friend," he retorts. "They both suck this year anyway, so who cares."

I like this guy, a lot.

We spend the next few hours practicing frozen drinks and studying the menu. The handsome Mike makes me comfortable and is a patient teacher as I fumble around a bit trying to learn the mai tai's and pina's.

"When you're behind the bar at Bryan's, don't forget one thing; you are the king!" Mike anoints me. "Everybody needs you. See all these cute little servers?" he asks, pointing to a couple of waitresses. "They need you. Same with the customers. They're all waiting for us Brother, we are the Kings! So who are you?"

"The King?" I reply meekly.

"Say it like you mean it, Yankee! I'm the King!"

I laugh and smile widely. "Yes, I'm the fucking King!"

"Now you're getting the hang of it! We've done enough for tonight, Brother. Meet me back here tomorrow, same time."

"I'll be here," I reply as we shake hands. "You need a nickname, too many Mikes in this place. I'm going to have to think of something. Anyway, thanks for all the help, it was nice meeting you."

"You got it, Friend. You're going to do great, I'll see you tomorrow." With that, I scoot under the bar top and out the front door. Feeling like a king.

Arriving back at the tower, I check our mailbox in the fancy lobby. Junk, junk, junk, something for Sara from her Mom, and lastly, a letter addressed to me from Faith Macalroy, the probation officer who had me locked up in New York. This should be interesting. I go back outside and sit down on the wall, holding the letter at the right angle to catch the street light so I can read it.

Dear Bryan,

I hope this letter finds you well. Getting right to the point, I want to let you know that I deeply regret the circumstances which led to your incarceration and wish on a daily basis that I could turn back time and change things. It was unprecedented in my short career that a judge ignored my recommendations on such an issue and as you know, I vehemently objected to your being jailed. I should have reached out to you and explained the seriousness of the matter before it got to that point.

I am writing this to tell you I am truly and deeply sorry. I pray for your continued wellness.

God Bless,
Faith Macalroy

I'm not sure if she wrote this letter to make me feel better or herself, but I've moved on and put the whole thing behind me, Faith, and you should too.

After another moment of consideration, I ball up the letter and toss it, aiming for the garbage can on the corner. My shot misses badly but is immediately scooped up by Sara, just arriving back home herself. She waves hello to me and then pantomimes a couple of dribbles on the sidewalk with the paper, now her imaginary basketball. Sara mimics a sports announcer describing the action.

"*Sara Addeo takes the pass from Ewing, one second on the clock, and puts it up.*" She shoots the crumpled letter and nails it into the garbage can from ten feet away. *"The New York Knicks are the Champs! Addeo has done it!"*

We share a laugh at her silliness and walk into the tower holding hands. I tell Sara all about my first day at the bar as we pass through the lobby and board the elevator. "It's still hard to believe we live here, that this is our home," I tell Sara, her finger pressing 16. "We're really doing this, Baby."

Sara smiles in return. "We are, Grayhill. Just me and you."

CHAPTER 32

FIRST DAY OF OCTOBER, A MONTH HAS PASSED SINCE SARA AND I touched down in Honolulu. It's amazing how fast life can change. We are fully enveloped in the day-to-day, both of us hustling to keep the team afloat financially. Sara is working days and I'm on nights, so that has been an adjustment. She doesn't want to work in restaurants unless it's absolutely necessary and is thinking of stopping in at a karate school to see if she could teach some lessons in her spare time.

Chief, the crazy dishwasher at Freddie's, did me a huge favor by getting me fired from there. I'm still bitter about it, but this gig at Bryan's is golden. I am loving the bar thing, much more so than I've let on to Sara, who gives me a third-degree interrogation daily about work. It's busy, I'm making good money and the girls are just flocking to this bar, especially the working girls (not that kind) that come in from other restaurants after they finish their shift. I'm very committed to Sara, but a little flirting never hurt anyone. Mike was right, we are the kings. He's in a relationship as well, so both of us are fighting off the ladies on a nightly basis.

I know most men perceive monogamy as a gift to their spouse and feel they should be applauded for not stepping out. In my case, I happen to agree with that philosophy. I'm pretty sure my significant other has already cheated on me, regardless of her denials, yet I'm out here in Hawaii, surrounded by gorgeous, willing women, and still staying faithful. Boyfriend of the Year right here.

It's a Sunday night, Mike and I are on the bar. After the dinner service is over at Bryan's Parkplace, the management team goes home, leaving us responsible for closing up, which is a big mistake. We charge for maybe half the drinks served after 11 and exchange the freebies for juicy tips. The late night customers all work in the biz, so they get it. And they give it, in abundance.

Mike and I have become fast friends, he's a good dude and makes me laugh. We usually sit around and shoot the shit after work, enjoying a few more drinks on the house. Sometimes it's with others but tonight it's just us. He's currently whining over Boston's World Series loss to the Mets a few years ago. Like most Red Sox fans, he knows in his heart that Boston is a loser sports town, and even when the teams there are playing well, Bostonian's never enjoy it, always in fear of the inevitable heartbreak lurking around the corner.

"I got a new nickname for you; I'm going to call you Mookie," I tell Mike. Mookie Wilson is the Met who hit the "*slow roller up along first*" that went through Buckner's legs, which famously ignited Boston blowing the '86 World Series.

"You're hilarious, Bro. Go ahead, call me Mookie, I don't give a shit. I've always wanted a nickname."

After a few more beers, we lock up at 2:30 and I head out on my walk home. I'm looking forward to the stroll, it's another perfect night. The fall provides no chill in Hawaii, a jacket is not required. I've got a new mixed tape ready to go with General Public, Fine Young Cannibals, Elvis Costello, and even some Madonna, not that I would ever admit that. I walk up past the arena and then Freddie's on my left. I'm singing FYC's "She Drives Me Crazy," as I give Freddie's, and the Chief, a middle finger salute.

It's late enough that I'm walking in the street, hardly any cars are out. Looking ahead, I keep noticing some movement on the road, almost like the psychedelic haze you sometimes see hovering over blacktop on a hot day. I can't figure it out, but as I get a little closer and with some help from a street light, I see that it's tons of huge roaches, all of them the size of my pinkie. They are running across the street, keeping a tight formation in both directions, it looks like a cockroach superhighway. Beautiful Hawaii: islands of Beaches, palm trees, pineapples, and fat-ass roaches. Frommer's guidebook never mentioned this disgusting detail.

I open the door to the apartment quietly so I don't disturb Sara, but to my surprise, she is wide awake and sitting in the dark living room as I get home. "What the fuck, Bryan. It's three in the morning on a Sunday night. I called that place ten times and nobody answered," she booms.

"Hello to you, too," I reply calmly, going to the fridge for a soda. "I was working."

"Yeah, 'till three in the morning on a Sunday? Give me a fucking break! I'm not stupid."

"What is your problem, Sara? I was talking with Mike for a while. What do you think I'm up to, huh?"

She jumps up off the couch and charges across the room, confronting me as I sit down in a bar chair. We are eye to eye. "Give me your hands," she demands.

"What for? You aren't making any sense right now."

She smacks the can of soda off the counter and it flies across the room, spilling everywhere. Sara takes both of my hands in hers as if we are at the altar, then lifts them one at a time to her nose, giving my fingers a big, fat sniff.

"I'm dying to know what you're doing. Please tell me what's happening?" I snicker incredulously.

"What's happening, Asshole, you wanna know what's happening? What's happening is I'm checking your hands for the smell of Lisa and her rank pussy, that's what's happening!"

I look at Sara like she's insane, which she is in the middle of proving. This is a side of her that I've never seen before. She's been mad, but right now there's a demon coming out. "What are you talking about? Who the fuck is Lisa?" I ask, in shock at this point. "Did you smell anything incriminating?"

"This is Lisa," she screams, holding up a business card and then smacking it down on the bar. "You left this in your pants from yesterday, Dumb Ass."

"Oh my God Sara, Lisa is Mike's girlfriend," I explain impatiently. "She's a model and knows a good photographer. Mike gave me her card to give to you because I had mentioned we want to take some pictures for the holidays to send home, you Psycho."

Sara does an impression of me, taking her voice deep and bouncing her head around like a moron. "It's just Lisa the model. I'm Mr. Innocent who comes home at 3 in the morning with a models phone number."

"Who the fuck are you to question me? Do I need to remind you that you're the cheater! Go ahead and call this chick, she's actually expecting you to call, and then you'll feel like the idiot you are."

"You're such a liar, Bryan, it makes me sick. I'm going to bed; I have to work tomorrow. Don't come in the room, sleep on the couch. This late night bullshit has to end, I won't sit here day after day not knowing what you're doing and where you are."

Well isn't this ironic? Shoe is on the other foot now, and Sara doesn't like it. "I'm working Baby, that's all I'm doing. You keep flipping out like this and there won't be anything left to talk about, because you're ruining everything with this jealousy. I'm the one that should be insecure, not you. Work on yourself more and stop worrying about fixing me!" I preach, as the bedroom door slams behind her with a thunderous boom.

Even though it's practically four in the morning, I take advantage of the time difference and call my sister Lauren in New York, who is wide awake on the east coast. She's been supportive since we moved out here and hasn't harped on her suspicions regarding my relationship with Sara. We bullshit for a few minutes about things going on in her world and mine, then I hone in on the matter at hand. After telling Lauren the whole story, she is less shocked than I thought she'd be.

"The sniff test, wow! That's a big league move by her. Knowing your history, I'm surprised you passed," she chuckles.

"Hardy har har," I pretend to laugh. "I'll have you know I've been a perfect gentleman out here."

"I'm sure you have, Bryno. Tonight seems a little extreme but give Sara a break. It's probably not easy being halfway around the world with absolutely no one. She's used to being with thousands of kids on campus at Penn State and now she's stuck in a tower like Rapunzel."

"That's a good point, I like your analogy; like she's waiting for her prince to come home every night."

"Yeah, and you ain't no prince," she jokes.

"Okay, let me get to bed. Thanks for the talk. I'll let you know how it goes from here."

Lauren continues on like I didn't say anything. "Don't get me wrong, that shit tonight was coo coo for Cocoa Puffs, but I'll give her a pass this time, even though she's by no means, my favorite person."

"Alright Lau, let me go. Take care and say hello to everyone."

"Love you, Brother."

Sara is kneeling beside me the next morning, running her fingers through my hair as I sleep on the couch. She's already dressed and ready to leave for work.

"Bry, wake up. I love you so much, I'm really sorry for last night," she begins. "You're the only person I have in the world. It's too much for my mind to handle sometimes. When I saw her card, it freaked me out. I'm so sorry, I feel terrible, and I believe your story. I know you love me, it's just—"

"Sara," I interrupt, "enough, I hear you. You're sorry, I get it, thanks. I'm not working tonight, I'll be here when you get home, maybe we can go to a movie or something. Whatever we do, these fights have to stop, it's not good. Why are we talking to each other like that? Like you said, in the end all we have is each other."

Sara shakes her head in agreement. "Totally, no more fighting."

"It's fine, I get it. Chicks dig me, I'm sorry it's such a problem," I joke.

"Yeah, you're a real stud, Bry, what can you do? Okay, I gotta go. Sorry again. Love you!" She kisses my head and is gone. By the time Sara is in the elevator, my eyes are closed for more sleep.

"She Drives Me Crazy," plays in my head, rocking me like a lullaby.

CHAPTER 33

ON THANKSGIVING, MY FAMILY CALLED FROM THEIR DINNER table in New York and they passed the phone around so I could say hello to everyone. Sara and I had cooked a little turkey ourselves and added some staples like stuffing, mashed potatoes, and some jiggly cranberry just for the fun of it. I'm not the biggest fan of turkey and our bird was particularly pathetic, but Sara and I enjoyed the dinner, proud of our first real culinary endeavor.

"We miss you so much, Honey," my Mom told me. "It feels so strange to not have you here. This is the first Thanksgiving that we haven't been together," she finished, and I could tell she was teetering on some emotions.

"I know, Ma, I wish we were there with you guys but it's too expensive to travel back and forth. We just got out here a few months ago," I explained. "Next year we'll be back."

"I can't even think about it, Honey. I'm hoping it all works out." Hoping? She is usually *sure*. Maybe Lauren got in Mom's ear and told her we were having problems out here.

"Okay Ma, get back to your dinner, of course it's gonna work out. We are really happy here, believe me, things are going great. Miss you and love you all."

It has been going great the last couple of months, ever since my fingers passed the sniff test. Sara and I have both settled nicely into our work schedules and when we are together, we're enjoying each other's company, without all the bickering and name calling that took place regularly during our first few weeks out here. We had been taking the uncertainty of our new environment out on each other and are both now really making an effort to be better.

Yesterday, Bryan's had an afternoon staff party in Ala Moana Park, a huge grassy area the size of several football fields, right next to the ocean. It's always teeming with locals and plenty of tourists as well. Natives cruise along in their low riding, tricked-out pickups, while foreigners invade the beach and joggers circle around it. The park is a melting pot of people watching.

"Hey, so nice to finally meet you, my friend," Mike greeted Sara in his affable way, giving her a hug. "I love working with the *New Yawka*, even if he does like the sorry Yankees."

"So happy to meet you too! I'm glad you've been such a good friend to Bryan."

"And this is Lisa," I chimed in, giving an introductory wave in Lisa's direction as Sara simultaneously reached out and hugged her too. As a local girl whose model face is on magazine covers around Honolulu, Lisa is intimidatingly beautiful to most women, but Sara is a beauty herself and they took to each other instantly.

The girls spent the next few hours chatting as Mike and I hung around with our co-workers. The restaurant had food and drinks set up, along with tug of war, volleyball, and lots of other fun activities. It was the first time Sara and I had been a part of something with people our own age, instead of just the two of us. We began doubling up with Mike and Lisa every so often. They were good company, and fun to be around. Sara and Lisa became pretty friendly, but they never got close, not like Mike and me.

The day after the beach party, Sara arrives home from work at four pm, another short shift at Sears. I am just getting out of the shower, readying myself for a night at the bar. We exchange greetings and a kiss in the bathroom. She closes the toilet seat and sits, while I duck down and shave in the mirror. The mirrors, door knobs, and such things are lower than usual in this building, no doubt because the designers were partial to the expected Asian tenants. I am King Kong in this place.

"They're screwing me on my hours at Sears, Bry. I'm always the first one they send home early."

"Maybe it's time to look for some restaurant work, start making some better money," I suggest. "Two or three nights won't kill you. I'd suggest trying my bar but I know they don't need anybody," I lie, protecting my turf.

"I'm going to look around," she answers in agreement. "Why not. I'm bored without you around anyway."

The number one recurring problem we are having in Honolulu is cash flow while walking everywhere or riding the bus is a close second. We flat out don't have enough money and are living day to day. Sara's Sears gig is okay, but we can definitely use some more dough.

"I was talking to Melody today, that Japanese girl I told you about at my job. She was telling me that she works a few nights a week at a club in Waikiki."

"Okay, what's the point? Can she get you in there?"

"Well, there's a little more to the story. So the job is as a hostess, but what she's really doing is sitting with and entertaining these rich Japanese guys. She's making amazing money, all off the books. What do you think about me trying that?"

"There's no way that's ever happening, I know you must be kidding. That's called being a prostitute, Sara. It's the oldest profession in the world, surely you've heard of it?" I ask calmly.

"Bry, I wouldn't be doing anything bad. Melody said it's just hanging out and flirting a little, but only if you want to."

"Yeah, that's how porn stars get their start, just a little flirting. Flash forward a month and you'll be standing on the corner shouting, "Me love you long time!""

"Oh yeah, that's me, Bry. You're so stupid!" she laughs.

"Please forget it, Sara. You don't have the patience for that kind of bullshit anyway, who are you kidding?"

"I know; just thought I'd mention it. I knew you'd think it was crazy, and you're right. When you're right, you're right. Love you," she finishes, then gets up and leaves the room, only to return a second later. Sara opens the lid and sits back down on the toilet again, this time pulling her undies down and whistling out some pee.

"Forget something?" I ask.

"Yes, another thing Melody mentioned was taking a class in Hawaiian language and culture, even learning how to hula dance. I could make some extra money working the luaus at some hotels in Waikiki."

"You'd want to take a class?" I ask.

She rolls up a ton of toilet paper, much more than seems necessary, and wipes, or dabs, whatever the ladies do down there. "It's quick, like three hours. They are very serious about their history and traditions here."

"Sounds like a possibility. Do they have a lot of Italian hula girls?"

"I don't know but they're gonna have one now!" she smiles, then stands up and breaks into her east coast honky version of the hula, which look pretty good to me.

"You're funny. I think underwear will be required," I laugh, pointing out the undies still down around her ankles.

"I might make better tips this way," she says while pulling them up. "So maybe I'll look into that instead."

"Sure, sounds interesting. Check it out."

Sara leaves again after a kiss, and I can't help but notice that our communication is improving. That conversation, especially the hooker portion, probably would have ended in a brawl not too long ago, so things between us continue to get better.

CHAPTER 34

WHEN I GET BACK TO THE APARTMENT THAT NIGHT AFTER WORK there is a newspaper splayed out on the coffee table. An ad for bartenders and cocktail waitresses is circled in black marker. Sara wrote over the other classifieds: "Found this! We are going here for interviews on Saturday!" I didn't know I was in the market for a new job but okay, sounds good.

Flash forward to noon on Saturday. Sara and I are lined up with other applicants at a cattle call for some place called "Hot Rods," a brand new club right in the heart of Waikiki on Kalakaua Ave. At least fifty kids around our age are standing around, waiting to be seen. The bar is filled with auto racing memorabilia, hence the name. Tables are designed to make someone feel as if they are sitting in an old-timey car. Shiny, bright-colored vinyl is everywhere. It's totally cheesy but may be just kitschy enough for tourists to come check it out.

Sara and I are separated by a few people in the long line. It's an open call for employment and we don't want it to be known that we're together. A mook named Tony interviews each of us. He fit right in with the corny decor, his shirt unbuttoned and a big Italian horn dangling from his neck, nestled in an overgrown black forest of chest hair. His IROC-Z is probably taking up two spaces in the parking lot.

Sara goes first. With her pretty face, the interview is just a formality. Tony asks her if she has any experience, Sara says yes, and that's that. He puts on the charm for a few more minutes, making small talk about himself (You Italian? Ehh, me too!) and this place, before sending Sara on her way. Opening night is next Friday and she's back in the biz.

I talk to her outside after their meeting and she tells me it was all soft questions and very easy. My interview is next and I don't get the free pass Sara got. Tony decides to be a hard ass with me, asking about drink recipes and even questions regarding wine and food pairings. I laugh internally as I imagine somebody sitting in the rumble seat of a goofy vinyl hot rod. I don't think they would care for one second about what wine goes with the "Carburetor Calamari," but I play along and answer. Spying Tony's dangling horn as he speaks, I pass the time by imagining myself jamming the little dagger in his eyeball and popping it out, blood flooding down his face. Thankfully Tony couldn't read my mind and I am hired for opening night next Friday as well. I'm scheduled at Bryan's already, but I'll get coverage for my shift there easily enough and check this place out. If it's good here, maybe I can find a way to fit it into my schedule. I wouldn't mind keeping an eye on Sara either, especially with Tony Chest Hairs lurking around.

We are back in Waikiki for training on Thursday night. With Hot Rods opening to customers the next day, they are doing this by the seat of their pants. Only one night of training for the entire staff is going to result in a shit show here tomorrow night, guaranteed.

"Baby, trust me, this job ain't gonna last," I tell Sara on the bus ride home, as we sway in unison from side to side.

"I know," she replies, "It's a total mess."

"It's going to be a free for all."

And it is. Friday night, the place is mobbed within an hour of opening. It's total chaos. Luckily for us, Sara and I are teamed up at the same register, meaning that I'm the bartender for her section. There are five bartenders, so it's the luck of the draw. Things are falling our way, for a couple of reasons. Firstly, we are relaxed because if we make any mistakes, we make them with each other, so who cares? Secondly, as her bartender, I am also her banker. Let's say, for example, Sara approaches the bar and asks me for her drinks. I make them and tell her it's twenty bucks, then I ring up only $15 and keep a fiver for myself. Cha-ching! A victimless crime, one being perpetrated in bars all across the world. Sara did nothing wrong; she didn't even know I was skimming. Keeping count of the pilfered funds, I'll stop around 75, no need to be greedy. I do have morals, after all.

I'm moving a mile a minute trying to keep up as the bar is three deep with customers, all waving frantically at me, cash in hand and crying out for drinks. It's so busy I'm just going from person to person and pointing at them, prompting them to order.

"Two Heineken!" a mustachioed haole desperately calls out from the crowd.

"Six bucks," is all I reply, no time for extra words, finishing the transaction and moving on. Next to get my attention is a heavyset Mom-type, who has one of the few bar seats, and several empty glasses in front of her already. I point.

She yells above the crowd accusingly, shouting, "I see what you're doing, don't think I don't see!"

Holy shit, is this really happening; this lady knows I'm skimming? And here I thought I was being slick. "Oh, you do, do you," I reply tentatively. "What's that?"

She just stares for a second, bringing me to a halt as I await her evidence. "You're trying to impress me, spinning those bottles around, looking so cool," is what she comes up with.

In your dreams, lady! "Yeah, you figured me out," I reply with a dismissive eye roll. Using my hands to stress the urgency, I push for her order, saying "Let's go, what can I get you, Honey, it's now or never." I slam another

Madres in front of her, refusing to make further eye contact. No more swiping dollars tonight, I've been scared straight.

At the end of the shift, we sit in a rumble seat and count our cash. Sara and I have been slinging drinks non-stop all night, we are wiped out. Between the two of us, we make over 500 bucks, including my ill-gotten 75.

"Well, that was even worse than I thought it would be," I confirm to Sara after we sit down for some food at Denny's. It's five am and we're beyond starving. Sara orders the classic "Moons over my Hammy," which makes me stop and think for a second. The last time Patty and I were at Denny's, he drunkenly told the waitress that if she showed him her "Moons over my Hammy," he'd show her the "Big Dipper behind my zipper." With lines like that, it's no surprise he's still a virgin.

Sara is too tired to ask what I'm daydreaming about, and I wasn't sharing. "I didn't see a manager all night long," she tells me, and then lowers her voice and scoots closer to me. "Bry, I started charging people an extra dollar for everything, on the down low. I probably made an extra 50 bucks! I should have done it right from the start!"

"Baby, that's stealing! I'm going to have to report you to Tony Bologna," I kid, then continue and explain my ruse. "You're not the only one on the take," I start my story. Thick as thieves, we are. Actual thieves is more like it.

We never woke up Saturday morning, sleeping until one in the afternoon. "There's no way I'm going back there tonight," is the first thing out of my mouth once I finally get up. "We'll never be able to stick with it, working all hours of the night like that. You were on your feet like 20 hours yesterday between the make-up counter and the bar."

"I know; it's not going to work. Too bad, it felt good to make some Cash-ola. I guess I'll talk to Melody more about the luau class on Monday," she says.

"That's a good idea. I'm not going to bother calling Hot Rods. That guy Tony doesn't know his ass from his elbow anyway, I doubt he'll even notice we're gone. Well, maybe he'll notice if his paisan doesn't show up," I tease Sara.

We stay in bed the rest of the day, doing what comes naturally. For dinner, we splurge on pizza and beer, then spend the rest of the night doing what we did all day. Naturally.

CHAPTER 35

SARA AND I WAKE UP BRIGHT-EYED AND BUSHY-TAILED SUNDAY morning, energized by our Saturday full of sleep, sex, and pizza. What's better than that?

"Good Morning! Love you more than anybody loves anybody, Bry Guy," Sara kisses me as she gets out of bed, sporting my Reggie T-shirt again.

"Morning. Love you too, Baby," I reply, stretching my arms over my head and rolling into her vacated area.

"I'm so glad we didn't go back to Waikiki last night. That place was the pits, I hated it there."

"Yes, agreed. No regrets on my part, either," I reply, although I do feel a little guilty about stealing the money.

"It was like slave labor," Sara continues. "We don't need to break our ass like that to pay our bills out here. I'd rather be broke than do something I hate."

"Totally with you on that."

"Glad we're on the same page," Sara replies as she lies back down and snuggles up to me. "Now let's go spend some of that money, Honey!"

Sara and I decide we want to take our 500 in Hot Rods cash and go to the Aloha Flea Market out at the stadium. I call Mike and ask if we can borrow him and his little Datsun pick-up truck for the day. We are hoping to find some used furniture to replace the rented stuff. It'll be crap in, crap out, but at least it will be ours.

Mike rings the buzzer at 10 am sharp.

Sara presses the intercom, singing in a silly tone, "Whooo isss it?" knowing already it's Mike.

"Yeah, Hawaii Five-0, this is Detective Steve McGarrett. We're after the notorious pimp Super Sugar Daddy Grayhill, heard he's holed up in your place. I'm coming in with a warrant."

Sara laughs as she presses the entry buzzer. "Push in the door, detective!"

"Holy shit my friend, I can't believe you live in West Shore Tower!" Mike exclaims upon entering our apartment. "Wow, perfect view of the mountains up here, too. I'm jealous man, totally jealous."

"Enjoy it while it lasts," I reply, squinting as cigarette smoke drifts into my eyes. "We won't be able to afford it much longer."

"I thought you were quitting those things," he remarks, pointing to the butt hanging out of my mouth.

"Someday he will," Sara interjects as she hugs Mike hello.

We all take the elevator down to the street and cram into his tiny truck's cab. It's a stick, so Sara has to sit on my lap, allowing Mike room to work the shifter. As he tries to get the finicky transmission in reverse and back out of his parking spot, the Datsun's gears resist him with a loud ruckus.

"If you can't find 'em, grind 'em," I bust on Mike.

"Keep talking Yankee and you'll be grinding a ten-speed Schwinn to the flea market," he jokes back.

Finally moving forward, we putt putt up to H1, the main highway on the island, and merge into traffic for the 30-minute ride. Suddenly a big fat roach climbs out of the air vent and onto the dashboard. It just stares at us, antenna twitching back and forth in contemplation as he prepares to pounce. Sara lets out a scream, followed instantaneously by Mike's hand smooshing the critter dead into the dashboard, a sickening crunch confirming the conclusion of its life. "Sorry about that, guys. Fuckin' things are everywhere," he offers casually, removing the carcass with his fingers. Yes, we know, all too well.

The Flea Market is a massive gathering. Hundreds of people trudge along looking for a deal on whatever tired junk they are seeking, making their way through the tents and folding tables set up in the parking lot of the stadium. We score replacement furniture for everything we had previously rented. Sara picks stuff out, I haggle down the price as a true New Yorker does, then we bring our purchases to Mike waiting at the truck, where he ties them down and stands guard, allowing us to continue shopping.

We are browsing around for more loot when a chubby little white kid bumps into Sara and falls backward onto his butt. Sara looks down and sees the blond boy already crying, his hand scraped from the asphalt.

"Watch where you're going, Stupid Ass," comes streaming out of a reed-thin, stringy haired blond woman. Obviously the wailing boy's Mom, she's ironically wearing a Bart Simpson shirt that says "Don't have a cow, Man!"

Sara helps the boy up, even wiping away his tears, as she speaks quietly to the Mom. "It was an accident. You don't have to be so rude, I didn't mean it."

But the mother was looking for a fight. "Just shut up and look where you're going, Lady!" the Mom spews back angrily.

This is usually where I would step in and lose my shit on somebody, but I was thinking of my little brothers, about the same age as this kid, and I don't want to make a scene or get him upset again. There is an ice cream cart right next to the accident site, so I lean down and give the kid a five-dollar bill. "It's okay Buddy, you're tough. How about a little ice cream to cheer you up?" The mother doesn't argue over the treat but still wears a scowl on her weathered face.

The boy is happily distracted by choosing which flavor to get, the trauma of his fall long forgotten. This gives Sara a chance to address his Mom privately, and she addressed the shit out of her. "Watch the way you talk to me, you fucking White Trash Haole Bitch," Sara menacingly whispers at the Mom as she towers over her. "You have no idea who you're fucking with," she finishes with an icy glare, Sara's finger in her face. The mother actually apologizes and then hurriedly disappears into the crowds with her kid.

"Wow Baby, where did that come from?" I ask admiringly as we walk to the pickup truck. I can't believe what I just heard, as I wonder to myself if Mr. Rogers would have chosen those words.

"Who is she to talk to me like that? It was a total accident; the kid is the one who wasn't looking! Nobody is going to talk to me that way, I won't accept that shit."

"Good for you, Baby! Hey, you know I love it!"

"Yeah Bry, I'm sure you do. Just don't go looking for trouble, that's all I ask."

The truth is Sara has a lot of angst built up inside, she's been holding that in for a while. The little kid's Mom opened her mouth and got more than she bargained for. Luckily Sara didn't break out some karate action on her ass.

"Don't say anything to Mike, Bry. I'm not proud of that," Sara instructs me.

"You should be proud, you handled it perfectly," I assure her. "I'm a little surprised you called her a haole, but whatever works."

"It just came out. When in Rome, ya know," Sara shrugs.

We return slowly to the tower, all of our new goodies hanging over the sides of the truck, looking like the Beverly Hillbillies rolling back into town. Mike and I unload all of the new stuff and then he helps me return everything but the TV to the Rent-a-Rama around the corner. "Mookie, my good friend! Thank you so much for the help today!"

"Ha ha, Mookie! Anytime, it's my pleasure, Buddy. I'll see you Tuesday at Bryan's."

"Yes, Sir," I reply and head back up to my lair on the 16th floor.

When I get inside, Sara already has the place set up. It looks about the same but feels so much more comfortable because it's ours. "Mike is so awesome!" she proclaims. "I'm glad you have a cool person to hang out with." Sara pauses and then adds with a pout, "I need a friend."

Little does Sara know, Mike is hardly my only friend. Over the last two months at Bryan's, I have become chummy with everybody, that's just the way restaurants work. Plus, a bunch of workers from other places that come into the bar at the end of the night, too. I haven't mentioned my new friends to Sara, choosing to keep this as my little secret. I don't want her to get jealous and I'm not doing anything wrong, even though I've had plenty of opportunities. I am committed to Sara, we came here together and I have a responsibility to not fuck it up, her Dad Angelo is counting on me. And things are going so well with us, at least that's what I thought. Turns out I'm not the only one with secrets.

CHAPTER 36

LOOKING OUT THE PEEPHOLE OF OUR APARTMENT, I GET A
close-up of a Santa hat outside our door. Suddenly Mike rises up and
shows his face. "Mele Kalikimaka!" he shouts, giving Sara and me hugs upon
entering. "That means Merry Christmas in Hawaiian, for all you haoles,"
he laughs.

"Thanks, Mookie. You've got pretty good Christmas spirit for a Jewish
kid from Boston," I remark.

"He's doing it for me," Lisa smiles as she trails behind.

"Yeah, I'm trying to get on her naughty list," Mike laughs, "So Lisa
does something naughty to me."

"That's not exactly how it works, but nice try, Buddy," Sara responds
to him with a playful punch.

It's Christmas Eve in Honolulu, but it may as well be the fourth of
July. Without the change of seasons Sara and I are used to in New York,
not to mention no family around, this just feels weird. A mini plastic palm
tree with a few lights and a picture of a surfing Santa Claus is all we have
for decorations.

"I'll be ready to go in a few minutes," Sara announces to the group, "I
just have to make a quick call home before my Mom goes to sleep."

"Hurry up please, this show starts at six," I remind her as she goes off. "Guys, let's do a shot while we wait." Tonight we are going to a Christmas luau at one of the hotels in Waikiki, Lisa got some free tickets from one of her modeling gigs.

"I just need to fix my face real quick," Lisa announces, disappearing to the bathroom while Mike and I sit around bullshitting.

"It's not easy being a girl, I guess, always something slowing 'em down," I complain to Mike.

"Ain't it the truth," he replies. "Takes me about ten seconds to get ready. Shit, I've been wearing this same pair of shorts since August."

Once Lisa returns from her tune-up, looking exactly the same as she did before she left, we get back to our shots.

"Cheers to the baby Jesus," Mike salutes us as we raise our glasses. "Here's hoping Santa brings you everything you asked for!" We throw down some Peach Schnapps just as Sara returns to the room, her face flush; she's obviously been crying.

"What's wrong, Baby, everything okay with your Mom?" I ask.

"She's fine, I miss her is all. I'll be okay, let's just go," she insists, heading straight to the door.

We packed in a cab and rode to the luau, which turned out to be the perfect way to celebrate the holiday in Hawaii, a good time was had by all of us not named Sara. She sat stoically all night, a step away from being comatose, actually. Her disposition worried me and I asked several times during the night if there was anything she wanted to share regarding her conversation with her mother, but she refused to discuss it, finally just imploring me to "let it go, please!" So that's what I did. The next week passed without another mention of it, and Sara slowly came back around to normal.

"Happy New Year! 1990 here we come!" I shout out gleefully at the stroke of midnight as fireworks fill the sky outside our window.

"We did it, Baby! We're Hawaiians!" Sara declares as we clank our plastic champagne glasses together.

"Love you! I love you more today than yesterday," I sing drunkenly, and then Sara joins in, and we both blare, "But not as much as tomorrow!"

It's a low-key New Year's party, just the two of us. Mike and Lisa have their own plans (after Sara's pity party at the luau last week, I can't really blame them), and that left pretty much nobody else. We called our parents earlier, collect of course, at midnight their time, which meant it was only six pm in Honolulu.

"I'm so proud of you, Honey," my Mom told me. "What you've done has been so brave. Both of you have been so brave."

"Thanks, Mom. We're having a great time," I told her and meant it. "Say Happy New Year to everyone. I love you, Ma."

I got my Dad's answering machine, which is exactly what I wanted. "Happy New Year, Dad! Give the boys a hug for me," I said in a cheery voice. "Call me anytime," not that I expect you will.

Sara called her parents while I sat on a stool by the kitchen bar, smoking a butt. My New Year's resolution is to quit the cigs, but who are we kidding, it probably won't happen. There was no more drama like last week when she spoke to her Mom, and we never did discuss it further.

January started gray and rainy, and it stayed that way for the whole month. You can usually count on a quick shower every day out here, followed by a bunch of rainbows as the sun returns, but this was different. For weeks, the sun hardly ever came out, and it just kept raining. The poor tourists were splashing through the streets of Waikiki with a look of hopelessness, and fortunes lost.

Sara still hasn't found another side gig to make extra money after the Hot Rods fiasco, which had closed mysteriously during Christmas week. Somebody came and padlocked the doors, a result of unpaid taxes or some other nefarious doings by ownership. A real shit show, from beginning to end.

Sara's hula girl aspirations didn't pan out, either. She tried it for a few days but wasn't comfortable being the only non-local. She did fall in love with the breezy, ancient Hawaiian sayings they taught in the class and still practices them around the apartment.

The sky brightened up considerably for the tourists in February and for Sara and me, the outlook was just as sunny. Unfortunately, just like my Dad had warned me about, a storm was brewing.

Mike invites us over to his place for a double date celebrating Lisa's 21st birthday on Saturday, February tenth. Pizza, beers, and a movie. He has a tiny second floor apartment in the University section of Oahu. Mike gave Lisa a VCR for her birthday and is having a little movie party, renting "Fatal Attraction" from Blockbuster.

Immediately upon our arrival, everyone smoked a joint, except for me. I don't have a problem with it but didn't partake either. Instead, I wait in the living room playing Sega baseball while they head off to pass the Dutchie.

"This is really good shit," I imagine them saying as they hand around some weed on the back deck.

Cheech to Chong: "*Hey Man, is my driving okay?*"

Chong to Cheech: "*I think we're parked, Man.*" Funny, but I don't ever need to be that stupid.

Fatal Attraction is intense. A guy's wife goes away for the weekend so he cheats on her and then the lady he was with starts stalking him and his family. "I'm not going to be ignored, Dan!" she threatens crazily. It's a little awkward between Sara and me as we watch a cheating husband and his wife deal with the infidelity. We've been down this road ourselves, though Sara has never officially copped to it. Thankfully nobody has died in our saga; not yet anyway.

We help Mike and Lisa tidy up and say our goodbyes. "Thanks for having us, Mookie! Better get rid of that chick on the side before Lisa stabs her," I joke, in reference to the movie. Sara hugs Mike and Lisa, then we walk a couple of blocks to the bus stop and jump on for the quick ride up to Chinatown.

"Sooo, I'm interested to know, how'd you like the movie?" I ask Sara as the bus lumbers down the road.

"It was terrifying, he picked a super scary chick. Hooking up with a stranger was his first mistake, you're guaranteed to get caught," she remarks.

"Hmmm. I thought it was a bad choice to cheat at all. I'm glad he got busted," I reply.

Sara rolls her eyes at me. "Don't start, Bry. I mean why did we watch that stupid movie, so you could quiz me on it?"

"I didn't choose the fucking thing. I'm just making conversation, Sara."

"Okay, well let's talk about the pizza. Let's converse about that instead," she snaps.

"I liked the pizza."

"Me too."

"Wonderful," I growl. "Good talking to you." Sara's mouth doesn't open again, but her eyes do the talking for her, warning me with a hard glare not to push it any further. I pull the cord and ding the dinger. "This is us."

Back upstairs, Sara washes up as I sit in the living room and light a butt, watching the news because that's what's on. "I'm going to bed," Sara shouts through the open screens of the lanai that connect the bedroom and living room.

"Coming too," I respond, dropping my cig in a can and heading for the bathroom. After brushing my teeth quickly, I snuggle up behind Sara in the bed, squashing any lingering weirdness from the bus. As always, I put my arm around Sara and sandwich my body against hers as we fall asleep. There is not a millimeter between us tonight. Little do I know that what will happen tomorrow is going to pull us apart, possibly forever.

CHAPTER 37

I'M UP SUPER EARLY THIS MORNING, "FATAL ATTRACTION" REPLAYing in my head as I stare at the mountains outside our window. Sara is still snoozing (looking pretty as ever), so I slide on my big shorts and slip out for the Sunday paper and some grub.

My customary New York breakfast of bacon, egg, and cheese on a roll has not been mastered by the Hawaiians. That goes for pizza and bagels as well, but I've found a delicious replacement for the egg sandwich. There is a little shop on the corner of Hotel and Maunakea that makes fresh doughnuts, which has become my new Sunday staple. They have a huge vat of oil boiling in the window, frying up dozens of floating doughnuts; it's a sight to see. I receive and pay for my bounty, light a smoke, and head back up the block. Little Mom & pop shops line the street, nothing fancy. I walk past a flower stand with fresh leis refrigerated in a glass case, before coming upon a parking lot with ten or so orange taxi cabs, all lined up and ready.

A bunch of drivers sit around in lawn chairs on the concrete, listening to each other "talk story," as the natives say, while they wait for a fare. "Howz it, Braddah?" I ask, in full blown local speak, to one of the guys I always see during my walks past here.

"Nother day, nother dolla," I get in return from the native, sitting in front his taxi. I'm fitting in okay, I think to myself.

Suddenly out of nowhere, Sumo the shirtless bully from my first day in Waikiki slides out from behind a cab. He spots me and immediately runs in my direction, all his blubber jiggling wildly with every thunderous step. I backpedal away casually, knowing this guy can't catch me unless he has a rocket up his ass.

"Manny!" shouts the local man I was just saying hello to, "get over here right now! What is the problem, Son?"

"This the Fucka' I told you about Poppi, he the one who hit and run on me that day at Kahuna Burger."

The older man chastises the Sumo loudly. "Good for him, Manuel. We both know you had it coming."

"Wait a second," I remark in disbelief. "This guy is your son?" Wow, another case study of how a father and son can be so different. It's the story of my life.

"He saving your ass Braddah, trust me on that!" the bully shouts as he tries to squirm out of his fathers' clutches.

The Dad has his back to me, keeping the baby bull from charging. "Listen, Manny," I begin, using the name his father shouted, "Believe it or not I feel bad about that day. I mean, you were an incredible asshole, but I shouldn't have smacked you. I'm from New York man, we don't take that kind of shit. I'm trying to be better these days; I've grown up a lot since then. Why don't we shake on it and call things even?"

Manny pauses as if contemplating my offer to make peace but instead dismisses it. "Fuck off Haole. Mothha fucka, you must be crazy!" he replies, but in a moderate tone, compared to his previous hollering. I think I'm getting to him.

His father gestures in the direction of the tower and addresses me. "Take off Brah, sorry for the trouble."

"I'll see you again, Haole!" Manny promises angrily.

"Not if I see you first, Manuel," I chirp back with a smirk, walking away backward.

Back safely in our high-rise nest, I'm sitting in the living room with my feet up on the coffee table reading the paper when Sara finally emerges from her slumber. She will never know of my relationship with the Hamburglar. I'm not sure what she would say, but whatever it is, I'm pretty sure I wouldn't want to hear it. Sometimes, for the sake of harmony, you just gotta leave stuff out.

"Morning Baby," she waves, on her way to the fridge. "You're an early bird today, I see."

"Early bird gets the doughnuts," I smile at her, pointing out the bag on top of the bar.

"Mmm, yummy. I love these things, thank you!" she says, emptying them onto a plate.

"One at a time, Piggy," I laugh. "Hey, guess what? Mike Tyson got his ass kicked last night!"

"You're kidding me! By who? I didn't even know there was a fight."

"Hold on a sec," I answer, looking back at the article in the paper. "Some fucking guy named Buster Douglas in Tokyo. Mike got his ass busted by the Buster, out cold in the ninth round!"

"Oh well, sucks for him," she shrugs, on her way back to the bedroom. "Taking a shower," she informs me. "I'll be ready in thirty minutes."

We are going to the beach this morning, enjoying an official tourist day for ourselves. I asked some of my friends from Bryan's where the best beach is and everyone seems to have a different opinion. We referred back to the good old Frommer's guide and chose Makapuu Beach Park, at the eastern end of Oahu. We've never been there before and found a direct bus route, so it makes the most sense. The ride takes close to an hour, but we are seeing all new things and besides, it's exciting to be on an adventure together for the first time in a while.

People think living in Hawaii is so amazing but Sara and I have not done much sightseeing or relaxing, we're on the run most of the time. Our most recent visit to an ocean together was last summer at Jones Beach in Long Island, NY. At Jones, you parked what seemed like a mile away from the shore and lugged your chairs and coolers across the sandy horizon forever, until finally getting near the water, which is a shit-colored brown. You're bathed in sweat by the time you get your towels down and stay overheated all day long in the humid New York air, sometimes getting bitten by ferocious man-eating flies as well.

Makapuu Beach is so beautiful, the exact opposite of Jones. Its landscape is breathtaking, with a backdrop of mountains and lush greenery. The Pacific Ocean water is turquoise blue, absolutely perfect. We set out a sheet on the sand for our cooler and towels, slather on the sunscreen, and then conk out for a few.

A little while later, Sara stands up and gently kicks my foot to get my attention. "I'm going in the water to cool off. What about you?"

I sit up. "Nah, I don't want to leave our stuff alone, I'll just watch from here. Those waves are no joke, Baby. Be careful."

She gives me a thumbs up and walks down to the water, at which time I do a little talent search of the beach and check out the local ladies surrounding me. As always, my girl is the best of the bunch.

Turning back around to face the water, Sara isn't out very far, but it's far enough that she can no longer stand, her head bobbing up and down. A breaking wave is closing in on her and she doesn't see it coming. I point it out, hoping she'll take cover, but she thinks I'm saying hello and just smiles back. I cringe as Sara gets absolutely destroyed by the surf. Disappearing under the water, she finally pops up a few feet away. Unfortunately for her, as soon as Sara is back above the surface, she gets pummeled by another breaker and is gone again. It happens just like that the next three times she resurfaces, all in the span of 45 seconds, as she slowly progresses back to the beach. She just can't evade these monster waves. Eventually, she makes it to dry land and serpentines up to our towels, like a drunken bum.

"Oh my God, you took a pounding out there!" I laugh.

"Leave me alone, Bryan, it's not funny! I almost drowned!" she chastises me.

"It's a little funny, seeing as how you lived and all. The fucking Titanic was more buoyant than you," I carry on.

Sara takes her towel and walks off, screaming, "Don't talk to me, leave me alone!" She sits 20 feet away, puts her head down, and cries into the crook of her arm. I amble over and start rubbing her back, wanting to apologize. Her body stiffens up upon my touch, coinciding with her looking me dead in the eye and slowly mouthing, "Go- the- fuck- away!"

"Maybe you'd like a little time alone," I reply sheepishly and slowly back off. I hadn't realized the severity of the episode and I'm feeling guilty for being so flippant with my jokes.

I decide not to brave the water myself, given her near-death experience. Sara took the test for me and failed miserably. Upon further examination, the only people out in the ocean are experienced swimmers, probably locals. I give Sara a little time to cool down and approach again.

"Hey Sara, I'm sorry Baby. I thought you would come out of the water laughing. From here, it looked funny. I didn't know."

"Well, you should have checked first before you laughed. I was being thrown around the bottom like a rag doll. I thought this was it for me, my time was up."

I give her a big hug, then stagger around the beach emulating Fred from Sanford and Son, holding my heart and bellowing, "I'm coming, Elizabeth! My time is up! It's the big one! I'm bringing Sara with me!"

"So funny I forgot to laugh," Sara grins, finally relaxing a little.

"Well I already paid for the bus fare home, so I'm glad you didn't drown," I joke again, but with a smile and a wink.

After our reconciliation, we laze in the sun a while longer and then wrap it up for the day; it's a long ride back. As soon as Sara sits down on the bus, she puts her head on my shoulder and closes her eyes, falling asleep immediately. Poor girl had taken a beating out there today.

"I'm glad you're okay, Love," I whisper into deaf ears. "I couldn't imagine my life without you."

As we ride along on the hot bus, I think of my brother Ed. He and I used to take a Greyhound from Rockland into New York City to visit our Dad. No supervision, just us boys, at the time only elementary school children. We would slide open the big oblong windows and squeeze our tiny heads through the little opening as the bus made its way into the Port Authority bus terminal, smells of New York City wafting through the air. Upon arrival, we had instructions to meet Dad at the lockers, sidestepping the sleaziest of what the city offered along the way. You would think a father would be on time to pick up his little kids from that hellhole, but he never was. Ed and I would stand with our backs to the lockers, holding hands and scanning the crowd of weirdos and freaks. We were always excited to see our father and had been too naive to be mad at him for making us wait. It was all worth it for us when we were little, Dad was our childhood hero and we always had fun with him.

Those memories with Ed seem like a century ago. Back then it was always Lauren and "The Boys." Ed and I were counted as one, not two, and we did everything together. Now we are a world away from each other; the only thing we share is the sun and the moon.

As Sara sleeps next to me, I push open the window for old times' sake, the distinct smell of the bus's fumes the same as they were in Port Authority all those years ago.

"Let's grab a pizza for dinner," I suggest to Sara as we exit the bus through the double doors in the back. "Whiskey, Partner," I instruct my imaginary bartender. "And one for the Lady."

We pick up a pie and walk the remaining two blocks home, loaded down with beach stuff, backpacks, a cooler, and the aforementioned pizza. Back at the building, everything needs to be unloaded because we have to rummage around for the key, then load it up again before heading into the lobby. A Chinese fire drill in Chinatown. Nothing to see here.

It's been a long day. Sara almost drowned, and in about an hour, I'm going to be wishing that she had.

CHAPTER 38

AFTER DESTROYING THE PIZZA, SARA AND I ARE NOW CUDDLED up on the couch, watching "Murder She Wrote" on CBS, but not by choice. We only get two channels on our TV, and the other is PBS, which is all nature documentaries. The "rabbit ear" antenna doesn't help with reception, and why would it? We're in the middle of the Pacific. Whatever is on CBS is what we watch, and tonight it's "Murder She Wrote."

"Hey Bry," Sara says as she turns to face me at the conclusion of the show. "I want to tell you something. A couple of things, actually."

"Uh-huh. What's up, Baby?"

"Well, first of all, I've never loved anyone like I love you, not even close. I mean, who would think this guy I barely knew in high school, I hardly even noticed you were there, could end up being the most important person in my life? And you are Bry, you're everything to me. You're my whole world."

"Wow, that's nice of you to say, Baby. What's the second thing, you want to marry me?" I ask with a grin.

"I know you're kidding, but I think about it. I would marry you one day. That's why I want to tell you the second thing, because I want to be an open book with you, and not keep any secrets." We've all been here before, at this exact moment. The proverbial war plane just flew overhead, the bomb doors are opening and Sara is getting ready to drop a nuke on me. She goes on, changing her voice to a childlike tone. "Remember that time that I said nothing happened with Chris, I just slept on the couch and we didn't—"

"So you fucked Chris that night, is this your breaking news?" I interrupt, surprisingly relaxed. "I know Sara, I've always known. I told you I knew, I told my friends I knew, I even told my mother I knew. I'm over it Sara, and have been for a long time. My question is, why in the fucking world would you bring it up randomly tonight? Things have been going so well with us, how can this *not* fuck it up? Back in New York, you told me not to sabotage things; now here you are coming at me like a suicide bomber. Please explain that to me. Why now?" I ask, still relaxed, although I'm not sure why. Probably because I've always known what happened.

She, on the other hand, is nervous. "I'm telling you now because when the phone bill comes this week, you are going to see that I called Chris on Christmas Eve. My sister Cara told me she ran into him, and he was real depressed—"

"Please stop. Don't feed me any more bullshit. I've had it up to here with your lying about this guy, I really can't believe this shit is still going on. You fucking lied to my face in front of our friends and said you were going to call your mother on Christmas Eve and you called him instead? Wow, this is a new low, I honestly don't know what to say. You two are obviously meant to be together, you certainly can't seem to stay apart. Maybe if we moved to the Moon or fucking Mars, I could get a little peace from this fucking guy!"

"Bry, don't say that," she pleads, "it wasn't a big deal. Didn't you hear all the things I said? How much I love you?"

My volume level is rising, and my popper is about to pop. "The only thing I heard that matters is that you fucked Chris Garvey, and you also called him from this phone on Christmas Eve, the phone that I pay the damn bill for, which, like I said, is what really pisses me off." I lift the large black rotary phone over my head and slam it down on the glass coffee table, shattering the cheap flea market crap into a million pieces. So much for being relaxed. This is inevitable, it's how I'm wired. I pick my Reds up off the floor, out of the pile of glass, and stomp off to the lanai for a smoke. "Leave me the fuck alone!" I turn and scream, shaking a bloody finger at Sara.

Leaning on the railing, facing the dark mountainside, it feels like (once again) this is over. I've always known in my heart of hearts that Sara cheated that night and I pretty much accepted it, but naively had thought the chapter was closed. To suddenly learn she's still talking to him after all this time is what hurts. Now I'm feeling this was always a lie, and I'm kidding myself believing we ever had anything lasting, or even real. She is older, hotter, and like I always say, out of my league. I liked proving to everyone that I could get this girl, but I never really had her, did I?

It hasn't been perfect, but we are giving it a go, the old college try. We have an address, a mailbox, a checking account, a phone, all of it. We're doing this, and she seemed happy. But now we are going to have to figure out how to undo it. I will not be out here scanning the phone bill every month, feeding my insecurities about this relationship. I guess my sister was right, as usual. Like Kenny Rogers sang, "*You gotta know when to hold 'em, know when to fold 'em.*" I feel ready to throw in my cards.

Sara cleaned up the broken glass and eventually fell asleep on the couch. I sat on the lanai for hours, then went to sleep alone in our bed. The next morning, I woke up with that same gutted feeling that I had after the night Sara didn't show up at my apartment in Rockland, way back when. I hear her on the phone as I make my way outside, amazed it still works after the shot I gave it last night.

"Yes, this is Sara Addeo, I'm sick today and won't make it for my nine am shift. Please call me back with any (adds in fake cough) questions." She hangs up.

"You should just go to work. I certainly don't want to sit here staring at each other all day," I bark, and then jump right back in it. "You fucking blew it, Sara! We were doing so good here, and you wrecked it. Save the tears for Chris, because I don't give a shit," I yell, as she begins sobbing. "I hope your little calls were worth it. What a joke you are! Do you think Chris is sitting in his room crying over you? He's not! He's grabbing every piece of ass he can, that's what he's doing. He'd probably throw your sister a bang if she let him."

More sobbing. "I'm sorry!"

"You did this," I continue, taking my tone down a notch. "You threw me in the garbage, Sara, and nothing you ever fucking do or say is going to change that." I'm not sure if I mean the things I'm threatening, but coming at her like this is instinctual to me. It's an eye for an eye mentality, that's what I've grown up believing.

She continues crying by herself on the couch for a long time, but I feel only a tinge of compassion, which is more than she deserves. You reap what you sow, Mom always said that. I let her reap.

CHAPTER 39

"I**'M WORKING LUNCH TODAY," I LIE TO SARA AND FEEL JUST FINE** about it. "Need to make some extra money. Your long-distance calls weren't in the budget," I add snidely. Adding insult to injury, I continue chopping her down. "Valentine's Day is coming up, how about dinner at Taco Bell?"

Sara doesn't say one word in reply, which is wise of her because she has no defense. I dress in work clothes to perpetuate my lie, then march out of the apartment. As the elevator reaches the lobby, I realize I forgot to bring my Walkman and head back up to grab it. I'm not sure what the day ahead will entail but know my music will be needed if I'm going to get through it. I get back to the apartment and upon entering, I can hear Sara on the phone in the bedroom. I put my ear to the door and listen in, sure it has to be Chris on the other end.

I pick it up mid-sentence. "—don't know when I'm coming home again, you'll just have to hold onto it for me. If you really care as much as you say, then wait."

Hold on to what? What's this all about? Holy shit, did Chris buy her a ring? My mother always told me that *"putting your ears where they don't belong will always give you an earache."* I know I shouldn't be eavesdropping, it doesn't feel good, but I can't help it.

She continues. "I took your advice and told him what happened with Chris over the holidays, and he did not take it well. Things were going so good, and I fucked it all up." Okay, so she's not talking to him, this much is clear. Sara continues with the mystery caller. "No, he didn't appreciate it. He practically threw me off the balcony." Sara is silent for a bit, then says, "Yeah, Chris said he loves me and can't live without me." Jesus, the guy said he still loves her? Man, I am such an idiot. Quiet again, then "No, I said I love Bryan now and told him to get over it. But Bryan will never believe me if I tell him that. Why should he? I wouldn't believe it either. I messed up a really good thing here, for no reason." More silence as the conversation continues from the other end. "He just has a bad temper; he would never hurt me. He's trying to work on it." Sara listens, then continues, "No, he went to work. I have to figure out how to fix this, but it's probably too late, everything's all screwed up. Hold on a sec, I need some water and the phone doesn't reach the sink."

This is my cue to exit stage left, grabbing my headphones and quietly backing out of the apartment. I'm not sure who she is talking to, probably a friend or her sister, but as long as it's not the old boyfriend, it doesn't matter to me. She loves me, she loves me not. I don't know what to believe anymore, it seems like she wants me *and* Chris. There's something about him Sara just can't get over and that's too bad because it's gonna kill us, or we're going to kill each other.

Outside the doughnut shop eating a cinnamon sugar, I swing the door closed on the pay phone and call my old reliable friend Mike. He answers groggily on the billionth ring. "Wakey, wakey," I sing into the phone while sticking my finger in the coin slot, trying to get lucky.

His Datsun rolls up ten minutes later, I get in and give him the whole story. "—and the fucking kicker is that she called him on Christmas Eve when you guys came to pick us up for the Luau, you remember that? They got into it on the phone and then she ruined the whole night for us, and blamed it all on her mother!"

"Every chick I've ever known has a secret, man," Mike declares, "but I really thought you guys were solid."

"It was all a mirage; I've always been waiting for the other shoe to drop. Things were going so good though, I stopped worrying about it. Whatever we had, Sara did her best to burn it down last night. Truthfully, it feels like she wants out. Why else would she admit to that after all this time? I wasn't even asking about him anymore; it was old news."

"Well listen, Brother, your girl might be a sneaky two-timer, but you can always count on me. Whatever you need, my friend. I know it's not a fancy tower, but you're welcome to crash at my place if you need to."

"Thanks, Bro, I appreciate it. You can start by figuring out how I'm going to waste this day. I've got nowhere to go and nothing to do."

"Dam, I gotta work at five but we can screw around for a while. Let's finish the series." We have been playing a best of seven Yankees vs. Red Sox on the Sega and left off tied after two games. Mike and I spend the next few hours lazing around, playing computer baseball on TV like a couple of ten-year old's. It keeps my mind off the reality of the situation with Sara. What's coming next with her, I have no idea.

"Dude, when do you work again? We haven't been on the bar together for a couple of weeks," Mike remarks.

"I know, I've been subbing out to Sherry here and there. Sara and I were spending some extra time together, which was a fucking waste. I'm working Tuesday through Saturday this week, you'll see plenty of me."

"You guys will be alright. They say time heals all wounds."

"Really, Bro? Every time this wound closes, Sara rips the scab off again. I've had enough, I'm cashing out," I claim in full bravado. "Fool me once, shame on me. Or is it shame on you? Whatever, you know what I'm trying to say; I can't take it anymore."

"Yeah yeah, I get it, no need to further pontificate. My point is, I still think you guys will work it out."

I'm caught off guard by his big vocabulary. "Pontificate? Brother please, just shut up and play the game."

Bob Stanley struck out Steve Balboni with the tying run on and Mike wins in seven games, the first time the Red Sox ever beat the Yankees in a big game. Hopefully, it'll never happen in real life. He drops me off in front of the tower at 4:30 in the afternoon. I'm not looking forward to dealing with any more of the Sara drama yet, or anytime soon for that matter. I feel trapped with nowhere to go so I sit down on the wall, exactly where I had listened to the karaoke party a while back, light up a smoke and watch the world go by. A work crew spreads smoking hot blacktop on the street in front of me, the pleasing smell of it intoxicating. Hands on my knees and head down, I stare at the sidewalk, wishing my problems away, then stub out the butt and go upstairs, expecting the worst.

"I'm back," I announce flatly upon returning to the apartment. What a difference a day makes. Yesterday, it was "I'm home!"

"In here," Sara responds in a normal tone. "Be out in a minute."

I am sitting on a bar stool when she emerges from the bedroom, eyes puffy, with a somber look on her face. Sara nuzzles into me and puts her arms around my body. I receive it and do the same to her, mainly because of the nice words I overheard about me earlier during the mystery phone call. We stay in the embrace for a long while. It was okay at first, but now I'm getting bored and ready to break the clinch.

"So?" I ask, looking into her eyes.

"Sew buttons on your underwear!" she jokes, smiling her pretty smile.

Don't give in Bry, I encourage myself. You're pissed man, stay pissed. "Ha ha ha, you're hilarious. So what have you been up to all day?" I ask. "Did you go to church and confess your sins?"

"Yes, I spent the whole day begging God for forgiveness."

"Why, did you cheat on God? I'm the one you need to beg."

"Bry, please don't start. I'm going to break down if we do this again tonight. Yes, I beg you. Forgive me!" she cries out, dropping to her knees in mock repentance.

"It's cool. I've said my piece on this situation and on that asshole Chris Garvey. I'm out of gas too, so I'm planning to sit and watch TV tonight, then I'll be working the rest of the week. We'll have plenty of time apart to figure our shit out."

"Fine, thank you," she replies, sounding relieved. "I went to Foodland today and got you some Totinos and some more soda."

Gee, thanks. Nothing says sorry I fucking ruined your life like some frozen pizza rolls.

CHAPTER 40

THE PHONE RINGS AT AROUND EIGHT THAT NIGHT, WHICH IS VERY unexpected as we rarely receive calls. Getting a call used to be exciting. Who could it be, we'd wonder? Now it's just worrisome and I can't help thinking it could be *him,* Sara's other boyfriend.

Turns out it's my Dad, of all people. It's always a surprise when he calls. "Hey Boy, how goes it?" he asks, extra enthusiastically.

"Dad, good. It goes good," I answer, even though it couldn't be going worse. I head out onto the lanai and light up a smoke. "What's this all about? It's like two am in New York. What going on, you're dreaming about me?"

"I'm in LA with your Uncle Bob, sitting on the deck with a bottle of scotch. We're on Hollywood time," he declares cavalierly.

"Ahh, I see. Well, you Swashbucklers stay out of trouble. To what do I owe the honor of this call?"

I hear my father's voice, but sounds like Johhny Walker is doing the talking. "Bob is telling me about...about the times you spent with him in LA, he says you're like the son he never had."

My inside voice: "Yeah Dad, I'm like the son you never had, too." *My outside voice:* "That's nice to know, Bob's the best. He's the most giving man I know," I blurt hastily, not being very considerate of my Dad's feelings.

"Well when you get back from your adventure out there in *Honoluau*," he pronounces hilariously wrong, "let's dig in and figure out how to be closher. If it's all on me that's okay, I know I need to try more harder," he stumbles, sounding both sincerely genuine and sincerely drunk.

I hold in my laughter. "That would be great Dad, I would like that, it's been a long time coming." I debate telling him what's happening out here with Sara but she's probably listening to me, so I just sum it up for him quickly, speaking quietly and in code. "Your weather prediction came true. That storm came to pass, and it was a fucking hurricane, but that's all I can say right now."

He whispers his reply, which is not necessary. "Oh, okay, okay, what storm is happening? Mum's the word from me," he carries on nonsensically, clearly not functioning at full capacity.

"Alright Dad, thanks for keeping it quiet," I whisper as well, wondering why I bothered. "Let me say hi to Bob," I ask, flicking the stubby cigarette butt over the side and lighting a fresh smoke.

"Oh, he went into the bed a long time ago."

"I see. Maybe you should hit the hay, too," I encourage him, and it is at this point I felt for the first time the pendulum swinging from father to son as the mature one in our relationship. "Good night Dad, I love you. I'm going to hold you to it, getting closer with me," I remind him.

"We did my boy, we will," he mumbles, barely holding on to consciousness. "G'nite, love ya," is the last thing I hear. Somebody's going to be hurting tomorrow. Whatever fueled his kind words, clearly it was the booze, hopefully, he follows through. I need him to.

Sara is gone by the time I get up Tuesday morning. No kiss on the cheek or fingers through my hair, no "love you more than anybody loves anybody." Just gone. Long gone, actually, because I slept until one in the afternoon. My body was telling me there is no reason to get up, so I didn't. Finally rolling out to the couch, I meander through Sunday's newspaper again. The Advertiser is full of Valentine's Day ads, and a special section on dining too, but I don't have to worry about that anymore. I sit around wasting time for a few hours, have some more pizza rolls for lunch, and am showered and on my way to work by four.

Tuesday is usually a pretty slow night at Bryan's Parkplace. As always, it starts off okay, the bar full with plenty of tourists drinking frozen mai tais and pina coladas. We serve a lot of food at the bar too, especially from the pupu menu. That's the appetizer menu, but they call it "Pupu" in Hawaii. To me, pupu means dog shit, not a tasty bar snack, and it doesn't sound right to me coming out of my mouth. A blinding sunset descends on the bar through the beach facing windows, signaling an end to happy hour and a thinning of the crowd. Around 10, the other restaurant crews start coming in.

"Yo bartender, who's the Chief Dick Sucker around here?" someone yells from behind me while I'm at the register. I look in the mirror and see my old buddy TJ, the friendly surfer kid from Freddie's. He has been coming in with some of his gang the last few weeks. We had a good laugh when he first spotted me behind the bar at Bryan's. TJ told me I'd left Freddie's a legend for what I said to the manager Paul the day he fired me.

"Whadda ya say, T?"

"Hey Dude, what's going on, Fly Guy? How's tricks tonight?" he asks, radiating his usual good energy.

"Pretty chill, man, everything's cool," I report, passing him his usual, a draft beer in a pint glass full of ice. No charge, of course.

"Listen up, Bro, one of our new dubs is hot for you. Look over my shoulder. See that killer local girl, the cutie with the white tank top? Bodacious, and really sweet too. That's Johanna, she's stoked to meet you! I told her how cool you are, and a New Yorker to boot!" he sells it enthusiastically.

"You're too much, Dude. Did you mention to her that my girl is here from New York too?"

"No Sir, I failed to mention that. Join us for a libation, that's all I'm asking. You won't be sorry!"

"Arright Man, maybe I will. Sherry is closing, so I'll be wrapping it up pretty soon."

Two days ago, this would never have been a consideration for me, but now, why should I care? Am I in a committed relationship anymore? That's a complicated question. Sara and I are bound to each other right now because we came here together and share a life, but our relationship is a car crash at the current time, and it seems like it's only going to get worse. I finish work an hour later and head toward a decision.

"Nice to meet you, Johanna," I grin, shaking her pretty little hand. "I'm Bryan."

CHAPTER 41

I WAKE UP THE NEXT MORNING TO SARA RUNNING HER FINGERTIPS along my forearm. "I have to get to work, Bry," she whispers, giving me a soft kiss on the cheek. "I left a little something for you on the table outside. Happy Valentine's day, I love you."

"Uh huh, you too. Guess I'll see you later," I mumble after her as she walks out the door. Jesus, this is awkward. I walk out to see what she's left behind, wondering if I should have gotten her something. Why the hell am I feeling bad this morning, I'm not the one who messed things up.

Sara left a framed picture of us, arms around each other with the ocean in the background. It's said that a picture is worth a thousand words, but only one comes to my mind; cheater! If the photo could talk, it would say in a thought bubble over Sara's head, "*I really love someone else!*"

It's boring sitting around the house all day and Sara's gift has made me even madder, so I shower and head off to work, getting there an hour early. I'm now relaxing in the break room by myself, eating a burger and going through an old newspaper. Wow, the Cowboys were 1-16 this year. That's pathetic, my brother Ed must be so pissed.

The door suddenly swings open, and Mike is holding the handle. Not my Mike, Curly Q Mike. "Bryan, can I talk to you for a second in my office?" he asks, his little blond curls shining in the sunlight.

"Sure, I'll be up as soon as I'm done here, is that okay?" I mutter with a mouth full of food.

"Let's do it now," he comments pointedly.

Aw jeez, what's this guy's problem? Take a number, man. "Right behind you." I stand up, suck down a slurp of soda and take one last bite of my food. This must be a scheduling issue, maybe a policy change or something. I've been kicking ass at the bar, so I'm not worried, though this is unusual. My level of urgency is low, as it too often is.

"Shut the door," he starts. Ohhkay, something's going down. Mike puts a long receipt tape on the desk and asks, "Can you explain this?"

I know what it is before he finishes asking, not a big deal. "Of course. The last time I worked, like three minutes before the kitchen closed, I sent this ticket in with a bunch of apps on it, just to piss the cooks off. I used to work in the back, so I knew it would get them mad because they were all cleaned up and ready to go. Anyway, I watched them get pissed for a second, then I walked down and told them it was a joke."

"So you rang in and then deleted almost one hundred dollars' worth of food as a joke?" Mike asks.

"I did. Just trying to give the guys a laugh. Like I said, I was just messing around with the cooks."

"I see," Q replies stoically. "How do you think it looked to me when I came across this computer chit today?"

Pause before you speak, Mom says over my shoulder. "I don't know Mike, what does it look like to you?"

"It looks to me like you're serving free food to all your friends and then voiding the check."

"No Mike, I would never do that. It was nothing. Just ask the guys, they'll vouch for me. No food was sent out."

An uncomfortable silence. "I'm not asking anyone. I'm only asking you, and unfortunately, your answer is unsatisfactory. We don't condone this type of behavior, especially out of the closing bartenders, who are supposed to act as managers. I'm sorry," Mike starts, as I picture the bomb doors opening once again, "you're off the schedule, effective immediately. You are relieved of your duties."

I pick up the long ticket from his desk. "Mike, I can see how this looks bad but you know I didn't steal all this food. I would never do that. You know me by now."

"I know you alright, Bryan. I know you smashed a full bottle of Absolut on the bar top last week trying to be Tom Cruise in "Cocktail." I also know you give away drinks to your pals non-stop. I know you better than you thought, don't I?" he asks with questioning eyes. "You know, I remember when I hired you, you said, "I won't let you down." Well, guess what? You did. I've already hired someone to take your place, and that's all I have to say on the matter."

"Damn Mike, you know my deal, man. I need this job so bad," I plead.

"We gave you the chance, and you squandered it. I didn't fire you, you fired yourself."

Wow, what can I say to that? When you're right, you're right. "Okay, Mike," I concede, and back out of his office, tossing the chit back on his desk. I have no fight left in me, and Curly Q is a truly nice guy who does not deserve my wrath. I've been defeated by myself once again.

I walk up to the bar area and tell my Mike, "I just got canned, call me later," leaving him standing there stunned. Sun still setting, I crawl home to the tower at a snail's pace.

So let's review. In the last few days, I've lost my girlfriend and now my job. The only thing left is my apartment, which we can barely afford when I *was* working, so that's next on the list to go. This is what my Mom would refer to as "Screwing the Pooch." This week, I'm fucking the shit out of the pooch.

Before going upstairs to face Sara with my latest dose of bad news, I need a little more time to myself, so I plop down on the cement wall in front of our building for a pit stop. This has become my sanctuary, I can sit here for hours watching the world go by, always accompanied by the awful music pumping out of the karaoke bar across the street.

As I languish, a taxi pulls to a stop at the traffic light in front of me, at which time I seriously consider hopping a ride to the airport and leaving this place, and that girl upstairs, behind forever. We've all heard stories of the husband who disappears without a trace, leaving the wife and kids to fend for themselves. Why not me? Nothing is waiting up in that apartment other than more lies, and crappy furniture.

I raise my hand and yell "Taxi!" then jump in the back and point, "To the airport, Braddah!" At least that's what I imagine myself doing, but of course, I stay glued to the wall, reminded instead of something I told myself before leaving New York. Troubles always stay with us, no matter how far away we go. Also, I still love Sara. I'm not a robot, I can't just turn it on and off. I'm mad, but also sad, and I miss her.

Walking into the apartment, I see Sara sitting in the saucer chair, talking on the phone. You're busted!

"Mom, let me call you back. Bryan just walked in."

"Was that your Mom?" I ask, "Or were you calling Chris for Valentine's Day?"

"Be serious," she replies dismissively, moving to the couch. "Before I forget, Pat Byrne called for you. He said call him back, it's important."

Maybe he lost his virginity, I laugh to myself while grabbing the phone to call Patty back. I get no answer. He doesn't even have a machine, so I guess it wasn't that important.

"Why are you home so early?" Sara asks.

"Because I got fired, that's why," I reply, then head into the bedroom to change my clothes, Sara up off the couch and following close behind.

"You must be kidding me? What happened that they fired you? Damn Bry, we need that money."

"Oh, *we* do?" I ask. "Who's we? What team are you playing for today, Sara? I need that money! Me. This is not a we problem, it's a me problem."

"Well, we share the bills, Bryan."

"Right, you worry about your half and I'll worry about mine."

"So that's how it's going to be?" she asks.

"Did you expect something else? How about if I cheated on you while we were together out here? Would you be okay with that? If I did then we'd be even, right? Yes, to answer your question, this is exactly the way it's going to be. Now it's you and it's me, it's not us or we. That picture you left me this morning, that's the old us. That's the calm before the storm, the fucking storm you brought in here for no reason!"

"You're cold as ice, Bryan. Sounds like you're looking for an excuse to get away from me."

Whoa, that's some master manipulation right there. "Yeah Sara, you nailed it. How did you figure me out?" I reply, sliding open the screen door to the lanai and walking out for some air. "I'm trying to remember, were Chris's balls in my mouth? No, I don't think so. Don't try to pass the buck to me."

She ignores my crude commentary, and impatiently asks, "Why did you say if you were with someone else we would be even? Were you with anybody?"

"Maybe I was. Do you want to smell my fingers again?" I ask, offering a hand.

"I don't mean today; I mean have you cheated since we've been here?"

I shrug.

"You're being such a jerk!"

"No Sara, I'm not the guilty party, I haven't done anything wrong," I remind her, sitting back down inside on the couch. "You're the only cheater here."

Which is true.

"Nice to meet you, Johanna," I grin, shaking her pretty little hand. "I'm Bryan."

"Hey Bryan from Bryan's," she replies with a smile that is cute as hell. But I'm not seeing Johanna. I'm seeing Sara.

TJ says, "I'm going to run to the cigarette machine, let you guys get to know each other."

"Actually T, I gotta split, just wanted to say hi. I'll have to catch you guys next time."

That's what happened last night. Nothing.

I go on, explaining to Sara, "I had a chance yesterday and passed up a sure thing. Hell, I've had a chance every night since we've been here, but I've never even thought about it because I have you. But you, on the other hand, have been sneaking around ever since we met. It's not just the cheating, or the phone calls, or whatever else I don't know about," I say calmly, "It's that I was never enough for you. This whole living together and team us, it was all a bunch of bullshit. Nothing and nobody has come across my mind since the day we decided to be together. You were enough for me. It's not a good feeling, knowing you need more."

"You're all I need, Bry. It was so stupid, and it meant nothing," she cries.

"Yeah, you're right, it was stupid, and now we need an exit plan, Sara. I want to go home. The only reason we are still together is that we're stuck here in the middle of the ocean. If I had any other place to go, I'd have burned rubber out of this mother fucker a long time ago."

CHAPTER 42

MIKE DROVE HIS ROACH COACH ACROSS TOWN THURSDAY NIGHT to have some beers with me. I bought a case of Sam Adams earlier, Mike's favorite Boston brew, and threw them in an icy cooler. We sit on the wall in front of my building for the next several hours, listening to karaoke and drinking. The cooler is behind the wall within our reach and we practically empty it as we sit there. I review the whole story of what transpired with Curly Q at Bryan's.

When I'm done, Mike reveals what happened after I left. "Dude, five minutes after you walked out, I shit you not, Mike's sister was training to take your place. Did you hear me, he hired his fucking sister! He was looking for any reason to get you out."

"Wow, that's fucked up. But listen man, I deserved it. I was giving away a lot of booze and should have been more careful. You better watch your back too, Brother."

"No shit, who you tellin'?" He pauses before changing the topic. "Anyway, Bro, I was telling Lisa about all this shit going on with you two over here. Lisa said she heard Sara on the phone Christmas Eve when she went to the bathroom, and had a feeling it wasn't her Mom. Sara was talking all low and secretive, definitely seemed like she was up to something."

"Huh, that's interesting. Why didn't she fucking say anything to me, or you?" I ask accusingly.

"What's Lisa gonna say, I was eavesdropping on your girlfriend and I think she's a liar?" Mike replies. "She just said that in retrospect, it all makes sense now."

"Yeah, you're right. A heads up would've been nice but I get it, I guess."

"So what now for you and Sara?" Mike asks, pointing up to our apartment as he tosses an empty into the cooler and reaches under the ice for another.

"Nothing now. Time to wrap this up, man. I can't fucking stay out here with no job, and everything's all kinds of messed up with her. I can't see how it's ever going to work."

"Dude, say it ain't so. That's some depressing news, my friend," he replies sadly.

"It's too much. We can't afford a car so we have to take the bus every-where. I have no job. Everything is so expensive. And to top it off, my girl can't stop thinking about her ex."

"Yeah," Mike agrees, "That's a lot right there. It's messed up, her calling that guy. Pretty dumb if you ask me. Doesn't she know the calls are printed out on the bill?"

"Of course, she knows, that's why I think she did it on purpose. But it's a lot more than a couple of calls. This guy Chris is like a skid mark in my underwear; he only pops up once in a while, but when he does, you know some shit's gonna follow. It's a never-ending pattern with those two. What would you do if some guy Lisa used to be with kept coming around?"

He doesn't hesitate. "I'd kick his ass. What you need to do is show this fucking guy who's boss so he stays out of your business once and for all."

"I hear you, Bro, but that's not going to happen. I'm embarrassed to admit he already tuned me up back in New York, the guy was born to brawl."

"Oh shit, that's not good," Mike shakes his head. "Man, I don't know what to tell you. Sounds like an ego trip Sara's on like she knows this kid's still burning a candle for her, and she digs it. It's human nature."

"Really, it's human nature, Confucius? Thank you for the heavy thoughts. I appreciate your deep analysis," I joke. "Bottom line is we're screwed."

"Well, I think you two can still get through this. You make a good couple man, and she's gorgeous too. You're going to have a hard time doing better than Sara. Cheers to that fine ass!" he remarks, holding up his bottle to clink.

I don't know if it's too many Sam Adams or if Mike is just losing his mind, toasting to my girl's ass like that. Not too long ago, we all went on a double date to Bobby McGee's, this dinner and dancing place in Waikiki, and Sara and I got into a huge argument that ended with us storming out of the place. She said me and Lisa were flirting, which we definitely were not, but I know she was flirting with Mike, I saw it. And now he's giving me these loose lips about her ass?

"Hey Buddy, where I come from, we don't talk about how fly our friend's girl is," I inform him, trying to keep it chummy, "so chill out with that shit."

"Dude, c'mon man, I love you guys. I didn't mean anything by it," he insists, offering up his bottle to toast again.

"Cheers," I shout, aggressively smashing my bottle into his. I can feel my Incredible Hulk trying to come out. *Don't make me angry; You wouldn't like me when I'm angry.* I quell the beast within, then reach over the wall and grab my cooler, ready to head back up. We drank most of the beer anyway and now all I can picture is Sara and Mike fooling around behind my back. That's why her phone calls to Chris are such a big deal because now I'm overanalyzing everything and everybody, even Mike, who's been a perfect friend to me.

"Love you, Mookie," I hug him, "and you're right, she has a great ass. No harm, no foul."

"Thanks, love you too, Brother," he proclaims, rising from the wall. "Get home safe."

"Asshole, I'm already home," I laugh, pointing up at the tower. "You get home safe in that shit box. And take off that stupid Boston hat."

"Bro, that will never happen."

"We need to get you a Yankee hat."

"Please do," he grins, "I can wipe my ass with it when I run out of toilet paper."

Heading back upstairs on the elevator, I'm feeling a little tipsy and sit down atop the cooler as I ride. Upon opening the apartment door, I see Sara sitting on the couch watching TV, whatever CBS has to offer.

"Hey," she mutters, without looking up. "I'm watching "Island Son," it's about a doctor here in Hawaii with that samurai guy Richard Chamberlain. You should check it out, I'm learning a lot about the island."

"Why do I need to learn more about a place I'm leaving?" I respond as I put down the cooler, then sit next to her.

"Bry," she replies, "we don't have to leave here. I know you still love me."

"*My love* has never been in question, Sara," I reply loudly, then drop to my knees and start pushing together a pile of hair and dirt that is below the now glass-less coffee table. We can't afford a vacuum so this is how the floor gets cleaned.

"Well I want to stay here with you," she declares.

"Pfft, no thanks," I state quickly, ten bottles of Sam Adams having eliminated my filter. "I'm fucking tired of running from my problems. We ran out here to get away from your reality, and it still didn't work. I don't want to find another job here. I miss my family and my friends. The novelty has worn off for me, anyway. It's a grind here just like anywhere else, so why should we stay, just to be away from Chris? I have an idea, how about we move back home and he can move halfway around the fucking world instead of us?"

"Wow. Anything else?"

"Yes, plenty, so glad you asked! I'm tired of walking everywhere. You don't have one friend. Groceries cost a billion dollars. I'm a fucking immigrant. I keep getting fired. Oh yeah, and I think you probably want to bang my only friend Mike too if you haven't already!" I head to the bathroom, still rambling. "I take the last one back, I'm a little drunk. I don't even want to talk about that one."

"You're babbling," Sara responds. "Come talk to me when you start making sense."

I walk away, raising my hand high, and throw up the middle finger.

"Fottiti anche tu, stronzo!" Sara screams as a little couch pillow whizzes past my head. She translates the Italian this time for full effect, still screaming. "Fuck you too, Asshole!"

A few minutes later, the phone rings. Who now? "Hello!" I answer angrily. It's my friend Pat finally calling me back, and he has a doozy of a story to tell. I head outside to talk in private. Funk ran into Chris Garvey again, and let's just say things went a lot better for Patty this time.

"Bro, when I saw him, we were online getting ice cream at Carvel Friday night, my blood started to boil thinking of that shit he pulled in the city, I just lost my mind. I've been trying to steer clear of him around the neighborhood, but he saw me on line and starting talking shit. He got too close and I got in a lucky shot, he just went down. Two hits; me hitting him, him hitting the floor!"

"Oh shit, just like Tyson! You're the Buster of New York! Patty, this is so crazy. What did you do, just leave him there? Have you seen him since? Is he alright?" I prattle on, peering in from the lanai to make sure Sara isn't listening. She looks up from the couch just long enough to flip me the bird (she stole that from me), then she goes back to watching TV.

"My older brother Tim was with me, they used to be friends when they were kids and played on the same Pop Warner team. He waited with him until he was okay, it didn't take long."

"Man, don't get in the way of Patty Funk and his ice cream," I joke. "Seriously, this is insane. Thank you, Funk, thank you!" I finish.

"Ahh, like I said, lucky shot," Pat humbly replies. "I didn't do it for you, Gay-hill, I did it for me. What he did to us that night was bullshit and I'm not going to walk around avoiding this guy for the rest of my life."

"You got nothing to worry about now," I assure him. "How did you guys leave it?"

"That's the craziest part, we shook hands and called a truce."

"I know you're making that shit up, Patty," I continue in disbelief.

"Seriously, my brother got between us and made us shake hands. Bro, you know Tim is twice my size, he's like EF Hutton; when he talks, people listen. Garvey said as far as he's concerned, it's done. Supposedly he's got a new girl now, so he said he's done with you too."

"Oh really? He may have a new lady, but he's still chatting up his old one, too. Me and Sara are in a huge brawl right now because she's been talking to him on the phone from out here," I tell him, lighting up a smoke and peeking in the window again.

"I don't even want to know, Dude," Patty replies, not interested in hearing our problems. "I'm still trying to figure out how you ended up living in Hawaii with Sara Addeo. To each their own, whatever works for you."

"Well it ain't gonna work much longer, I'm pretty sure of that. Maybe I'll hit you up on a ride from the airport in the next couple of months, who knows."

"Say the word, I'm always around, Gay-hill," Funk assures me.

"Aright Patty. Nice job slaying the dragon, you truly are a badass!" I commend him, flicking my cig onto the parking lot below and hanging up the phone.

Back in the living room, Sara and I are now in a cold war, exchanging icy glances, neither one of us willing to soften. I start. "Word from back east is that your ex took a beating Friday night."

"Bry, what the fuck are you talking about? You haven't been making sense for like a week now, maybe you need to see a doctor," she replies.

"I'm not the one who needs the doctor, Chris Garvey needs one, he got KO'd by Patty Byrne on Friday."

"I doubt that's true. I've seen Chris fight," she comments, not as alarmed as I thought she'd be. "I really don't give a shit what's happening at home, I'm trying to figure out how to make my life work here."

"Oh, I think we're done here, Sara. Did you not get the memo?" I inform her in a snarky tone.

A tear rolls down her cheek. "No, I didn't get it," she answers quietly, rising off the couch. She runs a finger down my arm and squeezes my hand, then walks into the bedroom and gently closes the door behind her. Sara's back on the emotional roller coaster, one minute flipping me the bird and the next seemingly wanting us to reconcile.

Round and round it goes, where it stops, nobody knows.

CHAPTER 43

"HEY MA, IT'S ME," I RECORD INTO MY MOTHER'S ANSWERING machine. "Some things have changed over the last few weeks. Everything's okay, but you'll be happy to know we're planning to leave here, for good, on April 1. I'm going to stay at the house for a while when I get back if that's cool. Give me a call, hope everything's good. Love you, bye."

"I guess that makes it official," Sara laments with a sad smile, sitting down on my lap.

"Guess it does," I agree.

It's March 1st. A couple of weeks have passed since all the shit hit the fan. I've decided to not exactly forgive, but at least move on, from Sara's transgressions. It's beating a dead horse at this point. I fight not to mock her every time she says I love you, and it's something I'll always question. Things are nowhere near where they were before her big reveal, or at least where I *thought* they were, but we are smiling and laughing together again. Hugging, kissing, and touching, too.

We have nobody and no place to turn to out here, so it's hard to just stay angry all the time. Humans need interaction. Sara and I had to figure out how to function, ignoring each other was not possible. This is a sticky situation, but we're making the best of it, and hopefully growing up a little in the process. Even if we've bounced back a little, I still think the Hawaii thing has run its course. For me, it's time to leave.

I'm working again so that has helped take some pressure off. Mike has a friend that works driving for a beer distributor downtown and he hooked me up last week with a job as a driver's helper. Nobody seems to mind that I'm leaving in a few weeks, they need all the help they can get. The job is located at a warehouse only a few blocks from the tower. It's seven am until whenever the route is done, sometime between four and seven each day. I run around in the morning loading the trucks with cases and kegs of beer, truly backbreaking work, then sit co-pilot with the driver delivering it all day.

The nights drinking with Mike and flirting with the chickadees at Bryan's seem like light years ago, but this is a good workout and I'm happy to be off the couch. Looking over the delivery schedule for the day, I notice that not only are we going to Freddie's but also delivering to Bryan's. I give the driver, some gruff old haole dog named Charlie, my backstory with our route today, telling him I'm not sure I will exactly be welcomed at either place.

"I don't give a rat's ass what your problem is, Kid. These are my big stops, so if you ain't up for the job, you can fuck off and I'll get someone else before we get going. Capiche?"

"Yeah man, I capiche, one hundred percent. Just wanted to let you know," I explain.

"Don't care."

I see that, you grumpy old fogy.

Our delivery to Bryan's is first. We are there at 11 am, so no reason to be concerned about seeing Curly Q or anybody else at this time, and if I do, so what? We make our drop without event. On to Waikiki, where we are making deliveries until early afternoon. Charlie schedules each stop to his liking, and I soon find out why. At about two o'clock he parks on Kapiolani in front of "Club Femme Nu," which has a big sign in the window reading "Non-stop live entertainment 2 pm-2 am."

"You know who Frank Zappa is, Kid?" Charlie asks as he shuts off the truck.

I shake my head no. "I've heard of Dweezil."

"Well today we're going to have a Frank Zappa lunch," he announces. "Titties and Beer!"

"I don't get it, Daddy-O. I wasn't born in the 1930s," I laugh at him.

"Yeah, I didn't think you'd know, it's an old Zappa song. And I ain't that old," he scowls as we cross the street.

Charlie's fat hand pulls open the door to Femme Nu and we are instantly enveloped by the dark. One lonely lady, her blond hair in pigtails, is gyrating for herself in the mirror as I follow Charlie to seats by the stage. Of course, this pervert has to be in the front row. We sit down and the dancer starts her engine, sauntering her way over to us, coming in for the kill. "*She's a Little Runaway*" by Bon Jovi is blaring, which seems fitting since there's a good chance she is a little runaway. I'm staring at some mid-west Dad's worst nightmare here, his daughter on the pole.

"Hey, Chuckie Baby," the girl smiles, sitting down on the stage in front of us, buck naked, the smile all she's wearing.

"I want to lick her like a Tootsie Pop. A one, a two," Charlie whispers in my direction, having mistaken me for someone who gives a shit. Seems "Chuckie Baby" is a regular, known by name thanks to his frequent pit stops. "Hello, Dolly, you lovely creature."

Oh, gross! Please, lord, don't let me be this pathetic in my old age. Charlie takes a wad of singles out of his pocket, clearly having planned for this. He throws two in front of me and puts one in his teeth while leaning forward. Ms. Birthday Suit shimmies a little closer and throws her legs up on Charlie's shoulders. She bends forward, scratching the floor with her natural Brillo pad. Big torpedo tits are coming in hot, aimed straight for the cash. Charlie's face disappears into Dolly's money makers and then he re-emerges, sans dollar. That's a lot of work for a lousy buck.

I pick up the two singles given to me by Charlie and toss them on the stage behind her, not wanting the whole goofy presentation, especially after dirty old Charlie desecrated her, not to mention himself as well. "Hey Man, how long you staying here?"

He looks at his watch and declares dramatically, "55 more minutes, not a second less."

"Okay Gramps, knock yourself out. I'll catch you back at the truck, I'm not in the mood today."

The old perv dismisses me without taking his eyes off the prize. "Suit yourself, College Boy."

Lunch with this little runaways' business in my face doesn't appeal to me. If I want to see a hairy beaver, I'll watch PBS for free at home.

I walk across the street and grab a beef and bean burrito at 7-11. Add in a cold can of DC and I'm happy sitting on the steps of the truck, waiting for Charlie to get his rocks off. As always with these stupid frozen burritos, I burn the roof of my mouth on the first bite, but when I get to the middle, it's cold and pasty.

Charlie stumbles out at three sharp, shading his eyes like a vampire leaving the coffin. We climb back into the truck as he growls, "Two more fucking stops and it's quitting time." Spending an hour with naked ladies had done nothing for his charming personality.

Last stop, Freddie's. This should be interesting. We park in the service bay next to the dumpster and ring a buzzer for the back door. A minute later, it swings open and there's Chief, of course, the mean eyes in his humongous head blinking wildly as he adjusts to the blast of sun coming down upon him. I pull my hat down low, grab a hand truck off the back of the rig and start stacking boxes of Heineken and Amstel. Four or five trips and we are all loaded in. Charlie heads back with the manager, not Paul, to count the delivery and get a signature. I walk through the kitchen and up to the front, looking for my pal TJ. I'm keeping a low profile, not wanting to get arrested or murdered.

"Hi, Bryan from Bryan's," comes from behind me. I know before even turning around it's Johanna, the beautiful local girl I met briefly with TJ.

"Hey, what's up? Johanna, right?" I unnecessarily confirm, as if I haven't been thinking about her every day since I first saw her.

"That's me," she answers giddily, and once again I'm shaking that pretty little hand. "So funny to see you, we were talking about coming in tonight after work. Will you be there? Are you delivering here?"

"No I won't be there and yes; I am delivering here. Looking to catch TJ, is he around?"

"Not now, but he's working later tonight."

"Oh okay, well I'll just see him another time. I'm not at Bryan's anymore, it wasn't working out. I'm moving back to New York in a month or so."

"Oh my God that's right, you're from New York, that's what I wanted to talk to you about at Bryan's before you ran off that night. TJ had told me that and I have an Uncle who lives there too. I was going to ask you about it because I'm considering east coast schools for my master's and would stay with him."

"Well, it's about 35 degrees there right now, are you ready for that? Where does your Uncle live?"

She holds her palms up and smiles. "Not sure, I need to check. I'm an island girl, it will be my first trip to the mainland. I hope I can handle the cold. I'll have to find a way to stay warm," Johanna says with a wink.

My, my, such a flirt. "Can I borrow your pad and pen?" I ask. She reaches into her apron and hands them to me.

"I'll be at my Mom's for the next few months, once I get back. Call me anytime and ask me anything. I'll be waiting by the phone," I finish with a grin and a wink back, handing over my number.

Johanna looks at the note and smiles, obviously approving of the smiley face and hearts I added. "I may just do that, Mister. Let me have a hug before you go." She proceeds to wrap me up like a long lost friend.

I'm more of a back patter than a bear huger, but I make an exception for the lovely Johanna and give her a good squeeze. "Nice to see you again, Johanna from Freddie's!"

"The pleasure was all mine Bryan who used to work at Bryan's," Johanna glows. "Here's hoping we meet again."

"I really hope we do. Don't lose my number," I tell her, thoroughly enjoying this flirty session.

Johanna gives me another hug and promises, "I'll guard it with my life!"

"Give my best to TJ, he's a good dude," I add with a wave goodbye.

We finally part and I walk back through the kitchen, brim low again to avoid recognition as I continue through the rear door and jump back in the truck. I'm sitting in the cab daydreaming of Johanna when I see Charlie in the side mirror as he plods through the open doorway. Chief follows him out, dragging a plastic can overstuffed with garbage bags. This is my chance for revenge. I briefly picture myself squaring up with him and knocking out a few of his teeth, but in reality, it would probably be me who gets their ass kicked. Either way, there's no point, that ship has sailed. Mr. Mature these days, I leave the Chief, with his garbage, behind forever.

CHAPTER 44

"**Y**OU WOULD HAVE BEEN PROUD OF ME FOR KEEPING MY COOL," I tell Sara that night, regarding my seeing the Chief again. She has made a delicious dinner of Sloppy Joe and white rice, her specialty. Sara wouldn't be as pleased with me for having given my phone number out to a pretty little local girl, so we won't be bragging about that. Nor do I mention that this Sloppy Joe on my plate reminds me of something I saw, ever so briefly, between somebody's legs at lunchtime today.

"Good for you, Bry," she says encouragingly. "A real man knows when to walk away."

How ironic coming from my cheating girlfriend, who I should have walked away from a long time ago. After giving Johanna my number today, I guess I'm a cheater as well. "That's pretty funny coming fr—" I start, and then the phone rings, probably circumventing another tedious conversation that goes nowhere. Saved by Ma Bell.

"Hello?" I answer with a question, not expecting to hear from anyone tonight.

"What's up, my friend?" Mike asks, no need to identify himself further. "It's the answer to all your prayers calling!"

"Oh really? You obviously haven't been listening to me pray."

"Dude, shut up and listen. My buddy Kyle is looking to move out here with his girl next month and—"

"Tell him he's making a big mistake," I interrupt.

"Let me talk already. So they were going to do it like you guys did, get a hotel then look around for a place. Anyway, I told him about your situation with the sweet pad and all in the tower. This kid is loaded, from a super-rich family, and anyway, Bro, guess what?"

"Spit it out, Mike, the anticipation is killing me."

"He wants to rent your apartment starting April 1st, and there's more. He will give you a thousand bucks for all the furniture. You just have to take your clothes and go."

So final when it's put like that. "Wow Dude, you're amazing. You've come through for us again," I tell him, as Sara mouths "What's going on?" to me. I hold the phone between us so she can listen.

"Tell the landlord you found someone to take over, and they're rich!"

"The only thing, Mookie, is we need the money as soon as possible, I can't wait until this guy gets here." It's so funny. Five minutes ago, we had no prospects for the furniture or the tenant, and now I'm being all bossy like I have tons of options. Truth is I'll take it any way they want to give it. This is a gift from the gods, or maybe King Kamehameha himself!

"Kyle said his parents would send a check tomorrow for the thousand, plus whatever security you have on the place."

"Hell yes, tell this guy done deal. Thanks so much, Mook, you truly are the best."

"Yeah, you keep saying that. Happy to help, my friend. I'll give Kyle your number, he'll probably call you tonight."

"Sounds good, we're here."

I hang up with Mike and fill Sara in on whatever she missed, which wasn't much as we were both huddled over the phone receiver for most of the call.

"Money, money, money........ money!" she sings, some old ditty that's in the back of her brain. Money truly does make the world go around. Here we are without a pot to piss in, as Sara and her Dad like to say, and now it feels like we just won the lottery. Whoever said money can't buy happiness, they should look in on us right now. We haven't been happier in a long time.

"So if my math is correct, that's $2,800 coming our way," I tabulate for Sara.

"It's not even the money, it's just not having to worry about it anymore."

"Yeah, because of the cash! Don't kid yourself, it's all about the money."

Mike's friend Kyle calls a little while later and confirms all the details. We promise him the building and the view is to die for, they'll absolutely love it. Probably wouldn't love the furniture, but it's better than having nothing like we had upon our arrival.

I'm thrilled to have this taken care of but am a little dumbstruck that everything just ended for us. All the planning and time invested, slowly building a little home, and poof, it's all gone. "This fucking sucks, Sara. I wish it didn't come to this."

"You're the one that wants to leave," she shoots back.

"Yeah I know; we have no choice. I'm just bummed it's over. You know that last day when we went to Makapuu beach? I loved you so deeply that day, and when you fell asleep on the bus I was looking at you and just felt so thankful we were together. I whispered in your ear as you slept, told you how much I love you and that I never wanted to lose you."

"That's sweet Bry, I didn't know that," she whispers back as tears roll down her cheek.

"Then two hours later, you basically dumped me. I'm not looking to rehash it all again, but it still fucking hurts. You helped me grow Sara, I was a little boy when we hooked up the first time, and I was on my way to being a grown man, right here in this apartment with you. I guess it wasn't meant to be."

"Stop Bryan, you're making me sad now," she frowns.

"Just know that I loved you here Sara, so completely. No matter what happens in our lives going forward." Now a tear slides down my cheek and onto my lips, an unfamiliar taste to me. I'm not a crier.

Sara wipes it away. "Don't cry, Bry," is all she adds before walking off. How nice it would be for her to reciprocate my feelings, but it's not going to happen. I'll take her silence over words that have no meaning.

The next two weeks are pretty mundane. Sara quit her job at Sears, she finished yesterday, the same day my beer delivery career ended. We are definitely both filled with nervous energy and even though we said we want to give it a go after getting back home, I'm not sure either one of us has much faith left in the relationship. I know I don't.

We debated splitting the money from Kyle and pocketing it for our return home to New York but instead chose to splurge on a quick trip to Maui. With a week left before our departure home and everything wrapped up, having no jobs and a pile of cash, Sara and I decided to treat ourselves.

Surprisingly, our four days here in Maui have been amazing. It is beyond beautiful, so tranquil and relaxed, like no place we've ever been. It's bringing out the best in us individually and as a couple. It feels like we're falling in love all over again (or maybe it's just the sex, like my sister warned me back in New York). Our hotel is the Hyatt in Kaanapali, right on the ocean. We aren't interested in group tours, whale watching, snorkeling, or taking the road to Hana. Quaint little shops, a few restaurants, and the beaches of Kaanapali are all we need. We've been running around for months in Honolulu, and besides a day off here or there, it's always been a hustle.

Sitting on the beach every evening and watching the sunset, it feels like a show being put on just for us. Four days in Maui and I am back in it with Sara, one hundred percent willing to make this work when we get back to New York. Sleeping late each day, we wake leisurely and just stay in bed laughing, talking, and touching, like we used to do. Not a care in the world, this is our best stretch in a long time.

Tonight is the last night here. After dinner at Moose McGillycuddies, a burger chain we also had visited in Waikiki a few months back, we head up to the outdoor pool on the roof of our hotel. After midnight, we have the pool deck all to ourselves. Sara takes it upon herself to get naked and jump in the water, and of course, I do the same and dive in right after her. We set up shop in the shallow water and get down to business, frolicking in lust, fueled by alcohol and the newfound feelings Maui has provided us. While getting out of the pool, we are only mildly embarrassed when I notice a security camera, meaning we probably had an audience for our show.

"I don't really give a fuck," I say, throwing up the bird.

"Hope you enjoyed the show," Sara waves to the camera, and we both walk off laughing.

The next morning, we still feel the warm and fuzzies. "Love you, more than anybody loves anybody," Sara purrs as we wake up on our last day in Maui.

"I know you do," I reply, and in my heart, I believe it. "I love you more today than yesterday," I quietly sing in her ear, for the first time in a long time, "but not as much as tomorrow." The truth is I don't know if I will ever love Sara more than I do at this moment in Maui. With the way things have been over the past month, who knows, today could be the last tomorrow we will ever share.

"We've been through a lot these last couple of months, Baby," I tell her during our quick flight back to Honolulu. "No matter what happens with us, I just want to say thank you. I've grown a lot since we've been together. I know I haven't been perfect by any means but at least I'm thinking twice before I make a bad decision, so that's something."

"You're still trending up, Bry," Sara whispers in my ear. "I should be thanking you. I'm the one who fucked this all up. I just hope you know you mean everything to me." Not everything. Something, but the lines are now forever blurred. These days in Maui are the first time I ever felt that I truly had all of Sara. It's probably too little too late, but once again, we pledge to keep trying.

A few days later, we are back in the tower, making final preparations for the trip to New York. I return to the apartment after lugging the TV back to Rent-a-Rama around the corner and we are now officially done with everything, all packed and ready. Besides the missing TV, nothing is out of place, as we are leaving everything except our clothing to Kyle and his girlfriend. May they have better fortunes than we did. Kyle is arriving fully funded by his Daddy, so that will alleviate a lot of pressure for them.

"Now what?" Sara asks, gesturing to the space where the TV used to sit.

I laugh and reply, "Now we wait," sitting down next to her with my hands on my knees.

"Ha ha, Dork." She elbows me in the ribs, asking "for the rest of the night I mean, and what's the plan for tomorrow?"

"For the rest of the night, there's only one thing I can think of doing," I suggest with a sly grin. "Why don't you come sit on my lap and we'll talk about the first thing that pops up!"

Sara looks at me blankly. "Your jokes are getting dumber every day; you sound like a fourth grader. I'm serious Bry, what's the plan?"

"I'm serious too! I know tomorrow I'm going to take my walk down to Hotel Street like every Sunday morning and get doughnuts. Then we need to bring the keys to the Tungs and be ready for Mike to drive us. The flight is at noon."

"That's it?"

"That's all she wrote. It's over, and the fat lady is singing."

"You're being weird," she replies. "Nice tan, by the way."

"You too. Took us six months but we finally look like locals."

"We'll never be mistaken for locals, Braddah," she cracks, and we both bust up laughing.

CHAPTER 45

OUR ALARM CLOCK GIVES OFF A SOUND THAT'S LESS LIKE TIME to get up and more like the end of the world is imminent. My hand crashes down upon it for quiet. This is it, our last day in Honolulu.

"What does your watch say?" Sara asks sleepily.

I lift the watch to my ear as if I'm listening to it talk. "It says go back to bed," I smile, and we start our last day off with a good laugh.

"I had the weirdest dream last night," I say, wiping some crusties out of my eyes. "We were looking out the window of the apartment, but there was only like two feet between the floor and the ceiling. So we're lying there with our faces up against the glass, and we are on like the two thousandth floor, the tower was super skinny and twisty and swaying up in the clouds. All of a sudden, George Jetson and Astro drove by in their little space ship and Astro kept saying, "You should stay, you should stay," in his dumb voice and pointing at us with his paw."

Sara looks at me skeptically. "You're making this up!"

"No I'm not," I grin, "let me finish! So you put your palms on the window and tears start pouring out of your eyes like rain, and your voice sounds just like Astro. "No Raastro, don't reave me. Raaaaastro!" you cried.

"You are so full of shit!" she interrupts, and both of us double over laughing.

"You're right, I made up the last part. But the rest is spot on, I really dreamt that."

"That's crazy! What does it all mean?" she asks.

"Who knows? Think about it and get back to me," I say while rising off the mattress. "I'm going to smoke a cig and jump in the shower." Never did stop smoking. Sara stands as well. Man, first thing in the morning and she looks ready for the prom.

"What?" she asks. "Why you eyeballing me?"

"You just look so pretty, I lost my balance for a second there," I respond.

"Cut it out, Bry! Give me a hug," she gushes.

After the shower, I head down to Hotel Street for my last ever trip to the doughnut shop. I get a half dozen powdered, pay, and then take one last whiff on the way out, never to return. Approaching the taxi lot where my most recent encounter with the Hamburglar occurred, I switch over to the other side of the street, hopefully avoiding any further confrontation.

"Howz it, Braddah?" comes from the direction of the cabs. I look to my right, Manny's Dad is waving me over. "Don't worry Brah, that crazy fucka not here today."

I cross back over the street and shake his extended hand. "Good to see you, Braddah," I greet him sincerely. Still holding the shake, he transfers his hand from the customary shaking position and goes for the weird hand clasp, like we are about to arm wrestle. This doesn't really work for me, it's too much, but I don't want to offend so I follow along clumsily. Of course, next, he pulls me in for a hug.

"Listen, I know my boy call you a haole but I don't believe that, you one of us now. I'm Manny. Manny Sr."

"Maholo Manny, that means a lot to me, I'm Bryan. I wish we started talking before, I'm leaving today, moving back to New York."

"Yeah Braddah, you act like you from there. Nobody never stand up to my son around here, but you do. You teach him one good lesson, he ain't so brave no more."

"We don't back down in New York," I brag, even though I did run away like a baby that first day.

"*Kahuna nui hale kealohalani makua*" Manny sings with the voice of an angel. "*Love all you see, including yourself. I*t's my family way, we tell Junior all the time, but he no wanna listen."

"He'll come around man, you'll see. Hell, I did. Me and your boy, we ain't that different."

Senior takes my hand again. "Aloha Bryan. Have a good life. *No keia la, no keia po, a mau loa.*"

I have no idea what he just said, but I know it's meaningful. I smile and turn away.

"*From this day, from this night, forever more,*" Manny translates as I walk off.

"Love it!" I declare, waving goodbye forever.

An hour later, Sara and I are lugging our five suitcases back out to the elevator, leaving behind the home we busted our asses for. We never did see another roach after that first night, for the record. Sitting on the little wall out front, we are waiting for Mike to show up in his Datsun and deliver us to the airport, and the next chapter of our story. This is my wall, but Sara doesn't know that. I've observed from here, drank, smoked, sung, and laughed from right here on this wall. Sitting and waiting, the city scurries by, living another Sunday, just like the last and the next. Meanwhile, today's a turning point in our lives, nothing ordinary about it. You never know what the guy next to you is going through.

"Hey, my friends from New Yawk!" Mike shouts through the open window as his little truck comes to a stop at the curb in front of us. We give him a wave and I throw our suitcases in the back, which is littered with empty beer bottles and cans, along with some swimming fins and a couple of bald tires. "No wonder you have roaches in this piece of junk," I say to myself as I ease our luggage on top of all the crap.

"I gotta' tie those down so they don't end up on H1," Mike declares as he hops out. Everything secured, we are rolling out, forever. Aloha, Honolulu. You worked me over good.

"Appreciate this, Mookie. Everything you've done for me," I thank him, slapping his knee.

"For us," Sara chimes in. "We couldn't have made it without you, Mike."

"You didn't make it," he comments, "We're going to the airport. Seriously though, it's been my pleasure man, even if you are from New York. Your good people, real good people."

Mike pulls up curbside at the terminal and shuts off the car. He jumps out and trots up to the sidewalk, chats briefly with the security guard or skycap, hands him something, and then joins me in pulling the baggage out of the truck bed.

"I gave that guy a ten spot; I'll be good for half an hour. He'll take care of the suitcases, just leave them here," he informs me, then we all head down a big outdoor ramp to the doors of the terminal. "Hey, check your pockets for cockroaches," he jokes to Sara, making her squirm one last time. We take a ceremonial last breath of Hawaii's tropical air and head inside.

I notice right when we walk in, there is a little group of ten or so people holding "good luck" and "Bon Voyage" signs, decked out in Aloha shirts and fresh floral leis. A couple of more steps and I start recognizing some faces, too. These are my friends from Bryan's, clearly here at Mike's behest. They lay the flowers around our necks with more pomp and circumstance than two basic strangers deserve.

"We miss you being around," Sherry my bartender comrade says as she hugs and kisses me.

"You're a solid dude, for a Yankee," a cook named Mark adds. "What they did to you at Bryan's was totally bogus."

Sara had slipped off after the initial greeting, running to the bathroom as I enjoy one more bullshitting session with the crew. More of the same chit-chat and well wishes, then we are off to the boarding gate.

"Mike, give me a hug, my brother. Make it fast, I hate goodbyes."

"Me too, Friend, me too."

He hugs us both and we watch him strut off. Mike's always going to be the coolest guy in the room.

"Must be nice to have made some friends," Sara frowns as we line up to board the plane.

"Nah, they're just acquaintances, Baby," I assure her, trying to ease the sting.

"It's okay Bry, I'm glad you came out of your shell." Oh, I didn't know I was in a shell. You're the one that made not one friend while we were here. I say nothing. I just want to get out of here, once and for all.

CHAPTER 46

WHEELS UP AND HEADING HOME, IT'S FULL THROTTLE FOR THE next ten or so hours. Sara has been wearing her "leave me alone" face since we said goodbye to Mike at the airport. She's an expert at turning it on and off at will. This attitude coming on now is reserved especially for me, but I'll try to break through as we settle into our seats.

"I was just thinking, Hawaii is the only state where you have to go east to get to California," I inform Sara.

She shrugs her shoulders and makes a face. "So what?"

"I don't know. It's like a fun little tidbit I just thought of."

"Fun for who?" she says, completely uninterested. Not for you, I guess.

The stewardess comes around and offers a set of headphones for the upcoming in-flight movie, "Field of Dreams."

"Five dollars, cash only," she answers when I inquire about the price. Jesus, what a rip-off for a six-month old movie on a tiny screen twenty rows in front of us, but they have us by the balls.

"I'll take one, please. Sara, you want?" I ask, pointing to the stewardess.

"No, I'm taking a nap. I'm not into a stupid baseball movie anyway."

"It's not so much a baseball movie, it's more about family an—"

"Not interested," she cuts me off again with a hand up. Why does she get so snotty every time we're on a plane? This is an unlikable trend.

"Fuck if I care. No need to get all pissy," I say under my breath.

"Goodnight, goodnight, goodnight," she yaps dramatically while pulling a sleeping mask down over her eyes.

"Okay goodnight, it's been a pleasure," I reply facetiously. "Oh and also, you look like Grandma Moses with that stupid thing on your face."

Sara slides the mask up onto her forehead and stares at me with a blank look for an inordinately long time, then begins slowly scratching the tip of her nose with her middle finger, making a show of it.

"I get it, fuck off. Real nice, Sara."

"Do you hear something? Like a baby crying?" she asks with a hand cupping her ear, "because I'm trying to get some sleep. I think it's in the bathroom, so if you happen to go and see a baby in the mirror, tell it to shut the fuck up."

Then for the coup de grace, she pulls the mask back down over her eyes, crashes back into the seat and pretends to snore, snorting obnoxiously. "ZZZZZZZZ." She stole that one from me.

I enjoy the movie as Sara and her rotten disposition sit idly by. The words on the screen are coming to life through my five-dollar headphones as one of the characters laments what could have been:

> *"You know, we just don't recognize the most significant moments of our lives while they're happening. Back then I thought, well, they'll be other days. I didn't realize that was the only day."*

Makes me wonder if anything of significance has happened in my life over the past six months.

Only time will tell. I know I've changed, if only a little bit. Sara has helped me be a more deliberate thinker and not so dangerously impulsive. I regret the night at Hot Rods, I've gone over it a lot since we stole the money. In the past, I'd never have thought twice about a move like that, so there's something I guess. On the other hand, she's made me a lot less trusting, or to be more specific, I don't trust her, not for a second. And of course, I've learned how to love, and lose love, then love again, and now, well, I hope she never wakes up.

Wow, maybe Sara really is going to sleep the whole way home. We are more than halfway into the flight and she's still out cold. "Wake up Sara, they're getting ready to serve dinner."

Her mouth barely moves as she grunts out, "Don't want it."

What's the deal with this chick? I peck at my food, smoke a butt, and then fall asleep myself. A bump of turbulence wakes me after two hours or so. Our roles reversed, Sara is now sitting up, and wide awake.

"Sup?" I ask.

"Nothing, I'm hungry. Give me the doughnuts from above your head," she orders. I reach into the overhead bin and throw her the grease-splotched bag, slouch back in my seat, and light a smoke.

"Oh my God, will you give it a rest with the fucking cigarettes?" she barks, a thick ring of white powdered sugar around her mouth contradicting the seriousness of her tone.

"First of all," I volley back, "You look like a clown with doughnut all over your face, and second, what is your fucking major malfunction?" I ask between gritted teeth. I've had enough of her bitching. She wipes her mouth, closes up the doughnut bag, and turns to me. Looks like she's getting ready to open the bomb doors again. Here comes another storm, Dad.

"I need a break from you," she starts. "You've been annoying the shit out of me since we got back from Maui, and what's with this bullshit, you having these girls waiting for one last kiss at the airport? It's all too much. That was the last straw for me."

I stare at her blankly. "Annoying the shit out of you?" I whisper, still gritting my teeth to keep from making a scene. "I've taken care of absolutely everything for the last six months, and you have done nothing but come along for the ride, all the while bitching and moaning at me non-stop. And about all these girls at—"

She holds up a hand to shut me down. "My sister is picking me up at JFK. I'm not riding home with you and Pat. Like I said, I need a break."

Well, I'll be a monkey's uncle, Sara needs a break. "YOU need a break? That is hilarious. So when did you make this little plan with your sister?"

"I called her while you were hugging and kissing your harem at the airport."

"Oh please. You've probably had this planned out for months."

"It doesn't matter what you think Bryan, I'm just letting you know what's happening when we land."

At this moment, for whatever reason, fear of being alone is paralyzing me. I can't live without her. Sara has a plan for her future in New York, and it looks like I'm not part of it. Who wants to bet she turns right back to Chris when we get home, I seriously doubt he has a new girlfriend. The truth is that she's spent much more of her life with him than with me. Sara is the love of my life, but Chris is the love of hers. In Hawaii, she begged for me, because she had no one else, but now she has options.

"Okay Sara, so what does this mean for us?" I ask softly, now in total pussy mode.

"It means we are both going home to our families, and we'll start to figure it out when we wake up tomorrow. What did you expect Bryan, things between us weren't going to change? I mean we're not going to be living tog—"

My turn to interrupt, I hold a finger to my lips. "Shhhhhh. Say no more." I still can't pinpoint when she planned this or what her end game is. There has been a serious shift of power during this flight, I am quickly becoming a lame-duck boyfriend. Feeling desperate and helpless, I break my silence imposed five seconds earlier. "Sara, I don't understand where this is coming from. I thought we agreed we were happy after Maui, everything was fine."

"You said that, I never said that."

Okay, here comes the old Eddie Murphy "wasn't me" act again. She's trying to pull a Jedi mind trick on me like she wasn't totally devoted to making this work three days ago.

"I don't get you, man, I don't. Make up your fucking mind already," I implore her, putting my headphones on for the last hour of the flight. We don't speak another word the rest of the way.

CHAPTER 47

AS SOON AS WE WALK OFF THE PLANE, SARA TRAILING BEHIND me like the stranger she is, I easily spot Pat among a sea of others eagerly awaiting their loved ones. He stands out, firstly because he's enormous, and also because he's holding a homemade sign that reads, "My boyfriend's back!" with hearts and penises drawn all over it. Sara's sister Cara is standing off to Pat's left. I'm not sure if they know the other is waiting, or if they even know each other at all. I give Pat a high-five and grab the sign out of his hand.

"Good to see you, Funk. You smell worse than ever."

"Thanks, Bryno. You look like Zorro the Gay Blade with that tan."

Sara is sharing a dramatic embrace with her sister. I nod "Hi" to Cara with a wave, then motion to baggage claim and start walking. Our luggage all gathered, Sara gives me some kisses and a long hug, our cold war on the flight temporarily forgotten.

"I'll call you later at your Mom's," she begins, then continues in a monotone robot voice, "Love you more than anybody loves anybody."

"Love you, too," I answer, then lean into her ear and desperately whisper, "You're the love of my life." But it felt over. DOA.

Pat slams the trunk lid on my bags and we inch out of the airport, finally merging onto the Grand Central Parkway. Our previous time leaving

NYC did not end well, I remind him. "Let's not get our brains beat in like the last time we were in the city."

"I handled my business with Garvey while you were gone, so speak for yourself, Grayhill, you're the one that got his brains beat in," he reminds me.

"It wasn't my finest hour, that's for sure," I admit as we ride past Shea Stadium on our right. "There's your shitty team's shitty stadium," I point out. "How are the Mets looking this year?"

"Ah, we'll see, man. Good pitching with Viola, Cone, and Gooden, if he's not sniffing glue or—"

Pat's Met analysis becomes white noise to me as we drive north. I can't stop shaking my head at Sara's curt and emasculating dismissal of me on the flight home. I'm being a real wimp, I tell myself. Stop being such a pansy.

"— and Strawberry is the only good hitter," Pat finishes, oblivious to my not paying attention.

"At least you guys have a chance. Yanks are going to lose a hundred games," I carry on, seemingly in step with the conversation. The lighter pops and I stick the red hot stub on the end of my cig, ferociously puffing to get it started.

"How's things with you, Dude?" I ask through a cloud of smoke. "Are you the king of the neighborhood now that you took down Garvey?"

"Nah, that's old news, man. Everyone's talking about your old buddy Billy Gorman now. He wrecked his work truck and got sent off to rehab last week, it was either that or jail for him."

"Fucking Billy," I lament, shaking my head. "Probably the best thing that could've happened to him."

Funkster finally pulls into my driveway and there's my Cutlass, sitting sadly on the lawn, a winters worth of dirt and debris covering it. Suddenly a feeling comes over me that I've accomplished nothing in the past six months besides wasting time. I'm right back at square one. There's a welcome home sign on the front door for me, Lauren got a chance to use it again after all.

Everyone in the house is still sleeping, as I knew would be the case, and that's just fine for me. Pat helps me get the suitcases inside the unlocked door.

"Thanks so much, my dude. Ed is out of town, otherwise, I wouldn't have asked you to do this," I tell him. "I owe you one."

"No problem, Gay-hill. At your service," he replies, bowing as if he's my butler. Funk hasn't asked me one question about my time in Hawaii or even why Sara and I are riding home separately. He is live and let live, Pat just doesn't care about the details. He gets back in the car and holds a Van Halen cassette case out the window for me to see, then cranks the volume up on one of our high school favorites, "*Hot For Teacher*," loud enough for me to hear as he backs down the driveway; "*I heard you missed us, we're back! I brought my pencil.*"

Jesus man, it's not even seven in the morning yet. Six months ago this would have amused me, but now it seems idiotic. Pat is still back in 1985. At this moment I realize that no matter what happens with Sara, I did keep the trend for myself moving upward during our time away, that is my accomplishment over the past six months, and I'm determined to keep it going, with or without her.

Back in the old house, Patty peels rubber out of the driveway as I make my way up the stairs, passing my life in pictures on the wall next to me as I climb. Mom has added the picture of Sara and me with the Hawaiian sunset behind us, which I remove and put face down on the table at the top of the stairs. My feelings of desperation and abandonment that I had toward Sara after the flight home are now being overtaken by acceptance and fortitude. I should have jumped a fucking plane back to New York the day she came clean about Chris. I crawl into bed by myself for the first time in over six months and it doesn't feel good.

It's always darkest before the dawn.

CHAPTER 48

I DIDN'T KNOW MUCH ABOUT WHAT TO EXPECT REGARDING THE effects of jet lag but holy shit, it's knocked me on my ass. I have no energy and it feels like an anvil is on my back as I struggle to get up, which I need to do before I piss the bed. Mom spots me as I try to sneak across the hallway to the bathroom. "Hi Honey, you're up!" she sings and comes at me with her arms open. I give her a hug and a pat on the back.

"Up for 30 more seconds Ma, I'm shot. Great to see you."

"Oh okay Honey, you have a little jet lag. Sleep it off and I'll be here when you're ready, we can catch up then. I'm so happy to have you home, Honey."

"Me too, Ma."

I finally manage to get out of bed a few hours later and go downstairs, but I could have stayed up there for a week. My Mom is futzing around in the kitchen. "Oh hi, Honey. How was your rest?" Not waiting for an answer, she continues. "I got you some snacks and soda from Grand Union and also a Chicken Sandwich from the pizza place, figuring to myself you'd wake up hungry."

"Much appreciated, Ma," I thank her, grabbing the hero wrapped in tin foil and shuffling to the table. "Anybody call for me?"

"No, no calls Honey," she replies, sitting across from me and drinking a to-go coffee in the iconic blue "*We are happy to serve you*" paper cup. "How are you Bry, how was the flight? How is Sara?"

"I'm exhausted, the flight took forever, and Sara is fine," I answer, never one to reveal any extra information.

"Why do I always have to pull everything out of you, Honey?" she asks. "What's going on with you guys? I saw you took the picture down when you came home."

I hadn't told my Mom much since we left for Hawaii and always tried to give positive reports, even after the cheating bomb was dropped by Sara. I didn't want her to worry about me out there and was also embarrassed to share. I fill her in on the latest details.

"When we're good it's good, but the bad is really bad. I'm not calling her, and she's probably not calling me either. Truthfully, I'd bet dollars to doughnuts that she's already called or seen Chris, her old boyfriend."

"Oh honey, I'm sorry," she whispers, rubbing the top of my hand. "Maybe it's time."

"It's been fucking time," I agree.

"Same thing happened with your father, Bry. Everything with him was an argument. Daddy was living a separate life, doing whatever he wanted. He always came back saying he would change and be better, but the more things changed, the more they stayed the same. I remember when I finally said no more, what a relief it was. He and I were at the subway in Grand Central, I was leaving the city to come back up here to Rockland and he was saying the same old crap, the same old promises, and I finally had enough. "I'm done! It's over, Michael," I told him. I'd never actually said that before and it felt so liberating."

"I should have done it a long time ago too, Ma. The timing is never right."

"It never will be, Honey. There's always something, Bry. A holiday, a birthday, whatever it may be."

"Yeah, you're right. When you're right, you're right," I declare, shrugging my shoulders.

"Give me a hug, Honey. We're so happy you're home," she beams. "It will all work out." Of course it will. I give her my patented one hand tap on the back with a half hug, then shuffle off to bed.

Three full days have gone by, and not a word from Sara. I'm in the kitchen reading the paper this morning when the phone rings. I let the machine pick up and hover over it to listen.

"Hey Bry, it's Lauren. Ed and I are going to take you out for a drink tonight so we can all catch up. Let me know if you're not around, otherwise, I'll pick you up at eight."

I snatch up the phone. "Yo, yo, I'm here, I'm here."

"Oh hey, cool. How are you? How's it being back at home?"

"It's pretty weird, honestly. I need to find a job and get out of here."

"I have one for you, we can talk about it tonight. You good for eight?"

"Yeah, pick me up, sounds fun," I answer. "Ed is getting back soon I guess?"

"Dad got him a limo through his work, it's picking them up from the airport at four."

"I see, interesting. It's not like I didn't just get off a plane three days ago with five huge suitcases or anything. Guess we know who the favorite child is."

"That's Dad for ya," Lauren quips. "Not that it's an excuse, but he's having trouble with Rita, their marriage is on the rocks. Ed told me she's become a total pain in the ass, driving him crazy."

"I'm not surprised. Hopefully, she packs her bags, I won't miss her. Anyway, talk to you later, thanks."

I hang up with Lauren and the phone immediately rings again, she must have forgotten to tell me something. I pick it back up and ask, "What else?"

"Bry. It's Sara."

"Oh, I thought it was my sister. So nice of you to call," I reply sarcastically.

She ignores me and proceeds, asking, "Is this a good time to talk?"

"Yeah. What's on your mind?"

"How are you feeling about being home? I still feel tired from the flight," she starts.

"Yeah, me too. I wasn't prepared for that." We are talking like acquaintances, at best.

"Okay, well let me get to the point," she begins. Go ahead and drop the bomb, Sara. If you don't, I will. "I'm sure you feel the same way (maybe I do), but I think it's best if we spend some time apart and try to figure out where to go from here. I know you're thinking this has to do with Chris (I'm sure it does), but that's not the case. I just need to clear my head and get back on track here."

"That's fine, Sara. It's totally weird being without you but you're right, it's time. It has been. We had a good few months out there," I add, "but it seems like a long time ago. Besides Maui, that was good too." I'm saying too much. This is ending today, end it like a man. You need to stay focused, Bry, this is not the time to get soft. Be Buster Douglas, go in for the knockout punch. "I don't need time to clear my head, Sara, I'm ready to move on… alone."

"Bryan, I know about that girl you cheated with out there," she proclaims out of the blue. The master of manipulation has returned.

Think before you speak, I tell myself. "Sara, there's nothing to know, I didn't do a damn thing. You're trying to pin this break up on me right now, and go ahead for all I care. But there's only one dog in the dog house, and it's you. I'm going to go; this is a pointless conv—"

Click. She's heard enough and hangs up in my face, and simple as that, our whole relationship is thrown out the window, just like the phone was six months ago.

I place the receiver gently back in the cradle, pleased to have followed through on my intentions. I immediately run a whole gamut of emotions; happy, sad, scared, free. Now I'm on the roller coaster. How is it even possible for the pendulum to swing so fast, and so drastically? One morning we rode on the bus to Makapuu beach seemingly more in love than anybody, anywhere, and by the end of that day, it was all but over.

I only know my side of the story, and it was genuine, but it takes two people for a love story to have a happy ending, and this one had three.

CHAPTER 49

LAUREN AND I ARE SITTING AT THE BAR WAITING FOR ED TO SHOW up, some joint called Lauderdales that recently opened in Nanuet, about 20 minutes away from the house. All bright colors and vinyl, it reminds me a little of Hot Rods in Waikiki. Hardly anybody is in the place, not a good sign for a new venture.

My sister hasn't seen her rocker boyfriend Jeff in almost six weeks, not because they're having problems, he has been touring the west coast with his band.

"Wow, your guy has been away for six weeks? And you're okay with that?"

"It comes with the territory," Lauren shrugs.

"That truly sucks for you. I don't know how, or why, you do it."

She shrugs again. "I'm just having a good time with the guy, not really worried. We all know how this will end. I'm not as invested as you think."

As usual, Lauren seems totally in control of her life. Good for her, that makes one of us. Ed joins us, looking almost as tan as I am, as he is just off a plane from Aruba. We exchange greetings and a big hug, then sit.

"Look at you two bronzed Stud Muffins," Lauren teases us.

"Oh my God, it's freezing here," Ed starts up while rubbing his hands together to accentuate the cold. "Aruba was baking hot on the beach.

Michelle got burnt to a crisp our first day there and we basically stayed in the room for the rest of the trip; it was total misery."

"I know, 45 degrees felt like zero to me when I got off the plane. Of course, I wasn't getting into a toasty limo like some people," I direct to Ed.

Right on cue, he affirms, "Well I am the favorite child. Anyway, what's up with you? Where's Sara Addeo at?"

I purse my lips and hold up my palms. "It's over, guys. Elvis has left the building."

Lauren and Ed exchange double high-fives and he says "It's about time."

"Dude, she was terrible for you," Lauren begins, "I told you from day one the girl has issues."

"And she gets around, man. I know a lot of dudes who explored that bush beside you," Ed snickers.

I shake my head at him. "That's not true. You don't know anything about her, that's all a bunch of gossip. And if you thought she was so bad for me, why didn't anybody say something?"

"You must be kidding me, Bryan. I did everything besides lay my body down on the runway to keep you from going with her. You guys seemed happy for a while there, I thought maybe I was wrong. Sorry it didn't work out, Brother." Lauren pats my back as she gets up to use the bathroom.

"I'm not happy about it, this whole thing sucks. We were going full tilt boogie until a few days ago," I tell Ed.

"Give it a week, you'll get over it," my brother promises, before adding, "I told you going out there was crazy."

"At least I tried, man. I don't regret it. No matter what anyone says, I know Sara is a good person, nobody knows her like I do."

As we are about ready to get into it, the Hawaii Five-O theme song blasts through the speakers and Lauren walks toward us doing a mock Hula dance. *Dah dah dant dah dah dah, Dant da dant da dah.*

"I dedicate this to you, Don Ho," Lauren says to me upon returning to the table. "Happy to have you back, Brother," she adds, raising a glass.

Lauren goes on to tell me that she is working for a new restaurant chain called Martinis. They have four places in Westchester, on the other side of the river, and need managers. She guarantees me jobs are available and I can be working by the weekend. Perfect, just what I need, as Freddie's is no longer an option. I hadn't just burned that bridge, I'd nuked it.

Checking the answering machine when I get home that night, Dad's voice informs me that he will be by tomorrow "around noon-ish" to "do some lunch and catch up." He has his own funky language. "Let's get the ball rolling," he said, I assume meaning us working on improving our relationship.

"Noon-ish" came and went the next day, and so did one-ish and two-ish. Why does this always surprise me, after all these fucking years? My Dad finally pulls up in front of the house at about three and honks his horn to summon me. He is leaning on the fender of his car when I come out.

"There's my Boy," he smiles as I approach from the driveway. "Give me a hug, Son," he says jovially, and when I gave him a meek man hug he encourages me to "hug me like you mean it!"

I withdraw from the lame embrace and look at him with dead eyes. "Dad, if you want to get the ball rolling," I began, using finger quotes, "then things are going to have to change. Sorry to be bitching right out of the gate, especially since I haven't seen you in so long, but you're three hours late today and that may be your way of doing things but I'm fucking sick of it, man. This has been going on forever and I should have said something a long time ago. It's bullshit, I've had it with you never being close to on time. It's going to be on your tombstone; HERE LIES MICHAEL. LATE FOR EVERYTHING."

"Hey Bry, give me a break, man. I got a lot of shit going on today." He doesn't say it like he is remorseful, he says it like he's about to punch me in the eye, but I hold my ground.

"Give *me* a fucking break, man!" I echo him. "It's not just about today Dad, it's about every day, it's about my whole life for that matter. If you want to make things better with me, this right here is the place to start. It's really not that hard; do what you say you're going to do, or don't say it. I've waited around for you more hours in my life than McDonald's has served hamburgers, and I'm fucking sick of it!"

My Dad stands there glaring at me. This is a landmark moment for us, it's the first time I've ever stood up for myself. The ball is in his court; I've said my piece. He nods his head imperceptibly slowly, downright menacingly, then he opens the car door and drives off without uttering a word. Classic Dad.

I go straight to my car and take off as well, in search of the lunch my father has deprived me of. After downing a couple of slices at Turiello's and going back to the house, I pull into the driveway and there's my Dad, leaning against his car again. He's come back to kill me.

"You're one hundred percent right," he begins as I approach him. "Being late is selfish and disrespectful, it's something I need to work on. I'm sorry it's been such a problem," Dad apologizes as he moves closer and reaches out for a handshake. "I'll do better. I want to talk about all the ways we can make this better."

"Thanks, Pop, I do too. Let me know if there is something you would like me to work on. I know I'm far from perfect."

We gave each other another hug, and this time Dad didn't say, "Hug me like you mean it," he could tell I did.

CHAPTER 50

I'M LYING ALONE IN BED ON A GORGEOUS SPRING MORNING, looking through the screen of my open bedroom window at our neighbor, a man I don't know, who's cutting the grass in his little front yard.

As he pushes his mower parallel to the white picket fence separating his lawn from ours, the man's young son proudly walks behind in his Dad's footsteps with a little Fisher Price lawn mower. I'm mesmerized by this and can watch them all day. The sound of the mower, the smell of the grass, and a summer breeze hitting my face. I feel happy for the boy. This is going to be a good day.

It's been just over two months since I've been home, today is June third, 1990. In the past couple of months, I've started an awesome new job that I absolutely love and recently signed up for culinary school so I can get going on the dream of having my own place one day.

I've also made new friends and reconnected with old ones. Spent a lot of time pondering past decisions and considering future ones, even spoken to a psycho-somebody or other who has helped me with my temper and self-confidence.

It hasn't been easy; I'm not trying to convey that it has. Just like a drug addict fighting to rehab and get well, I know I'm doing what's best for me.

I've also reconnected with my Dad, or maybe I should say connected. For the first time, we are finally connected.

I'm reuniting with my first true love today, we've been apart too long. Everything feels and smells the same as I remember like it was yesterday that we last visited. Today I will close the loop on the one last thing that's been missing in my life these past two months. I turn and face the front, not wanting to miss the start of this. My body gets goosebumps as the music begins. The organ plays its last note, and as the man in the black uniform takes his rightful place, onlookers buzz with excitement. "Play ball!" the umpire shouts.

Pinstriped uniforms, bright green grass, the huge Marlboro billboard in center field. It's all here, Yankee Stadium is just as I'd left it. Mattingly dribbles a single up the middle to score Roberto Kelly and give the Yanks a lead in the bottom of the first, but it doesn't last. They'll lose today, and it looks like this will be one of the worst seasons in their mostly glorious history. They may stink, but it's okay, I'm not mad. Like I said, this is my happy place.

I've had a lot of strong moments in the last couple of months, and some pathetic ones too. Sometimes I miss Sara with an ache and sadness that is profound, but those moments are fleeting. I'll never go back, not that she wants me anyway. I don't know what happened with her, but I'd bet the farm on a reunion with Chris. I've heard some things but really wasn't interested. I've moved on, learning to take the positive experiences in and expel the negative, instead of dwelling on them. My psycho person taught me that.

I can't give my therapist all the credit for keeping me on an upward trend. As bad as things got with Sara, I value most of the time we spent together and truly believe that in many ways, she made a man out of me. I'm not sure if we were ever really in love, it was more like a whirlwind of lust and newness that, of course, didn't last. "*It never do*," to borrow a line from my old cuz Junior. She also got me on track with my Dad, not to mention taught me how to make a mean Sloppy Joe. No regrets. Mahalo, Sara!

Needing to pick up the paper and some food, I stop in town on the way home from the game to grab the Daily News and a sandwich. I cut to the front of the line at the deli and drop a dollar on the counter for the Sunday paper. Upon exiting, the old bum who's always standing out on the sidewalk approaches me and pleads, "Hey man, lemme get a cigarette?"

"Sorry friend, I don't smoke. That shit's no good for you," I reply proudly. It's only been a few weeks since I quit but it's been a big part of my reckoning since I've been back.

I pull the Cutlass up to our house and park in the driveway, grab my food off the front seat and tuck the Daily News under my arm. I shoulder the still damaged door of the car open, sympathizing with my old jalopy as she groans in disrepair. "We've all got some dings," I say out loud. My Olds got a tune-up and some new tires after I cashed my first paycheck at the new job. I'll continue to work on her, and work on me. We're both trending up.

"Hello?" I ask while going through the big red front door, receiving no reply. I put my stuff down on the kitchen table, the late day sunshine streaming in the windows as I check the answering machine, see a red "1" blinking, and press play.

"Hi, this message is for Bryan from Bryan's. Aloha, it's Johanna from Hawaii—"

I had a feeling when I woke up this morning that this was going to be a good day. Spring is all about the possibilities of what's to come.

JUNE 2019

"**HEY POP**," **MY SON MIKEY CALLS OUT FROM ACROSS THE ROOM** as he holds up a box of photo slides, dozens of my Dad's memories from the Sixties and Seventies. "What should I do with these things? What the hell are they anyway?"

"Hold one up into the light and look at it," I instruct him. "What's the date printed on the bottom?"

"Oh man, this is so cool. June 15, 1969. It's Grandpa sitting on an Oldsmobile. It looks like ours, and he looks like you!"

"That's the Cutlass, Mikey! My Dad bought it 50 years ago, that picture is at the dealership. He gave it to me twenty years later after it was all rusted and busted."

"And then you fixed it up?" he asks.

"It was a big job, took me a long time."

"I bet. Good thing you're so mellow yellow."

"Yeah, that's me, Mr. Patience. Let's finish cleaning this place out," I reply, proud of myself for breaking the long line of temper tantrums and impatience that runs in my family. Mikey is free of this affliction, I made sure of it.

My father died suddenly last month. Dad went to sleep and never woke up, leaving me heartbroken. He and I spent the last thirty years in constant contact, and we had both long ago gotten past the bitterness and petty bullshit that had divided us so often when I was a kid. In my eyes, we had more than made up for all of that time lost. We lived life in the present, not the past. Dad made an effort to be involved my entire adult life, and it felt like he cared. What more could I ask for?

Nobody could have ever predicted my father was capable of that back in the Eighties. We all grew up together. Dad never did figure out how to be on time, and he died still not knowing shit about baseball. Nobody's perfect, right?

My only child Mikey benefited from my Dad's early foibles, as my mother had predicted all of those years ago when I was a boy. Mikey is everything to me and of course, I give him double the love, while always careful not to make the same mistakes that hurt me when I was young.

"Alright, time to go," I tell my son. "Uncle Ed can take care of the rest. He's going to be here later for a walk-thru with Grandpa's landlord. Mom's meeting me outside, we have to get to the airport. Hug me like you mean it, and be good while we're gone. Drive around to the front and say goodbye to your mother." This August marks 25 years of marriage for my wife and me and we are going back to Hawaii to celebrate.

While I stand outside waiting to be picked up, my thoughts drift to decades earlier, when Sara and I waited outside our apartment in Honolulu for my friend Mike to take us to the airport, ending our Hawaiian life. I can still hear him like it was yesterday, shouting out the window. "*Hey, my friends from New Yawk!*" Mike stayed in Honolulu and raised a family of Red Sox fans; I'm looking forward to seeing him next week for the first time in three decades. Now that I've sold my restaurants (yes, I made the bar exactly like Bryan's Parkplace) and retired, I have nothing but time.

My wife parks and gets out of her van. She smiles sympathetically, softly saying, "Hey Bry. I'm sorry, I know it must be tough going through your Dad's stuff."

"I'm okay, Babe, thanks," I reply, giving her a big bear hug, just as tight as the first one I gave her thirty years ago.

Our son Mikey rumbles up to the curb in front of us with a big smile, his high school graduation present sparkling in the sunlight, same as it did on the lot 50 years ago. "Hey Ma, have a great trip! Stop worrying about everything, It'll all work out!" he grins, then waves goodbye. We watch as the Cutlass roars off, tail lights fading down the boulevard.

His mother turns to me. "Love you, Bryan from Bryan's," our inside joke from days gone by.

I take her pretty little hand in mine. "Love you, Johanna. More than anybody loves anybody."

I stole that one from Sara.

ACKNOWLEDGMENTS

THERE MAY BE ERRORS AND THEY ARE ALL MINE. WRITING A STORY based in the late 80's, I included language and phrasing that is clearly unacceptable in today's world but was part of the everyday vernacular back then. The story would not be a true representation of the times had I left that out.

This is not a memoir, most of the anecdotes in this book did not happen. My father is a kind-hearted man who has woken up every morning for 81 years and counting. The character Sara and the things she does and says in this story are a fusion of many people and experiences I've had in my life.

Thank you to Kiki for encouraging me to write, hearing all my ideas, and giving me some great ones as well.

Thanks to my parents and siblings, who read this multiple times without complaint. Their input was invaluable to building this story and encouraging me to continue. Family is everything to us.

To everyone else who contributed: John M, Izzy, Bob, handsome Mike, Debby, Stephanie, and anyone else I may have forgotten. Thank you for the valuable input, I'm sure you will notice the changes related to your suggestions.

AUTHOR BIO

RYAN CAHILL GREW UP IN NYACK, NEW YORK. HE HAS ALWAYS been an enthusiastic storyteller and after many years of people suggesting "You should write a book," here is his first, "Too Late To Turn Back Now."

When he's not writing or reading, Ryan's fast-forwarding through the Yankee game at midnight or driving his kid somewhere, hopefully with the top down. Like most of us, he is a work in progress.

Ryan has three daughters, each one his favorite.